Passion's Fire

Cataloging-in-Publication Data is on file with the Library of Congress.

Paperback ISBN: 978-0-9913338-4-4
E-book ISBN: 978-0-9913338-5-1

(Previously published in 2002 under ISBN 1930928378)

1

The noon sun beat on Jacqueline Cardew's back as she fought the kitchen door's jammed lock. Why did things always go wrong when she was wearing a suit and heels instead of jeans and sneakers? Knowing it would mean a dry cleaning bill, which she couldn't afford, she smashed her hip against the faded green door.

With a snick, the catch clicked free and the door groaned inward. Jacqueline lost her balance and grabbed the doorjamb to keep from falling into her kitchen. Momentum twisted her so she ended up looking at the charred concrete block and rubble; all that remained of the research facility's laboratory. She shivered as she stared at the sooty foundation and withered cacti, which surrounded the black memorial to the past.

Fire.

Death.

Ashes.

A breeze wafting across the desert bringing the stench of smoke; a vivid reminder of the horrible inferno, which had consumed the laboratory and her husband, Adam.

She whirled away from the sight, until cool air from the adobe's dark interior rolled over her face. Feeling stronger, Jacqueline fled into her kitchen's shadowed sanctuary and slammed the door against the past's horrors. She kicked off one shoe, then the other. The navy heels clattered into the shadow of the ancient round-topped refrigerator. Jacqueline still smelled the ashes, but now the heavy sweet scent was stronger. As she headed toward the sink, something moved in her peripheral vision.

She whirled to confront it. An intricate origami crane and a plumeria flower lay in a pool of sunlight, at the center of her old Formica tabletop. She looked from the paper bird to the window, where a broken shutter created a spotlight for the bird. Her gaze darted around the dim kitchen, as she listened for any sound that would betray the intruder's presence, then a puff of air made the wings tremble.

Jacqueline stared at the yellow paper and tropical flower, which had no business being in her home, and shuddered. Someone had been in her home – perhaps still was in her home. Chills coursed over her; fear made her shake so hard she grabbed a chrome-backed chair for support.

She only heard her thundering heart.

Jacqueline tiptoed to the old, out-dated wall phone and pressed 9. The last time she'd found an origami animal and plumeria blooms on her welcome mat, the burly, crew cut police officer had laughed in her face. Though her forefinger trembled over the 1, she pushed it.

Being laughed at for fearing a paper seal and wilted blossom had been humiliating, but it wasn't as bad as finding the officer's notes tossed into the prickly pear cacti next to her front steps. Jacqueline's face heated at the memory.

She turned and glared at the crane's delicate yellow wings.

For all she knew, the officer had left it and all the other whimsical shapes with their menacing messages. Jacqueline quietly put down the receiver, took a deep breath and forced her legs to move back to the table.

What would the hidden message say this time?

Another threat?

A declaration of love?

Whichever tone the note expressed, for Jacqueline, the crane and flower were omens of doom and violation. Yet in the three years she'd been receiving them, not a single person had taken her fears seriously. Jacqueline gritted her teeth and reached for the fluttering yellow wing.

"It's only paper, it can't hurt me. It's only paper. It can't hurt me," she whispered the chant, "It's only paper, it can't hurt me."

When the first note had arrived, her nerves had been reeling from her first serious quarrel with Adam. The yellow origami tulip had declared:

> Burning desire.
> Heat of the night.
> Passion's fire.
> Give them back.

Charmed by Adam's apology, Jacqueline forgave him, but the following morning, he'd denied writing the "foolish drivel." Worse, he'd accused her of having a lover and gone into a rage. Still, she'd harbored the certainty that her husband was hiding a romantic streak.

Jacqueline knew she'd never grow beyond five foot two. Her hair would always be ash brown, and her eyes would always be the gray-blue of a stormy sky, and corpses did not send flowers much less hide messages in origami.

Paper wings pulsed beneath her fingers in a silent demand to be opened. Fingers trembling, she unfolded the legal paper until she could read the blood-red ink.

Scorching strand.
Inferno of infatuation
Inferno of endearment
Inferno of desire
Inferno of love
Inferno of passion
Inferno of ardor
Inferno of delight
Passion's Fire
...all mine.
You won't bring them to me.
I'll take them.

When she covered her mouth to stifle the welling scream, the paper fluttered to the floor.

Who kept writing these notes?

Did the brawny police officer get his jollies from terrorizing strangers?

With Adam dead and only wildlife for miles, who else could it be?

She rushed to the door, secured the deadlock, then leaned against the aged timber, finding comfort in the wood's gentle warmth. Glaring at the table, she noticed the shaft of light now spotlighted her pepper mill.

How quickly the light moved.

Yet the crane had been spotlighted, when she arrived... A distant squeak made her gasp. Had she just locked herself in with a lunatic?

Heart pounding so hard her ribs ached, she darted across the cracked linoleum, grabbed a butcher knife, then, blade poised to slash, Jacqueline tiptoed down the narrow, dark hallway whispering, "...though I walk through the shadow of death, I will fear no evil, for thou art with me." Unable to recall the rest of the passage, she repeated it, but as she approached the doorway to her bedroom, the sound came again. Louder this time.

Taking a deep breath, Jacqueline burst into the room, knife at the ready, looking for her harasser.

Squeeeeak.

The faded pink curtain billowed into the room. She whirled. *Squeee-* the wooden ring moaned against the pine rod. Then, as if exhaling, the bulge receded. *Eeeak.*

Squeee- faded fabric swelled into the room, again.

It had never moved before.

Jacqueline's fingers tightened on the knife's haft as she inched forward. Whipping the bulging fabric aside, she slashed downward. The blade sliced through hot glaring light and arid desert air spilling through the open window, then its tip embedded into the once-white enamel sill. "What the—" She gawked at the window frame, where layers of paint had been sliced and gouged.

In the distance, a motor gunned. Knuckles white around the knife's haft, Jacqueline yanked the blade from the dry wood. She squinted past the mesquite hedge. An old blue pickup truck fishtailed onto the dirt road, trailing a plume of billowing dust.

Jacqueline slammed the window shut and locked it.

Knees shaking, she sat on her bed and wondered if the police officer drove a truck. She told herself the man deserved the benefit of doubt, but aside from Adam, who was dead, the officer was the only person she could think of who had exhibited any sort of malice toward her. Lately, the news had been rife with accounts of police officers committing crimes and firemen turned arsonist. How accurate were the reports that listed the lab's destruction as an arson-suicide?

Adam would never have killed himself. Nor would he have destroyed their project.

Had her stalker lit the match?

With a shiver, Jacqueline pushed her long hair out of her face. Drastic measurers were needed.

2

Link Gavallan squared his broad shoulders, straightening his spine to his full six-foot-two, and opened the door to his office. Mavis looked up from a stack of mail. Her piercing gray-blue eyes matched the color of the Valdez sky outside the window and her hair matched the snowy clouds. She rose, a lethal-looking letter opener gripped in her raised hand. He'd previously seen a slight shift in her grip send that replica antique Celtic sword hurtling at impudent roustabouts and pin their hats to the wall.

Drops of perspiration trickled down Link's spine, just like they had when Mother Superior had caught his six-year-old self reading a Playboy at recess.

Mavis' militaristic posture defied her petite stature. Her gaze never wavered, though the corners of her mouth turned up. "So, you finally decided to do some work." Had that been warmth in her tone?

Doubtful.

Link had never felt like Mavis' employer. "Good morning, Mavis. How've you been?"

She sat down. "Fine, except for this infernal contraption of Mr. Bell's." She stabbed the telephone with her letter opener.

As if in pain, it shrilled.

Mavis jabbed it a second time, then put down the miniature blade and grabbed the receiver. "Linkstone." Her forehead furrowed as she listened. "I'll call you back."

Mavis slammed the receiver down and turned her full attention on him. "You owe me."

"That's right."

Mavis raised an elegant white brow. "I didn't think you'd admit it." The corners of her dainty mouth turned up, but her wintery blue eyes remained frosty. "Did you do it on purpose?"

He shook his head.

"That's the second time this month." She picked up her letter opener and twirled it between her fingers. The blade flashed round and round in a mesmerizing whirl. Link swallowed. "Are you still going fishing?"

He nodded.

She actually smiled. "And you're taking your sister and her beau." The blade flashed faster. He nodded, again.

Her smile widened.

His stomach churned.

From what Carmen had said about Phillip, he seemed like an unlikely candidate for a wilderness camping trip. "Plus Tempest. That means you'll be taking two canoes."

The satisfaction in Mavis's tone was giving him an ulcer. Worse, he felt like a dashboard Madonna.

Mavis's smile could have belonged to the Cheshire cat. "Therefore, you have room for one more." In the entire decade he'd known her, he'd never seen her look so pleased. Why? Surely she didn't want to join his trip. He imagined Mavis canoeing down an icy Arctic river, making his life a living hell for two weeks. Link's stomach rolled. What with his sister's intended, his partner's step-kid and now Mavis, this was sounding less like a vacation every minute.

He'd need a vacation after this vacation, assuming

he survived it.

Mavis settled back in her burgundy leather chair, the picture of a contented woman. "My granddaughter will be arriving from Arizona tomorrow. I want you to take her with you."

Link blinked. Mavis had a family? She had worked for Linkstone since they opened a decade earlier, and her expertise accounted for much of Linkstone's success, yet this was the first he'd ever heard of a family. Of course, until last week, when Carmen's phone call had begun the destruction of his vacation, he'd never mentioned his sister to Mavis, either. He cleared his throat. "You have a granddaughter?"

"Jacqueline." Mavis proudly thrust the photo of a young girl at him. "She's on route here as we speak."

He examined the small oval face, which was dominated by thick glasses, a mouth full of metal, all topped by a wild mop of brown hair. "Nice looking kid," Link lied as he returned the photo.

"This was taken a while back." Mavis caressed the air above the image. He'd never seen such a tender look on her face.

"The Sheenjek isn't a safe river, especially when the person doesn't know how to survive in the wilderness."

"Jacqueline will be fine and she needs to get away from … things."

Link squinted at the photo. The kid looked younger than Tempest. Worse, Mavis, who could handle anyone wanted to be rid of the kid as soon as she arrived.

"You will take her." Her wintry gaze chilled him.

It seemed like Mavis, Carmen, Stone and Ariel were conspiring to turn his vacation into a survival expedition for troubled teens and mis-placed nerds. Ariel and Stone had told him that Tempest had been packing for a week and she still wasn't ready. Link grasped the possible reprieve. "If she can get ready by the time I head back for Fairbanks tomorrow, I'll take her."

Mavis gave him a radiant smile. "You won't regret it."

Wrong - he already did.

~0~

Jacqueline purchased a bag of chips, a can of cola, and a pair of binoculars, then dodged vacationers clustered around the tables of rustic souvenirs and headed out of the tourist trap. Pausing on the porch, she inhaled the clean, thin air of the Rocky mountains. Grateful to be out of the overcrowded log structure, she leaned against a totem pole, which resembled a parrot more than a native American carved eagle as it supported the porch's tin roof. Moving cautiously, she peered past the bird's lime colored wing and studied her mud covered Jeep Cherokee, which was barely visible behind the row of stately pines.

No one was near it.

Her spine relaxed against the bird's crimson talons and she sipped her drink while admiring The Rocky Mountain's snowcapped peaks which gleamed above the pines. Her gaze wandered downward to the boughs caressing the ground as they cloaked the lower slope and perfumed the air with their fresh scent. Best of all, the boughs hid her Jeep from the road and her stalker.

A pair of tourists left the trading post, the woman preening in her new moose ball necklace while the man ushered the woman toward a mud-spattered sedan as if she were wearing the crown jewels. The sight of someone proudly wearing varnished moose feces was nearly too much. Eyes watering with suppressed laughter, Jacqueline watched the pair leave. Beyond them, a distant flash of familiar blue made her forget to breathe.

She adjusted the binoculars, impatient for the first glimpse of her stalker, but long blond hair streaming out the old pickup truck's window, whipped in the wind, hiding all features. Her jaw tensed as she tracked the truck's progress toward the store. When the muddy vehicle turned into the Trading Post's graveled parking area, she slipped behind the bird totem. The old truck pulled into a spot next to a Winnebago. After a final chug, its engine became silent. A moment later, the door creaked open.

Jacqueline pressed against the bright blue tail and held her breath. The soft pitter-patter of footsteps approached. Thunk, a foot hit the first step. Thuckity-thunk-squeak. He was on the porch.

Now or never.

Jacqueline's legs wouldn't move.

Hinges squeaked as the door opened. "Hey, Cody. What's doing?"

"Nu'tin much," said a voice from inside. "How'z it wit you'n Lenny?"

Embarrassment heated Jacqueline's neck. She must be totally paranoid to believe anyone would pursue her more than four thousand miles. Jacqueline leaped off the porch, jogged to her filthy Jeep, vaulted in and slammed the door. When Jacqueline leaned forward to start the engine, she glanced in the rearview mirror and saw a shaggily bearded face peering around the Trading Post. In a blink, the face vanished.

She craned around, but there was no one. She shook her head, amazed at the lengths her imagination took. Then she saw a tiny yellow origami sailboat lying on the passenger seat.

3

Link glanced at the small, sullen female he'd picked up at Mavis' home. She hugged the passenger door and looked out the rear window every other second. Her body language made him think her camouflage cap and jacket were more armor than fashion. He gritted his teeth and drove toward the airport. What had Mavis told her about him to make her so hostile? Her tension grew until it permeated the Dodge Ram's cab and her ponytail bristled. Ms. Jacqueline Cardew acted like he was Jack the Ripper incarnate.

Link pointed toward the glistening white expanse on the right and kept his tone calm. "That's Chugach." Jacqueline ignored him, her mirrored sunglasses remaining on the traffic behind them.

And he'd thought Tempest had impossible days.

Link glanced at the rearview mirror. A quarter mile back, a shiny black sedan bobbed over the centerline, looking for an opportunity to pass a rusty Volkswagen. Father back, an old blue pickup kept a sedate pace.

Normal traffic.

Why did he make Jacqueline uncomfortable? Why did she distrust him, or did she distrust all men?

"Can I ask you something?" she asked. He nodded. "Why are you taking me on this trip?" Her antagonistic tone confirmed his worst suspicions.

"Do you have a problem with me?" Link kept his

attention on the road and tried to sound relaxed.

"I don't know anything about you, and frankly, I like it that way." She pulled her mirrored glasses halfway down her nose and peered over them. Her eyes were the same shade of hostile blue as Mavis' eyes. "I came to see Grandma and to find a job, not to go camping. Grandma forced me to come with you." Jacqueline jabbed her index finger toward a seedy motel. "Pull in there and drop me off."

Mavis would have his guts for garters if he left her grandchild at the sleaziest pickup joint in Valdez. He shook his head. Jacqueline yanked the steering wheel to the right. The front tire dropped off the pavement. Link slapped her hand, slowed and merged back onto the road.

"Take me there." She balled her fists.

He tensed for a strike. "No."

She looked out the back window. The fight evaporated and her expression turned to defeat. "I don't have time for camping." No wonder Mavis figured taking the kid along was adequate payback. Still, if something happened to her granddaughter, Mavis would spend the next decade inventing new and ever worse forms of torture for him.

"Don't worry, I'll show up at Grandma's front door when you're supposed to be back and regale her with tales of wonder and excitement."

"Don't you understand the word no?"

Her lips thinned. "Grandma told me you usually camp alone."

"So?"

"Leaving me here gets you off the hook."

"Bull."

"Bull." She mimicked his gruff tone. "As long as

neither of us tells her, she won't know." He knew better than that. She flashed him a seductive smile. Link gripped the steering wheel tighter. Why did she want out so badly? And why that motel? Was it the lure of drugs?

Something else illicit?

Jacqueline took several deep breaths, then resumed her efforts in a calmer tone. "Just why are you so stubborn about taking me?"

Her grandmother knew the company books ten times better than he and Stone did. If Mavis quit, their business would suffer. Worse, he would have to do the paperwork. Link rubbed his temple. "Tempest can be quite a handful. I need help." He gave her a lopsided smile. "At least a female's perspective in dealing with her."

"Grandma said your sister and her guy were going to be there. Why do you need me?" Jacqueline seemed genuinely confused, and for the first time her attention focused on him.

"Tempest is sort of a child prodigy." She gave him a 'so what look'. He cleared his throat. "Sometimes I have a problem getting her to listen. You seem levelheaded." *May God spare me for lying.* "And you're young enough to understand Tempest." Link felt invisible quicksand envelope him.

"You think I'm a kid?" She laughed while she shook her head. He risked a glance, and found her expression filled with incredulity. Jacqueline pushed her ponytail back over her shoulder. "I'll be twenty-five in November." Link grinned at that whopper. "Grandma lied about her age, huh?" She pointed to a billboard proclaiming a motel a half-mile further. "Let me off there."

There'd been two murders there last week. Link accelerated. "What's so important that you can't put it on hold for a couple weeks?"

"You wouldn't understand."

If she was that determined to go to a motel, he did not want to understand. "In the past ten years, Mavis has asked me for one favor." He paused significantly. "I figure she's got a good reason for it and I, for one, do not intend to argue with her." Jacqueline glared at him. He stared at the road.

The silence became oppressive.

Though his attention was on traffic, he could feel her angry gaze. Dammit, why had everyone decided to ruin his vacation? *If only he'd never answered the phone when Carmen had called.*

That had been his first mistake.

Why the heck did Carmen want to haul Phillip all the way to Alaska, when it would be so much easier to take him home to meet the folks? Why was it so important to her that he be the first to meet her fiancé? Link's jaw clenched. Then, when he went next door to see if Ariel could give him any insight into the female mind, Stone had suddenly seen his vacation as a wonderful opportunity to dump Tempest on him so he could take Ariel on a second honeymoon. Within an hour, he'd not only given up his solitary vacation to chaperone his sister and her geek boyfriend, but he'd agreed to bring along Tempest.

Mavis had found the perfect revenge, too.

He gritted his teeth.

Jacqueline continued staring out the back window. Maybe Mavis had destroyed the kid's plans by sending her camping, but plans involving sleazy motels needed wrecking. Link swerved into the airport's private entrance, parked the Ram, then gestured to Linkstone's company plane. "Decide. Are you coming with me willingly, or do I need to phone Mavis for permission to use force?" He flipped his cell phone open.

"Why didn't you say we were flying?" Jacqueline suddenly looked cheerful.

Link suspected a trap.

4

When the Cessna's shadow crossed a wide river, Link flicked switches, adjusted dials, then requested landing instructions in Fairbanks. Jacqueline glanced at the altimeter and sighed. So much for her unexpected reprieve. She needed to decide how to circumvent her grandmother's well-meaning plan and going on Link's canoe trip would be a bad idea. River's only flowed one way, so her stalker would have time to regroup after being outmaneuvered in Valdez.

After following her most of the way across the continent, she hated to imagine what motivated her stalker.

She needed to use this opportunity to break his trail, and disappear for a year, or however long it took for him to lose interest in his perverted game.

Jacqueline glanced at Link. His thick blond hair reminded her of rich honey and his gentle brown eyes made her think of chocolate. Except for treating her like a kid, he seemed like a good guy. Too bad he seemed so single-mindedly determined to bring her along on this trip.

From the air, Fairbanks looked larger than Valdez. A bigger city offered more places to disappear. Best of all, wilderness surrounded it.

Moments later, Link eased the Cessna 185 onto the runway. "Did you hear the one about the brunette who spent 20 minutes looking at the orange juice box because it said 'concentrate'?" He turned onto a taxiway.

"When I heard that one, he was blonde."

Link laughed.

As the Cessna taxied into the hangar, a big dark-haired man met them. He opened her door and helped her out. "Welcome to Fairbanks." Then he reached in, grabbed her duffel and tossed it over his broad shoulder.

"That's mine." Jacqueline hoped her panic didn't show as she reached for her duffel.

"You'll do enough hauling in the next couple weeks." He patted the strap. "The least I can do is help now." He turned to Link. "Did you take the scenic route?"

"You were concerned?"

"Hell, yes. We took Tempest on our first honeymoon, I will not take her on the second." Jacqueline tried to make sense of the bizarre situation, then realized the man didn't act like an airport employee; he had to be Stone O'Banyon, Link's partner. Oh, Lord, it was going to be harder to get away than she had anticipated. Link laughed and punched Stone in the biceps. Then the two started walking toward the exit, making it worse.

Jacqueline trotted behind them, two paces for their one, and focused on how to retrieve her bag, which contained all her necessary paperwork, including billfold and passport. With every stride Link and Stone made, her escape plan seemed more impossible.

By the time Stone parked his Suburban behind some townhouses, her lungs felt like they were full of soggy cotton candy.

"Link's spare room and den are full up, so you'll be staying with us." Stone ushered her into his condo and introduced her to his wife, Ariel, a petite willowy blonde woman with a ready smile and an energetic manner.

Introductions complete, Stone took Jacqueline's duffel upstairs.

"I'm so glad you're going with Link." Ariel gave her a big smile.

Jacqueline watched her possessions disappear and faked a smile to cover her panic. Just then, a younger version of Ariel stomped down the stairs, blonde ringlets bouncing on her shoulders with each step and frosty blue gaze centered on Jacqueline. "Tempest." Ariel's tone held a warning. "Jacqueline will be sharing your room. Would you take her up?"

"It's my room, and you can't tell me who sleeps there."

"Actually, I can," Ariel said.

Tempest's hostile glare fixed on Jacqueline; it felt as if icy venom washed over her. Jacqueline cleared her throat. "There's been a misunderstanding," she began.

"Shut up and come on."

Tempest couldn't have been better named. "I don't think so." Jacqueline calmly turned her back on the unreasonable teen. "Ariel, I appreciate your hospitality, but I never intended to stay the night, much less go camping. There's been a misunderstanding. Grandma manipu— "

Ariel touched her hand. "You don't have any place specific to go, do you?"

Jacqueline shook her head.

"You look just like Mavis," Tempest snarled. "Old as dirt."

First Link treated her like a child, then the kid said she looked ancient. Jacqueline choked back a laugh. Tempest stormed upstairs. Ariel touched Jacqueline's upper arm and steered her through an archway into the living room, then nudged her toward the burgundy leather sofa, all while shaking all over. "Are you okay?" Jacqueline asked.

Ariel nodded, but her watering eyes contradicted her. A distant door slammed. Ariel sat down with a thump and burst into laughter. Jacqueline looked from Ariel to the archway framing the stairs.

Above them, where her things had disappeared, the kid was pitching a screaming fit. Crash. Bang. Something heavy hit the floor. She hoped the obnoxious brat hadn't touched her things.

Jacqueline half rose, but then heard the low tones of Stone's voice speaking beneath Tempest's screeching. With resignation, she sat on the sofa's edge and steepled her fingers.

Ariel looked at the ceiling. "The look on her face," she snickered. "You're just what Tempest needs."

The feeling was not mutual. "Grandma forced this on me. I want out of her plot."

Ariel sighed and looked downward. "You've come so far. Is it Tempest?" Jacqueline shook her head. "Then why?"

"There was an accident where I worked, and the lab office building burned. I need to get my life back on track, find a job, a new place to live." Jacqueline sighed. "I came to Alaska partly to see my grandmother, but mostly because there are many grants available for biologists, here." She sighed. "The last thing I need is a vacation."

There was movement in the foyer's shadows. Link appeared in the archway, his expression wary. "So it wasn't something I said or did?" Jacqueline shook her head. "I hate keeping records," Link said. "Without Mavis." He rolled his eyes toward the ceiling and shook his head.

"I'll tell her you said that," Jacqueline said.

His eyes widened. "Don't."

Ariel laughed. "Link and Stone both hate office work."

"Adam did, too. He always said that he needed a hundred pounds of paper for every sheet he actually used, and that the government needed all those to justify purchasing the one sheet he needed."

"Who's Adam?" Ariel looked interested.

Jacqueline wished she'd never mentioned him. "He was my husband."

"Your husband," Link echoed.

"He dumped you, huh?" Tempest appeared on the stairs. She moved purposely toward Link and possessively looped a slender arm around his waist. Though Link didn't seem to notice the adolescent hanging on him, Jacqueline suddenly understood the source of the girl's hostility and her mother's eagerness to have an extra person along.

Jacqueline looked Tempest in the eye. "Adam burned to death."

Tempest glared at her. Jacqueline glanced at Link. What made the man think she could help him with this hellion? Could anyone manage such a venomous kid?

"I expect Mavis felt that you needed to get away," Ariel said. "You must go. You'll have a wonderful time."

Tempest gave Ariel a withering glare, then stomped toward another door. Ariel and Link ignored the behavior, but gave each other defeated looks.

What if this trip wasn't her grandma's idea? What if Link had ordered Mavis to find someone to help him? Her refusal could cost her grandmother her job and her dignity. Jacqueline's throat constricted. If her suspicions were accurate, that would explain why Link and Ariel were so adamant about her acquiescing.

Ariel sighed. "Tempest is intelligent, but sometimes her personality makes sandpaper seem like silk."

"My Mom called it PTS. When I was younger, I had a terrible case," Jacqueline said.

"PTS?" Link straddled the sofa's arm. "It's not contagious, is it?"

Jacqueline shook her head. "Pre Teen Syndrome is when adult hormones start being produced and previously sweet, adorable children turn into raving lunatics." She used her solemnest tone. "I believe either Dr. Jekyll or Mr. Hyde patented the formula."

Link laughed. "She's seventeen and too old for that."

"I remember going through that stage." Ariel sighed. "It was horrid to live through and it's embarrassing to remember."

Jacqueline's tension eased. "That's the truth." She glanced at the empty archway and decided she could afford to take a short vacation more easily than she could financially support her grandmother, now that she was unemployed. Despite Tempest's mood swings, she would go on this trip. Maybe she could use the time to plan her next move.

Later that night, she followed Tempest upstairs to her Mickey Mouse theme room. Tempest climbed onto a black lacquer bed topped by a red quilt with a huge silhouette of the famous rodent. The girl settled cross-legged on the center and silently studied her. The fire building in Tempest's eyes proclaimed a brooding rage ready to burst into an inferno.

Jacqueline went into the adjoining bathroom and changed into her nightshirt. When she returned, it appeared as if Tempest had not moved so much as an eyelash. Jacqueline climbed between the crisp white sheets of the spare bed.

"Link is mine." Tempest hissed.

Jacqueline had hoped to avoid a direct confrontation. "You can't own another person." Tempest's face paled and her eyes enlarged with hatred.

"He's mine. Stay away from him, you piece of shit."

"I'm not interested in a relationship with Link or anyone else."

"Why not? Isn't he good enough for you?"

Had she ever been this impossible? "I don't know him well enough to have an answer to that. Regardless, I don't want a relationship." Yes, in some ways, Link attracted her, but she needed to find herself, not live in another man's shadow.

"If you're lying, I'll kill you." Jacqueline shrugged, plumped her pillow and hoped for beautiful dreams. "Aren't you worried about sleeping in my room? I could kill you while you sleep."

Though she hid it well, the sheer absurdity of the threat amused her. "No man is worth committing murder over."

"Link is."

"Fine, he's yours. Keep him. I already told you that I don't want any man in my life."

After a moment's silence, Tempest demanded, "How come you don't like guys?"

"I like them." Jacqueline plumped her pillow again, and tried not to remember that her stalker killed his competitors. "Right now, I prefer to be alone."

"Why?"

Heaving a sigh, Jacqueline rolled onto her side and propped herself up her elbow. "For the past few years, I lived for my husband's dream instead of my own. Now that he's dead, I want to live my life my way."

"Did you murder him or something?"

Jacqueline shook her head. "Somehow, after we married, I lost myself in Adam's ambition. His wants always seemed more important than my own. I didn't even realize what had happened until after he died." Gooseflesh rippled over her as the truth she had never verbalized before echoed in her ears.

Tempest's expression was a cross between suspicion and hostility. "You really aren't after Link?"

"Nope." Jacqueline snuggled into her pillow. "I don't care if I ever fall for another man."

"Don't talk down to me. I'll start college soon."

"What's your major?"

"Zoology." Tempest rolled onto her side and propped herself on her elbow. For the first time, her eyes held something besides malice. "Why did you change the subject?"

"I didn't realize I had. When I started college, I had no idea what I wanted to do with my life. I'd never taken time to think about what I liked."

"Why didn't you?"

Jacqueline shrugged. "I guess I always took things for granted." Tempest grunted. When the silence lengthened. Tempest looked at Jacqueline expectantly. "When I enrolled in college, I chose nursing, to follow my mother, and I earned an LPN degree. But Animal Psychology interested me." Jacqueline chuckled. "Actually a certain professor intrigued me, so I changed majors to take his classes." Jacqueline shook her head at her own foolishness. "I was so naïve, that I spent the last few years trying to be who the person I loved thought I should be." She raised her chin. "Now that he's gone, I need to find out who I am and what I want."

"You were real dumb," Tempest said.

"Exactly! Now, do you understand why I'm not interested in a relationship?"

"And you agree that Link is mine?"

"Whatever bond you have with him is your business." Jacqueline studied Tempest remembering how she'd publicly pawed Link and how everyone had accepted the behavior. She frowned. Link seemed like a nice man, but the worst child molesters were often members of the victim's own family. She wrapped her blanket tighter and remembered that her grandmother talked about Link as if he walked on water. Who was Link? A great guy who didn't know how to tell a kid to behave or the monster of her suspicions?

Jacqueline cleared her throat. "Tempest, is there some special reason why you think Link belongs to you?"

"He just does. And don't you forget it!"

Jacqueline hoped the obsession was in Tempest's mind. She felt like naming her pillow Link, then punching the stuffing out of it.

5

Link took a bite of blueberry pancake just as Phillip walked into Ariel and Stone's dining room, while reading something on his iPad. His shoulder collided with the archway separating the dining and living rooms and he fumbled with this iPad, more concerned over dropping it than the spectacle he made. Link sighed. All Carmen's previous boyfriends were athletic, why the heck had she decided to get engaged to one who couldn't even walk straight? In the wilderness, lack of attention could be the difference between life and death.

Was camping with two hostile teenagers, a klutz and a tense sister some sort of test?

Ariel stifled a snicker, then began toying with her fork. Stone excused himself, quickly vanishing out of the room.

Oblivious to everything but whatever he was reading, Phillip settled into a chair at the far end of the table. A few minutes later, Jacqueline slid into the seat across from Link, looked around the table and whispered, "Is something wrong?"

The fresh fragrance of her scent wafted over him. The next two weeks would be purgatory instead of vacation. "Everything is fine," Link said. Except the thought of mollycoddling a nerd, babysitting Tempest and fighting the absurd fascination he had with a kid, who acted like she was fifteen going on thirty.

Thank goodness his parents had convinced him to teach Carmen camping skills when they were kids, at least he would have some support.

Ariel laughed. Carmen's high-pitched voice and nonstop chatter had been as welcome in his childhood fort as a polecat. He frowned at the memory.

"Oh, so you're one of those." Jacqueline sipped her orange juice.

"One of what?" Link snarled.

Phillip peered at him over the top of his iPad and Ariel raised an eyebrow at his harsh tone.

"Sorry." Jacqueline's smile widened. "My father is one and so was Adam. From now on, I'll only speak with you after you've had your coffee." With a smug smile, she took a bite of pancake and never told him if she'd just complimented or insulted him.

"Oh, for— " Link clamped his jaws together and counted to ten. He was one of what? Without ever taking his attention from whatever he was reading, Phillip meticulously spread jam on his toast.

Carmen slid into the seat between Jacqueline and Phillip, then leaned as close as possible to the food. "Morning. Mmm, this smells wonderful."

After twenty years, his sister was still a magpie.

"They taste even better," Jacqueline said. "It's been a long time since I had pancakes made with wild blueberries."

"You can tell the difference?" Carmen asked.

"Taste for yourself." Carmen obediently ate a bite off of Jacqueline's proffered fork.

"Mmm. Oh, these are wonderful." Carmen licked her lips.

Tempest slid into the chair beside Phillip and fixed her gaze on Jacqueline. "So, what type of guy do you go for?" Her thumb motioned left. "A computer geek like Carmen's Phillip, or," her hand caressed Link's shoulder, lingering on his biceps, "a macho stud like my Link?"

Link ignored the possessive hand, hoping it would leave.

"Phillip seems intelligent and pleasant," Jacqueline said. "I can see why Carmen loves him."

Link gripped his fork until his knuckles turned white. "That's the type you go for?" The words burst out before he could stop them. "Scholars?"

"Not necessarily." Light twinkled in Jacqueline's eyes.

Carmen glared at him. "Phillip is smart and athletic." The man being discussed remained engrossed in reading.

Jacqueline grinned. "Ah, an intelligent jock. Someone like Link."

"You think I'm like Phillip?"

"You are obviously fit," Jacqueline said. "Furthermore, a dummy couldn't pass the pilot's test or build a company like Linkstone."

"Maybe Stone simply let me come along for the ride."

Ariel guffawed. Jacqueline smiled and slowly shook her head.

"What did Mavis tell you?" Ariel asked.

Jacqueline shrugged. "She just insisted that I come on this trip. No reason for her request, but then, that's my grandma. She figures that as head of the family, she doesn't have to give explanations." Jacqueline fingered her glass of orange juice. "I based my opinions on my experience with animals. Sentient creatures with similar interests and intellects gravitate toward each other."

Ariel nodded in understanding. Tempest looked up,

her gaze narrowed on Jacqueline and Link wondered if all kids used terms like sentient and gravitate.

"No matter how much some individuals would like to deny it," she continued, "Homo sapiens are animals." When she noticed Tempest's hostile expression, Jacqueline grimaced. "Sorry. I'll put my soapbox away." Jacqueline rubbed her temple and turned her attention back to Link. "You and Stone own equal parts in Linkstone, don't you?"

"Yes, but it would never have gotten off the ground if Stone's family hadn't loaned us the start-up money."

"Do you resent that?"

"Not anymore." Link crammed a forkful of pancake in his mouth, hoping that she wasn't rude enough to continue with the inappropriate questions.

Later, as Link placed his plate into the dishwasher, Jacqueline quietly asked, "I get the feeling that you don't think Phillip is good enough for your sister."

Did the kid always bring up topics people didn't want to think about, much less discuss? "If Carmen marries him, she has to live with him." He shrugged. "I only have to spend the next couple weeks with him."

Jacqueline nodded knowingly. "And you don't want to spend it with him or Carmen or me."

"Not exactly." He rubbed the knotted muscles at the back of his neck.

"I'd appreciate knowing your reasons." Jacqueline put her silverware in the dishwasher. "You act like you want to be left alone, yet when I try to bow out, you won't let me."

"Phillip packed a solar charger and some ziploc bags for his iPad plus a can of pepper spray, how about you?"

Jacqueline blinked in confusion. "Pepper spray?"

The corners of his mouth tilted up. "He believes it'll work against a bear."

The corners of her mouth twitched. "Pepper spray." Link nodded. Jacqueline put her hand over her mouth to hold back the laughter that twinkled in her eyes. "He isn't planning on spraying himself, is he?"

Link grinned and tilted his head toward Phillip, who was visible through the archway separating the rooms. "He thinks pepper spray will repel bears and be more humane than a gun."

"I can see it now." She dramatically pointed to the refrigerator. "A twenty-foot-tall grizzly approaches. Phillip, our knight in shining armor, valiantly steps forward to save us. Lifting his hand, he sprays." With theatrical gestures she pantomimed the story. "The wind grabs the spicy mist and it envelopes us. We all fall down, overcome by the fumes. The bear dances a jig of triumph because it loves spicy food and now has enough to last until Christmas."

Link laughed. "Thanks. I needed to have my perspective adjusted."

She winked. "Glad I could help."

"Uncle Link." Tempest shoved between them. The force of her impact rattled the contents of the dishwasher and propelled Jacqueline backward against the counter. "How soon do we leave?" Tempest hugged him, then held on like a burr. "Do you think we'll see a bear this time? Maybe some caribou?" Her constant squeezing focused his attention on her upturned face. "Are you going to let me paddle? Can we stay longer than two weeks?"

"Tempest," he warned in a futile attempt to stem the flood of words.

"Can I— "

"If you want to leave, you have to finish eating breakfast."

"I'm not hungry."

"I can fly you down to stay with Mavis while we're gone." Her face paled, then she scurried into the dinning room and began forking huge amounts of food into her mouth. He turned back to Jacqueline, but she'd disappeared sometime during his confrontation with Tempest. He headed for the door.

As he crossed the foyer, Ariel caught his wrist and pulled him close. "Tempest has a crush on you," she said softly.

"Me?" Her expression attested to her seriousness. "But I adopted her as a niece."

"I know that." She sighed. "You know that... Everyone knows that, except Tempest."

An uneasy feeling crawled up his back. "I never gave her any reason to think that I cared for her in any way other than as an uncle." Link shifted uncomfortably. "Did I?" He recalled the way Tempest liked to touch him and sit on his lap. Things that he'd always viewed as harmless suddenly took on a new and sinister meaning.

"Don't get upset." Ariel kissed his cheek while she patted his upper arm. "I'm not accusing you of anything." She gave him another pat, then took a step toward the dining room.

He caught her arm. "I'm not willing to wonder what you meant by that remark and why you're telling me now, when I won't see you for the next two weeks."

Ariel sighed. "Last night, I overheard Tempest threatening Jacqueline and claiming you belong to her."

"You've got to be kidding."

Ariel shook her head while she ran her tongue over her lips. "Tempest told Jacqueline that you are her personal possession."

No, this couldn't be. As if reading her thoughts, Ariel nodded. "Why would she say something crazy like that?" Link demanded.

"I only know what I heard." Her fingertips touched his hand. "I thought you should know."

He nodded in agreement. "What did Jacqueline say?"

"She basically told Tempest that one person couldn't own another. I had the impression that she initially thought the subject was ridiculous."

"Smart for a kid."

"Then Tempest started being very specific." Ariel chewed her lower lip. A chill settled in his stomach. "I don't know what to say to her, especially since she's leaving." Ariel's voice trailed off.

"It's always best to know what you're up against." Ariel nodded, her manner glum. With an effort, he changed the subject, "What do you think of Jacqueline? Gut reaction, no holds barred."

"Anyone who has patience with Tempest scores high in my book."

"There's a but."

"Sometimes I wish you didn't read me so well." Ariel sighed. "But there's something about her that reminds me of me."

"And that's bad?"

"Maybe. Maybe not." Ariel frowned. "Do you remember when Tempest and I met you?"

"Sure."

"Back then, I thought of myself as the Queen of Paranoia." Her eyes closed momentarily, as if she was remembering the person she'd been, when she and Tempest were being stalked. "You know why."

"Yeah," he agreed.

"I noticed a hunted look in Jacqueline's eyes." She paused as if her statement held significance. "It's the same look I used to see in the mirror."

He shrugged. "She's tense. Probably from marrying way too young and being widowed." How old had she been when she married? Ten? Twelve? Had she attracted some pedophile or something?

"That is a possibility, but don't you find it odd that Mavis was anxious to send Jacqueline away?" Link shrugged, again. "Did Mavis tell you why she wanted her gone?"

"No," he admitted.

"That's what I thought. Think about this: until a few days ago, I didn't know Mavis had any family. Suddenly Jacqueline shows up with her hunted expression, and Mavis packs her off to the wilderness quick as she can."

Link weighed Ariel's words and remembered how Jacqueline had kept watching the road behind them, how she had only relaxed after they were airborne. "You think someone is after her. Or that Mavis never mentioned having kin because of complications."

"I could be wrong."

"You're usually right."

"What if Jacqueline is some sort of felon? What if she's a deranged killer and she murdered her husband? What if she kills all of you and— "

He tickled her under the chin. "Ariel, you're still the reigning Queen of Paranoia."

Her face colored even though she tried to laugh away the truth. "But I'm usually right."

"Mavis likes to antagonize me— "

"Link, get the lead out, or we'll leave without you," Stone yelled from outside.

"Coming." He leaned close to Ariel and added more softly, "No matter how much I piss her off, Mavis would never do anything to endanger any of us." He kissed Ariel's forehead, then grabbed his duffel bag.

"You're right, she wouldn't; at least, not knowingly." She blew him a kiss. "Take care."

"I will. I'll try to set Tempest straight, too, though I don't know how. What's she think I am? A rock star or something? Isn't that what girls are supposed to have crushes on at her age?"

"If she's going to fall for someone, I'd rather it was you than some weird singer." She shivered. "Some of them look like they eat their young."

Link walked out the door wondering what else could possibly go wrong with his vacation. Instead of fishing and kayaking with buddies, or better yet, alone, he was canoeing with Phillip. Worse, he was the focus of Tempest's infatuation. Something told him things would get worse before they got better and he was not looking forward to the coming weeks.

6

The Cessna's window felt cool against Jacqueline's forehead as she watched the plane's shadow caress the vast unbroken miles of stunted trees interlaced by lakes and rivers without any mining within sight. "The way eco groups talk, Alaska has been ruined by oil and deforestation."

"Hype," Phillip said, "is the best way to get donations. They love to howl about the dangers of nuclear energy, too and it's pretty darn safe."

Jacqueline twisted to face him. "What's your profession?"

"I design computer games."

"For children or adults?"

"Both." He chuckled. "Especially when the adult is in touch with his or her inner child.

"Interesting."

He glanced at the backs of the heads of the other passengers, and readjusted his seatbelt, as he turned toward her. "Graphics initially make or break a game." As he warmed to his subject, he leaned closer. "But the strategy and the ability to draw the player into the game are what keeps them coming back for the latest and the greatest."

"Fascinating," Jacqueline said. "I've always thought of my computer as a tool." More like a fancy filing cabinet that was capable of printing out copies of reports when they were needed.

"I do strategy. You see— " Eyes shining, Phillip leaned even closer. Jacqueline soon found herself absorbed in the subject and realized video games were far more complicated than she would have imagined.

When the plane began losing altitude, she noticed they'd flown so far above the Arctic Circle that there wasn't a tree, road or dwelling in sight. Stone landed the Cessna 185 near a gravel bar in the river.

Link hopped out of the copilot seat and made a sweeping gesture of greeting. "Welcome to the Sheenjek." His grin made him appear boyish. He gestured to the northward, toward rugged, snow-capped mountains, which pierced the pale blue sky. "The home of the snow that spawns rivers." He helped Carmen disembark.

Jacqueline marveled at the sheer exuberance in Link's voice and demeanor. Adam had hated desolate areas, and had only agreed to do the desert study because he viewed it as a stepping-stone to a lucrative spot on the lecture circuit and stays in five star hotels. She stood on the Cessna's pontoon looking at the crystal-clear water, remembering other streams that had been lovely and frigid like this one – streams that her parents had pulled her from when they moved to the city. A wave of homesickness burst over her with such force that her vision blurred.

"Right," Carmen's laugh sounded loud and somewhat forced. "I hope you don't expect anyone to believe that whopper.

"Seriously, the Sheenjek is spawned by glaciers at the continental divide." Link gestured toward the river. "The water is cold as all get out, so I hope you don't plan on a lot of swimming."

"Playing fish isn't on my list of goals," Carmen said.

Stone helped Tempest and Phillip deplane, then while they unloaded gear, Jacqueline worked next to Link in silence until she could trust her voice not to quiver. "What do you like best about the river?"

"It's not apparent right now, but this is designated a wild river. I love putting on a wetsuit and riding it." Jacqueline studied the placid water surrounding the gravel bar and wished he hadn't just mentioned one of her favorite things. The way he seemed to enjoy the things she loved seemed eerie. He tweaked her ponytail. "Don't worry, this isn't the season for a rough ride."

"Is the scenery like this the whole way?" Carmen asked.

"Mountains for now, then forested foothills just before it joins the Porcupine," Jacqueline said.

"Ouch." Carmen said, as she pretended to pluck out a quill.

Link looked at her in surprise. "You know this river?"

"I've studied maps." And fantasized about canoeing it when the water ran high.

Eyes filled with laughter, Carmen rubbed her backside and mimed pain. "Please tell me it doesn't have quills."

"Do you classify rocks and an occasional log jams as quills?" Link teased. She pouted and nodded. They both laughed.

"Hey, are we going to finish offloading this bird so I can get out of here, or what?" Stone demanded.

"Offload," the three said in unison.

Link lightly touched Jacqueline's arm then indicated she and Carmen should carry the gear to higher ground. The casual contact warmed her. As

Jacqueline trudged up the slope, she wondered if a person could transmit their inner tenderness by a simple touch.

After the Cessna was only a tiny speck in the sky, they erected two dome tents. Carmen and Tempest immediately deposited their gear. But the air smelled fresh as a sunrise and the sun felt warm as life, so Jacqueline climbed onto a nearby boulder and turned her face to the breeze. Closing her eyes, she soaked in the harmony of nature.

"No way I'm sleeping next to her." Tempest's angry voice drifted from inside the nylon dome. "Last night was enough. She ... she... she snores!" Jacqueline looked to see who had heard the exchange. Link looked up from connecting the propane cylinder to the camp stove. When he glanced from the tent to her, Jacqueline's face heated. Link smiled. She shrugged, but her face still felt hot.

"Fine," Carmen said, "I'll take the middle."

"She'll still be in here."

"Which side do you want? Left or right?"

"Listen to me, bitch," Tempest screeched. "I will not sleep in here."

Jacqueline squeezed her eyelids tight closed. Why hadn't Adam told her she snored? Jacqueline stood up, brushed off her pants, then headed back to the gravel bar. When she heard footsteps behind her, she braced for another round of verbal assault.

"Do you know how to inflate canoes?" Link's voice came from the proximity of her elbow.

"Of course."

Link tilted his head toward their gear, his posture an invitation. How loudly did she snore? It must be thunderous to generate so much hostility. Jacqueline felt her burning cheeks heat as she unbuckled the gear bag. Tempest emerged from the tent, glared in her direction then gave Link a sunny smile.

When she'd fled from her unseen stalker, she hadn't appreciated how peaceful quiet could be. Tempest sashayed over to Link as if she didn't have a care in the world. The girl hunkered down next to Link and proceeded to speak softly and giggle.

It was going to be a long two weeks and probably not particularly quiet or peaceful. Jacqueline sighed and began inflating the first canoe.

"Carmen and I are going for a walk," Phillip announced, his can of pepper spray clutched in his right fist. Jacqueline's lips twitched so hard, she turned back to finish inflating the canoe before anyone noticed. "Anyone want to come along?"

Tempest started shaking her head but when Link stood up and brushed his palms on his jeans, she scrambled up, saying, "Me! I want to go." She jogged to Phillip and Carmen.

Link ducked into his tent almost immediately reappearing with his rifle. While he sauntered toward the others Tempest shifted from foot to foot in anticipation, then he handed his rifle to Carmen. Tempest's look turned confused when Carmen shouldered the weapon as if she'd carried one before. "Be careful," Link said. Carmen nodded and took a step toward the game trail. Link picked up his fishing pole, then moved in the opposite direction. Tempest took a step after him. He grabbed her by the shoulder and gave her a soft shove toward the others.

"No, I want to stay with you," Tempest yelped.

Link shook his head. "Not this time." He gently pushed Tempest toward his sister and Phillip. When she became agitated, Link leaned over and whispered, "They need your good eyes to keep them out of trouble." He made a shooing motion. "Go." Mouth flat, Tempest sulked after the others. Before she got caught watching, Jacqueline turned back to her project. A shadow blocked the thin light. "I want to explain about Tempest," Link said.

"Don't bother, she explained everything last night."

"I see." Link hunkered down and sat back on his heels. "What was her version?"

His presence made Jacqueline's hands shaky. "Don't you have something to do?" She looked meaningfully at his fishing rod.

"I heard about the threats Tempest made to you, and— " He looked at the kid's rigid shoulders. "You see how she acts." He tried to get her to look at him, but she evaded his gaze. "Mind listening to my side?"

"What do you want to tell me?" she asked, focusing on the canoe as if it required total concentration.

Link stood up, paced to the riverbank, thrust his hands into his back pockets, then stared at a distant snowcapped peak with as much attention as she'd given the canoe. "Ariel thinks Tempest has a crush on me."

He thought this was news? Jacqueline wiped her sweaty palms on her denim-clad thighs. "What do you think?"

"At first I wanted to laugh because the idea was so ridiculous, but then..." Link shook his head. He cleared his throat. "I've always thought of Tempest as a niece." Link turned and looked her in the eye. "I love the kid, but not like that."

"Why are you telling me?"

"I need your help," he said. Jacqueline blinked in surprise. "Distract her," Link said. "I need time to figure out a way to set her straight."

Jacqueline stifled a laugh at the preposterous idea of the kid accepting her help. "In case you haven't noticed, she hates me. There's no way I can help with her. Ask Carmen."

"I already did." He gave the hikers a significant look. "Your interests are similar to Tempest's, you could- "

"Link, stop avoiding the issue. Be blunt. Tell the kid how you feel. Then tell her again and again and again. However many times it takes until she hears what you're saying." He took a step backward, as if she'd slapped him. She straightened and followed him. "Don't just tell her with words; if … no, when, she does something that irritates you, tell her right then and there. Do not put up with her attitude in either word or action."

"I don't know if I-"

"Do not tell me you can't." She glared at him. "You can do it. You did it with me when I wanted to be left in Valdez."

"Sorry."

"Don't apologize." She took a deep breath and admitted, "You were right. Ignoring things only makes them worse."

His expression looked worried.

Jacqueline took a deep breath and softened her tone. "When I was young I hated it when people tried beating around the bush or hiding their feelings."

"I wouldn't want to hurt her."

"Then quit letting her believe a lie." She messaged her temple. "You're the adult. The one in control. So, quit letting her manipulate you. By doing so, you're hurting both her and yourself." He shook his head, she signaled him to be quiet and hear her out. "You're repressing your true feelings. That's never good." Seeing his expression, Jacqueline sighed. "Sorry. I'll put that soapbox away."

"Don't apologize for saying something I needed to hear." He studied her. "What else do you think?"

He appeared serious. "I like Tempest," Jacqueline lied. At least she could tolerate the kid for two weeks, maybe even without tipping her into the frigid water. "Obviously, you do, too." He gave a curt nod, making her wonder how badly the kid was getting on his nerves. She took a deep breath of the crystal clear air, then asked, "Which is easier: facing the truth after a month of delusion, or after years?"

He scowled as if he didn't like that idea. "You're right," he said, though his tone did not sound convinced.

"When I was young, I was obsessed with an actor." Heat crept up her neck.

Link grinned. "Who?"

"No one I'll admit to." Jacqueline fanned away her embarrassment. "Anyway, my mother discovered I was writing this guy." Link looked amused but mystified by her confession. "I wrote him a passionate letter every day." It felt very hot under her collar.

"And?" Link's eyes twinkled with amusement.

"Mom read a letter I hadn't had a chance to post." Jacqueline cleared her throat. "Specifically, Mom read it out loud, using a breathless tone." Her entire face burned at the memory of her mother's rendition and how asinine her overblown prose had sounded. It had been the most humiliating five minutes of her teenage life. Jacqueline shook her head at the memory, then with a laugh, transformed her embarrassment into shared amusement. "My sentiments sounded incredibly absurd." She fanned her face. What an innocent she'd been. "Mom then pointed out the difference between an actor and the part." Heat crept farther up her cheeks. "You see, I'd been posting love letters to a fictional character. The man who played the part had a reputation for being an obnoxious drunk and bully."

"I guess we all had experiences like that."

"You wrote love letters to a fictional character, too?"

He laughed as he made a 'sorta' motion with his hand.

A bush plane passed low overhead; Link glanced up and waved. "Looks like we won't have the river to ourselves."

Jacqueline shrugged off the irrelevant comment. "My point was that my mother loved me enough to tell me the truth and I'm certain it was better to learn the truth as soon as possible rather than continuing to act like a fool."

"Do you have any ideas about how I can change her attitude? Your mother's solution was great, but I don't think it'll work for me since I am who I am, not some Hollywood hunk of fiction."

"How do you want Tempest to think of you?"

"As an uncle."

An uncle … from what she'd heard, a vast majority of pedophiles preferred that title. She eased back to study him. "What does she do that violates your interpretation of how an uncle should be treated?"

Link uneasily glanced down the path the other three had taken. No one was in sight. He grimaced. "She likes to hug me and kiss my cheek." He hastened to add, "But she does that to all of us, so I guess it's just her way." He shrugged. "She's always done it." His brow furrowed. "It didn't bother me when she was younger, but now..." He shook his head. "And then there's the touching." Link couldn't meet her eyes.

Her blood chilled. "Touching?" Sensing the next few comments could lead her to the heart of the truth, Jacqueline used her softest, calmest tone. "Pinching?

Punching? Fondling? Tickling? Petting?"

"All on occasion. Did you watch her just now? How she grabbed my sleeve and tugged on it to get attention. The way she always seems to have her hands on me is getting to be a pet peeve." He scowled. "Plus, she likes to sit on my lap. She does it to everyone, but mostly to me."

"So what you're saying is that Tempest is a touchy-feely person and since you aren't, it irritates you."

He frowned. "I never noticed until Ariel pointed it out. Since she did..." A look of revulsion crossed his face.

Okay, so perhaps he wasn't a pedophile, or he was one, who was trying to mask his true nature by claiming the kid was the problem. "You've known Tempest since she was small, and while you still see her as a kid, she no longer sees herself that way. Does that about cover what you're trying to explain?" Link looked at her as if she held the answers to the mysteries of the universe and nodded.

"Pretty much."

"Tell her," Jacqueline said.

"What should I say?"

"Whatever you feel in your heart."

Link closed his eyes and shook his head. "I don't think I can."

Or he didn't really want to. "You'll have to sooner or later." At least he would if the kid was actually the only one pursuing the touching. "Sooner is best."

"Like honest is always best?" She nodded. He grimaced. "But how do I talk with her about this without hurting her feelings?"

"First off, you're probably going to hurt her feelings one way or the other, so accept that as a given. Secondly, why are you willing to hurt your own feelings? Are they less valuable than hers?" Or was his excuse with the expectation that she wouldn't see him for what he might be? "Wait until she does something that makes you uncomfortable, then speak up right then and there. Tell her she's growing up, and the behavior is no longer appropriate."

"Put that way, it sounds simple." He studied her. "If someone you'd had an infatuation with had said that to you, would it have worked?"

"I'm not sure," Jacqueline admitted. "It would now, and I don't think I've changed that much since I was her age." The corners of his lips twitched in a way that made her clench her hands. "But I'm not Tempest. I've always appreciated honesty, no matter how blunt and direct it is, but I don't know what will work with her." Link's warm brown eyes begged her for a more precise answer. Was he trying to make it look like she'd be the guilty one if something happened … assuming it hadn't already? "You know her better than anyone else within a couple hundred miles. What do you think will work best?"

"Hitting her with a 2 by 4 would be efficient," he joked.

"Well, if you prefer blood and guts to hurt feelings…" Jacqueline made a big production of looking around their campsite. "Sorry, we didn't bring any lumber and it's too far north for driftwood." To her surprise, Link laughed and hugged her. After so many lonely months, it felt wonderful to have strong arms around her. Before she thought about it, Jacqueline hugged him back. His arms tightened for a moment before he let her go.

As she stepped back, Jacqueline had the compulsion to pat her hair and smooth her clothing. She hadn't worried about those things in years.

Obviously, Tempest wasn't the only touchy-feely one in camp.

7

Tempest shrieked, "Uncle Link!" He felt his body tense as he looked over his shoulder. Agile as a cat, the kid leapt over a rock, then hurtled down the narrow, rugged path, which mountain goats probably considered a superhighway. Carmen and Phillip, who were several yards behind, waved. Link waved back.

He turned back to Jacqueline, but she was walking away, as if trying to put as much distance between them as possible. He wanted to follow her, but her advice still rang in his mind, 'You'll have to sooner or later. Sooner is best.' With a sigh, Link positioned his feet to withstand the inevitable assault, but didn't put out his arms to catch her.

Tempest checked her momentum a fraction of an instant before she leaped at him. Her thin arms clamped around his ribs like the jaws of a bear trap, binding his arms to his sides. Her embrace felt completely inappropriate. Wrong. Nothing like the quick, friendly hug he'd given Jacqueline.

Arms glued against his side, Link wondered how long it would take Tempest to understand his unspoken message to stop. Link looked down at Tempest's wind-whipped hair, hoping for a miracle. 'What does she do that violates your interpretation of how an uncle should be treated?' The better question was 'what doesn't she *do?*' Jaws clamped against a tirade of frustration, he raised his gaze to the horizon where Jacqueline was skipping pebbles across a calm expanse of water. 'When I was young I hated it when people tried beating around the bush or hiding their feelings.' Link swallowed, then wrenched his arms free, gripped Tempest's narrow shoulders and thrust her away. Burrs came off easier. "We need to talk." Something in her eyes reminded him of a wild animal sensing danger. Tempest shook her head and tried to regain her hold on him. "Stop it."

"No." She lunged for him, but he was stronger and managed to hold her at arm's distance.

She looked over her shoulder. When she turned back to him, fury filled her expression. "She poisoned you against me. I hate her."

"Who?"

"That bitch, that's who." Tempest's face turned purple with rage, her hands fisted, as she whirled out of his grasp and leaped toward the gravel bar.

Link lunged, barely catching her before she did something totally stupid. "Jacqueline has nothing to do with what I want to talk about."

"Yes, she does." It was like trying to hold a wildcat. "Everything was fine until you brought her home."

"What are you talking about?"

"Her. I warned her I'd kill her. And I will."

"Whoa up there." Link tried to figure out what Tempest was screaming about. "I like hugs. But you are growing up and your hugs make me feel uncomfortable." Tempest clawed at his hand, as if it scorched her shoulder. "I'll let you go when you promise me you'll leave Jacqueline alone."

Tempest's ears turned crimson. "You have to leave her alone, too!" She swiped at her eyes. "Don't think I didn't see you!"

"You need to listen to what I tell you." Her body stiffened. "We need to talk about our relationship." She looked from him to Jacqueline. "Tempest, I love you. You know that."

"Yes." Her wooden tone implied an unspoken 'but'.

Carmen and Phillip's footfalls were nearing. "This is between you and me. No one else." He released one shoulder and held out his hand. "Let's take a walk." Tempest smacked his hand away, then turned to face him; her expression bespoke an internal battle. He held out his hand, again. Finally, she gave a jerky nod, but her clenched fists remained at her sides. Sensing that he no longer needed to hold her, Link relaxed his aching fingers.

Tempest took a step away from him. Her jaw jutted up. Link sighed. "If you want me to say what I need to tell you in public, so be it."

Tempest's eyes widened and she gulped. "No!" Tempest fled back up the path that, moments before, she'd trotted down with such gleeful abandon.

He sprinted after her.

When she dodged around Phillip, Carmen stepped off the path. Tempest stumbled as she dashed past. Link's longer legs closed the gap, and he nearly had her in reach when Carmen caught his arm. He tried to wrench free, but she yanked him off balance. "She isn't going anyplace," Carmen said. Again, he tried to pull free, but her grip held, her nails biting through his thick denim shirt. "Take a minute to think. What will you say when you catch her? Figure it out now. Then, in a minute, when you catch her, don't sugarcoat it."

"It's not your business."

"The circumstances make it— "

"You asked to come."

"Because I want your help."

"With what?"

Carmen gave Phillip's back a significant look, then leaned closes to him. "Making a decision. Facing truths." In a soft whisper, she added, "My problem can wait for a while." She tilted her head toward the hilltop. "Hers can't." Carmen smiled. The pressure on his arm decreased. "Her problem is puppy love, but you'll never convince her it's not the real thing. She probably won't understand for years." She sighed. "Maybe ..." Carmen made a helpless gesture. "I mean, how do you tell which sort of love is which?"

"Beats me. Maybe you should talk to Jacqueline. For a kid, she's damned bright about relationships. One warning though, she asks questions you're afraid to think about." He sighed. "They're also the ones that you need to know the answers to."

Carmen gave him a lopsided smile. "Sounds like a chat with her is just what I need." She handed him the rifle. "Go to Tempest and tell her what you must."

How he could have forgotten something so basic when he was in bear country? "Thanks." Link slung the carbine over his shoulder and jogged after Tempest.

He caught sight of her quivering emerald shirt a short distance up the trail. It looked like she'd dumped her clothing on top of a boulder. When he squinted, he realized she was bent double. Worse, her shoulders were heaving as if she were crying her eyes out. "Shit." Emotions weren't like mechanical problems that could be fixed by repairing or replacing a part. Link kicked a clump of lichen and wished people were more like emotionless machines.

Link took his time climbing the rest of the way, then

leaned against a rock near Tempest and waited for her to get over her hysterics. Her sobs intensified. Something told him that the platitudes he'd used in the past had helped cause the current problem and if he voiced one now, it would prolong the ordeal for both of them. He gazed at the distant horizon's jagged peaks, trying to block out her tantrum.

Tempest wept louder. A chill ran down his spine and the hairs on the back of his neck quivered. Link gritted his teeth and willed himself to endure her theatrics. Tempest howled loud enough to melt bone. Her voice echoed off the rocks and boulders in a chorus of misery. The mountains in the Brooks Range were created during a cataclysm millions of years before. Had the harsh landscape resulted from one of Nature's adolescent tantrums?

He shifted against the uncomfortable rock.

Tempest's caterwauling gained a desperate tone.

Link rubbed his arms. "Cold wind." He doubted if Tempest heard him over her wild, theatrical weeping. "When I like someone, I touch them."

"Aaaugghhh."

The gut wrenching sound skewered every cell in his body. He forced a calm tone. "I slap Stone on the back, or punch his biceps. I give Ariel brotherly hugs and kiss her on the forehead."

"Aaaaaaeeeeuugghhh." Tempest quivered as if she'd gutted herself.

Talking in a low, gentle pitch was harder than facing down a grizzly. "Even though we aren't technically related, I think of you as my niece. You've known that for a long time."

"Aaaeeeugghh!" She let out a piercing scream, which left his eardrums humming.

His patience snapped. "But if you keep acting like a raving lunatic, I'll disown you."

Her head shot up. Her eyes blazed with fury above dry red cheeks. The rotten imp had been pretending her heart was broken, trying to wrench his heartstrings. Trying to manipulate him. His jaw tensed so hard that he bit the inside of his cheek.

"Raving lunatic!" Tempest shook a balled fist at him. "How dare you call me that?" Perversely, Link felt like laughing in her face. "Take that back."

He shook his head. How could he take it back, when every word and gesture proved the remark?

"How dare you call me a raving lunatic!" In the distance, a flock of ducks took off in apparent panic. Drops of water fell from their legs and briefly glistened in the sun. "You think I'm a raving lunatic?" He arched a brow. Hands fisted, Tempest vaulted from the rock. He hardened his stomach muscles a moment before first punch landed. She pummeled his abdomen and arms, one hit per word. "How dare you. I hate you. I hate, hate, hate you." Link absorbed the hits and kept his hands at his sides.

She shook her fist in his face. "Answer me, dammit. Tell me you don't really think I'm a raving lunatic!"

Link grabbed both of her hands with one hand of his and her chin with the other. He tilted her head back until he could look her in the eye. He wished he could fly away like the ducks instead of deal with this wild child. "Do you think I like people who scream and hit?"

"Aaaeeeeeuugghh!" Tempest's bawl vibrated every cell of his body, severely testing his resolve. Then, her legs gave way and she landed on the ground in a dejected-looking heap.

Sensing that she needed time to calm down, he forced himself to remain calm and quiet. It was the hardest thing he had ever done.

She rubbed her cracked, red knuckles.

She sniffed.

The tension slowly ebbed from his body, replaced by a strong sense of concern for the kid, who'd had a miserable childhood. He offered her his hand. In a blink, Tempest leaped at him, trying to claw his face. He fended her off. Fists pummeling, she punched his chest. This time, her punches held more strength. Perspiration streamed down her face. He grabbed her wrists, again, and held her away. She fought like a marlin. Finally, she gave up, but was this another sham or the real thing?

"Are you done?" Dear God, let the answer be yes.

"No." She gasped for breath. "Not until you take that back."

"How can I take it back when every scream and assault reinforces the observation?"

She kicked at his crotch.

Link barely managed to evade the blow, but in the process of protecting himself, she got her hands free. Her fist connected with his left shoulder, and he fell back against a boulder.

Enough was enough.

Link grabbed her hands and held them in a crushing grip.

She screeched with real pain and struggled for freedom. "From now on, you'll get treated the way your actions deserve. Right now, that's a rabid dog or a raving lunatic," he said between clinched teeth. "What I'd really like to do is spank you, but I won't, because I refuse to lower myself to your level."

This time, Tempest's wails sounded real.

Link closed his eyes and counted to ten. The crying continued, as did the frantic wiggling. So, he continued on to twenty, Link fought the urge to slap some sense into Tempest, but the more he fought the desire, the more he wanted to. In self-defense, he pushed her away.

She stumbled backward a few steps, then came at him again.

He grabbed her wrists, again, but as he noticed the bruising was already beginning to show, he held her as gently as her behavior made possible, which wasn't soft enough to avoid more damage. "What is wrong with you?" he demanded in frustration.

"I hate you."

"Stop acting demon possessed or I'll give you a spanking you'll never forget."

"You wouldn't dare."

"With the way you've been acting?" He snorted. "If you were an animal, I'd have put you out of your misery by now."

"You mean you'd have shot me?"

Never taking his attention from her, he gave a decisive nod. "In a heartbeat." Tempest's eyes widened until the irises were islands in a sea of white. The silence after all the caterwauling seemed eerie. "Sit down." Link released her and pointed at the rock she'd previously occupied. "Listen to me. And don't make a sound. Got it?"

She shifted her feet uncomfortably.

He glared at her.

She hopped onto the rock. The expression on her face indicated that sitting on the boulder was equivalent to lying on a nest of vipers.

Link took a deep breath. "Tempest, I've never been more ashamed of anyone than I've recently been of you."

Her mouth flattened into a thin angry line. "Last year, I didn't think anything of the way you threw yourself at me." Her gaze darted to him, then quickly moved away. "But now you're becoming a young woman." Link rubbed the rigid muscles at the back of his neck. "You've stopped dressing in the baggy crap and started dressing like an adult, it's time to dump the little kid routine, too."

She stiffened, until her spine was more militaristically straight than Mavis'. And if she'd had Mavis' letter opener, it would now be lodged in his heart.

"When you throw yourself at me, it makes me uncomfortable." He took a deep breath. "Women don't hug men that way unless they..." He threw up his hands. "They just don't. Now that you're more of a woman instead of a child, you need to act like one." He looked her in the eye. "Do you understand what I'm trying to say?"

Mouth pressed in a thin, angry line, Tempest gave a short jerky nod.

"Would you like to say something?"

"You told me to shut up," she snarled.

While he was certain he hadn't used that specific phrase, Link suspected he might as well have. "Now that you've listened to me, I'd like to hear what you think."

"That Jacqueline bitch put you up to this, didn't she?" Tempest glared down the slope, at their camp. "Didn't she?"

"Why do you keep bringing her up when this is between you and me?"

"She's jealous of us. I saw it in her eyes when I first met her." Tempest faced him. The anger in her glare made his stomach clench.

"What's there to be jealous of?"

"You can't be that stupid."

"You're my niece, why should she care?"

"Niece!" Tempest's mouth worked as if she were chewing filth.

"Okay, so we aren't technically related. But I never thought that mattered."

She spat toward the camp. "That's what I think of her. I don't know why you had to bring her along."

"I wasn't thrilled about that at first, either, but then I wasn't happy about— " He didn't dare finish the thought.

"You didn't want me?" Fear and disbelief fought for dominance.

"This was supposed to be a guys only trip, focused on fishing." *'When I was young I hated it when people tried beating around the bush or hiding their feelings.'* Jacqueline's statement echoing in his thoughts, Link declared, "This definitely isn't the vacation I planned or wanted." A tear fell from the corner of Tempest's eye. The bitterness he'd felt since Carmen and then Stone had guilted him into asking her and Phillip along shimmered like an invisible barrier between them.

As the silence lengthened, Tempest's face turned red. "Ariel and Stone didn't want to take me with them either."

Was that the core of the problem? Did Tempest feel like no one wanted her? Or was this just another way to play his emotions? "Growing up is tough," Link said. "Suddenly, we aren't little kids that people dote on, and we have to stand on our own two feet."

She sniffed as she lowered her gaze. "Uncle Link, I love you."

He stepped forward and stroked her hair. "I love you - as a niece. If I didn't care, I wouldn't bother talking to you. Understand?"

Her lower lip trembled. "Yes." Fast as the Sheenjek

flowing past their camp, tears streamed down her cheeks.

Link shifted his gaze to the distant gleam of the river. Were these tears another form of manipulation? Was Tempest testing every feminine trick in her teenage arsenal on him? He silently counted: 1, 2, 3, 4, 5, 6, 7, and on. At 50, the tears finally stopped. He continued to 75.

He shouldered his rifle. "Ready to head back to camp?"

"No." Tempest sniffed. "I'll be along in a minute."

"Don't be long. Polar bears might have been attracted when you sounded like a wounded buffalo."

She looked around with interest. Link doubted if any game was left in a three-mile radius of her tantrum. In fact, he suspected her howling could have scared off the devil himself, but he wasn't about to admit that, nor, after all the roll-playing she'd done and her swift jumps between love and hate, was he going to give her his rifle.

Which meant that he needed to stay nearby to protect her.

But not too near. Dealing with her emotional explosion had drained him, so Link started walking toward camp, grateful to have the worst hysterical episode he'd ever imagined behind him. As he rounded the first boulder, he came face to face with Jacqueline. She held her finger to her lips in a shushing gesture. Link had seen hundreds of people put their finger over their lips, but when Jacqueline did it, it appeared erotic. Without thinking, he gathered her into his arms, and kissed her. Warmth burst through his frozen flesh and a bright shimmering cascade of relief tumbled through his mind.

Link clasped her closer and intensified the kiss.

For a tantalizing moment, Jacqueline's lips opened in response to his need for solace, then she stiffened and pushed against his chest. "Stop." Her lips moved softly against his own. "If Tempest sees you, she'll think the worst."

Every whispered syllable caressed his lips with tiny bursts of air. He hugged her tighter. Jacqueline pushed him harder.

He kissed her harder.

She stomped on his instep. A moment later her knee started toward his most vulnerable spot. Link reflexively moved.

She leaped away, her expression suspicious.

Good God, what had he been thinking kissing a kid that way? "Sorry," he said, "I don't know what came over me." Or why he still wanted to kiss her. Hold her. Find himself in her.

Jacqueline watched him, as if expecting an attack. Fearful that his need to touch her would overcome his common sense, Link shoved his hands in his pockets. Her wariness decreased, but his arms felt empty and his soul felt as barren as the windswept rocks.

"Why are you here?" he whispered.

"I heard -" She bit her lower lip, then started again, "I thought someone was being murdered." She patted the handgun tucked into her waistband. "By the time I figured out it was just a tantrum, Tempest had quieted down, and I was afraid to leave." Jacqueline's cheeks flushed an endearing shade of red. "I didn't intend to eavesdrop."

Link rubbed his ear. "Loud as she was, I expect some seismologist in Washington State is analyzing the strange readings on his Richter graph."

Jacqueline's posture relaxed as she smiled. "That was the worst case of PTS I'd ever heard, but you handled her well."

A rock shot past, missing Jacqueline's shoulder by mere inches. Jacqueline jumped away, gave Tempest a hard look, then headed back toward camp.

Tempest made an ugly face at Jacqueline's back.

Link wondered if anything had been resolved.

8

Hearing a stealthy noise, Jacqueline pirouetted while drawing her Walther. A clump of wind-blown grass trembled in her sights. She glanced around to see if anyone had observed her. Thankfully, Tempest was ignoring her, and Link appeared to be lost in thought. Jacqueline shoved the gold damascened pistol back into its place, next to her spine, then ran the tip of her tongue over her lower lip. She tasted Link.

Gooseflesh danced across her body. She told herself Link's kiss had not meant anything to her. High above, a raven shrieked. Its taunt seemed to say 'nothing to him, everything to you'. Link had kissed her with mind-numbing passion to release tension. She wished she could erase the tactile memory.

She had two weeks before she returned to Valdez.

Two weeks to think and plan.

Two weeks to find a way to to release herself from her faceless stalker's terrorizing influence.

Two weeks before her stalker could pick up her trail; she should use this time to get her thoughts in line so she was in an emotional position to regain control over her destiny. She squared her shoulders. She would not waste her time on her grandmother's poorly disguised matchmaking scheme, no matter how well Link kissed.

No longer would she think of this trip as a waste of time, it would become an opportunity.

Jacqueline glanced at Link. The last thing she needed during the next two weeks was to get distracted by some stud-muffin of a possible pedophile, who treated her like a kid half the time and like the lust of his life the rest of the time.

She inhaled deeply and tasted Link. Wild, primitive emotions cascaded through her until her forehead beaded with perspiration. She gritted her teeth and willed her legs to move away from him. Relief grew with each step she put between herself and temptation.

You're acting like you've never been kissed.

Her hiking boot connected with a rock. The stone skittered down the trail, then thudded against a boulder and stopped in a tiny cloud of dust. She wished the tactile memory would settle as quickly as the dirt. What was wrong with her? She wasn't some ditsy teenager.

She wished her grandmother had never suggested this trip.

Wished Link had let her stay in Valdez to deal with her stalker.

Wished she'd never thought to run to the security of the person, who had always made her feel safe. If it hadn't been for the faceless origami folder, she'd still be looking for a new home and job, but at least she'd have access to her contacts and a cellphone signal. Jacqueline wished the stalker didn't exist.

She shook her head. If she was going to wish for something, she should go farther back and wish that the lab-office building hadn't burned and Adam hadn't died. But wishes were for children watching shooting stars. What she needed was to turn this into a positive situation and spend the coming weeks figuring out a plan for her future; one that she wanted, not one Adam had chosen.

A breeze brought Link's calm voice wafting across

the tundra. "When we get back to camp, you can help me cook." Her perspiration chilled.

Jacqueline hurried into their camp, past Link's tent, hopped over Phillip's legs, as he sprawled near the campfire, reading on his iPad, then spotted Carmen, who was sitting near the river, gazing into the water, as if it held the answers to all life's questions. Adrenaline gushed through her system giving her a jittery feeling. Jacqueline jogged to the shoreline, then veered away from Carmen and followed the river's course upstream. Her body hadn't felt this alien since she'd had her own case of PTS. She arrived at a peaceful sandbar, and paused. A chill gripped her. She wrapped her arms around her stomach then began pacing the bank, while she centered her emotions.

"I take it that my stupid brother and the brat are okay." Carmen, who had crept up behind her, grinned as she whirled to face her. "Too bad the kid is okay."

"Why?"

Carmen's warm look reminded Jacqueline of brownies fresh from the oven and full of delicious heat. "If the brat is anything like I was at that age, she only views this howling match as a minor setback."

"Been there? Done that?"

"Oh, yeah." Carmen sighed.

"Me, too." Remembering some of the more foolish things she'd done when her own hormones struck, her neck heated. "It's a wonder someone didn't strangle me."

"Sheesh, when I heard that kid…." Carmen hugged herself while craning her neck, as if she was looking to see if anyone else might be listening.

Jacqueline sighed. "It was a loud tantrum."

They glanced at the trail, where Link walked as if deep in thought, and Tempest kicked pebbles, as if trying to pulverize them. Carmen chewed her lower lip. "At first I liked the kid, but now I'm wondering why he brought her." Carmen's mouth flattened. "Maybe I'm just being selfish."

"How?"

"I wanted Link to get to know Phillip, but it looks like he's going to have to spend all his time dealing with that juvenile delinquent."

"You're serious about Phillip."

"I love him. And I want to marry him." Carmen's tone sounded defeated. "But you don't need to hear about that. I guess I'd better get back to camp."

Jacqueline fell into step with Carmen. They traveled the short distance to the front of their tent before she asked, "What's the problem?"

Carmen shrugged and dropped her voice to a conspiratorial level. "If I knew the answer to that, I wouldn't need Link. I figured he could give me the male perspective." Jacqueline had to lean close to hear her. "But he hated Phillip from first sight, so— " Her eyes watered. Unable to continue, she ducked into the tent.

Jacqueline followed her into the canvas cocoon. "Can I help?"

Carmen wiped away a tear and gave her a lopsided smile, then whispered, "I don't think anyone can."

Jacqueline frowned. "Can you define the problem?"

"I'm not sure." Carmen wiped away another tear. "Phillip and I have been going together for months. Doesn't that sound adolescent? Going together? That's Phillip's term for it, not mine. We're both twenty-seven, not seven or even seventeen. I want a husband and children, not some childish relationship. And I want Phillip." Her eyes filled. "It seems so hopeless."

"What did you expect Link to do? Hold a shotgun

against Phillip's back while he repeats vows?" Jacqueline widened her eyes to show that she was joking. "I mean this is Alaska and things get done sorta rough up here. Why I hear some hermits still order mail-order brides."

Carmen's laugh ended in a sniffle. "I want Link to get to know Phillip, and tell me if I'm wasting my time waiting for him."

"I don't understand."

"Phillip is different from anyone I've ever dated. He's serious. Practical. Creative. Cautious. While I'm a happy-go-lucky, romantic, impetuous and the most creative thing I've ever done is stick silk poinsettias into the Christmas tree for ornaments after I dropped the box of glass ones" Carmen sighed and knelt next to her duffel. "Maybe I'm desperate. Maybe my biological clock is ruling my mind. I don't know."

"And you figured Link would know?" Carmen nodded and began rocking on her heels. Jacqueline blinked, unable to imagine asking her brother for relationship advice. After all, Rory had detested Adam from the moment he'd met him. "You should know what's right for you better than anyone else."

"Link said you were smart for a kid."

"I've told him I'm twenty-five." Jacqueline shook her head in disbelief. "He still called me a kid?" Was that how he thought of her? Gooseflesh rippled across her body. He wouldn't be the first who didn't believe how old she was... If he was a pedophile and honestly thought she was a kid, it would explain why he treated her the way he did. She dug into her duffle bag, extracted her wallet and pulled out her driver's license.

Carmen squinted at the birth date. "Don't ask me why he called you a kid, maybe it's just some expression he picked up. Some days, I don't know why I do or say something, let alone why anyone else does."

Or maybe he just liked kids… she had to get Link and his possible issues out of her mind and deal with her own life, but Carmen's problem baffled her and unless she understood that, she'd never be able to properly focus on her own issues. "Do you think your maternal instinct is kicking in, telling you to reproduce?" The canvas undulated.

Carmen dabbed the corner of her eye. "Until I met Phillip, I never wanted to settle down or start a family. I don't know if I feel this way now because he's my Mr. Right, or if it's just a timing coincidence with my biological clock."

"Until you met him, you never wanted kids?"

"Never." Carmen sighed. "Of course, I never dated anyone like Phillip, before, either. I'd always dated jock types. I understand them, because they're so much like my father and brothers."

Jacqueline chuckled at the idea of Link being considered a jock. "My image of jock is nearer Neanderthal; a guy wearing his favorite team's jersey, while screaming at the ref on Sunday football and stuffing his face with chips and beer. What's your definition?"

"Someone whose body is as active as their mind."

"I call those guys well balanced."

"Call them whatever suits you. In case you're interested, Link's jersey is from Texas A & M and he prefers nachos over chips, but his favorite beer is Bud, though I've often heard him joke that he started drinking it because he thought the frog on the old commercials was cute."

"Hmmm. I always liked their Clydesdales." Carmen's expression turned from amused to strained, so Jacqueline changed the subject, "How did you meet

Phillip?"

"I had a flat tire. I'd just gotten out to fix it when he jogged by." A gentle smile lit Carmen's lips. "Being the gentleman that he is, Phillip offered to repair it for me." Carmen glanced out the tent flap. "He didn't know how to change a tire and he kept trying to take off the lug nuts by tightening them. It was sorta funny and endearing." Carmen put her fingers over her mouth, but the chuckle escaped. She shook her head. "Phillip had the greatest legs I'd ever seen, so naturally, I didn't tell him why the bolts seemed so tight. When it looked like he was frustrated enough to leave, I suggested that maybe lug nuts were like mayonnaise lids, which turn counter clockwise to come off. Then I pretended to be amazed when my suggestion worked."

It felt good to laugh. "How long did it take him to change your tire?"

"At least half an hour." Carmen's eyes glinted with amusement. "I could have had it done in twelve minutes flat. Pun intended." She winked. "Phillip talked the whole time, and I liked listening to him. I still do."

"But your initial interest in him was due to a false impression," Jacqueline said.

"What do you mean?"

"You said that you liked jocks. You met Phillip when he was running. Naturally, you must have thought he fit the profile. He added to that image when he insisted on being macho and changing your tire."

Carmen shook her head. "All this time I've been thinking..." She shook her head. "Underneath all that intellect, he is a jock. Isn't he?" Since Phillip would never fit any box except 'academic' in her mind, Jacqueline shrugged. "I've been looking at him all wrong." Carmen's tone warmed with happiness. "Since he doesn't play football, or any of the rough and tumble sports, I must have started thinking of him as something less than a man. That and the fact that he doesn't pressure me for..." Her face flushed. "You know."

"No Russian hands or Roman fingers?" Jacqueline asked. Carmen's face flamed as she nodded. Jacqueline knew Phillip's type: the academic sort, just like Adam. Since it wasn't her place to warn Carmen about caring for scientists, who valued their work more than the people who loved them and expected others to set aside their own goals, which seemed inferior, Jacqueline bit the insides of her cheeks.

Tempest burst into the tent, saw them and stopped so suddenly she shuffled her feet to maintain balance. "Where's Link?"

"He was with you," Jacqueline said.

Carmen smiled. "Knowing him, he's off with his fishing rod trying to catch our dinner."

Tempest's nose wrinkled in acute distaste. "Fish."

"Yep," Carmen agreed. "He loves fishing better than anything I can think of. Always has. When we were little and Mama couldn't find him, she'd go down to the creek and he'd be sitting under the weeping willow trying to catch dinner. He caught a lot of bass, so we ate fish practically every day. For a while, I thought I'd grow gills."

"Gross," Tempest said.

"Grandma told me he's spent years trying to catch a prize fish." Jacqueline looked at Carmen.

"So much has changed, yet he still loves fishing, but it didn't start out as fun," Carmen said. Tempest moved as far away as she could, without exiting the tent, then back to the curved wall, settled down to listen. "When I was ten, Dad had an accident. At first no one expected him to survive, but he did." Carmen swallowed,

"Except he's a paraplegic." Tempest's face showed a trace for boredom, as if she'd heard this all before.

"I'm so sorry," Jacqueline said.

"It's okay now, but for a long time, it was rough. Really rough. All our lives changed. Link started fishing to put meat on our table. If he hadn't, we'd probably have starved because money was that tight. Mama had been a traditional stay at home mother, but she started cleaning houses and doing anything she could to feed and shelter us. Things were tough and a family of six was a burden. We all knew that, and each of us tried to help as much as we could." Carmen shrugged over her matter-of-fact tale. "Link delivered papers and mowed lawns. He spent all his money on food, and what he couldn't buy, he caught." Her expression was wistful. "I wanted to work too, but I was too young to baby-sit, except for the twins, clean our own house and cook simple stuff."

"But surely that helped," Jacqueline said. "Otherwise your parents would have had to find time to do it or pay someone."

"Funny." Carmen's face twisted into an odd grin. "Lousy as I thought my efforts were, I never looked at it that way. Maybe I did help, at least I got efficient at cleaning and learned not to confuse baking powder with backing soda." Tempest gave her an odd look. "Trust me, there is a huge difference and you do not want to substitute one for the other."

"Like an explosion of something?"

"No, thank goodness! Just the worst possible taste." Carmen shook her head. "We'd have starved without Link."

Tempest's brows knit into a small ridge. "So, Uncle Link was sort'a like your father, because he took care of you?"

"He turned into a petty tyrant, who thought he could tell everyone what to do and how to do it. He was the spitting image of my dad. Thank goodness he grew out of it."

Tempest gave a loud snort.

Jacqueline bit her inner cheeks.

Carmen glanced out the flap and her eyes lit up. Jacqueline turned and saw Phillip, pepper spray tightly gripped in one hand, iPad in the other, apprehensively scanning the horizon. Carmen surged to her feet. "See you later." She ducked out of the tent.

Jacqueline wondered if her eyes had gleamed with love when she looked at Adam.

"You dress like Indiana Jones." The tent amplified the vicious quality of Tempest's words.

"Thank you." Jacqueline slowly turned to face the child, and she prayed for divine guidance to defuse the situation.

Tempest growled. "You look like what you are. A Car Dew. One bitchin' big drip that'll evaporate." Though the words were said with hatred, they struck Jacqueline as hilarious. She felt her lips twitch. "Your jeans are totally grungy," Tempest added. "You look like you've slept in that ugly old shirt for the last year— "

"Actually about the last three years," she interrupted. Tempest's mouth shut like the bite of a snapping turtle. "Since you're interested in zoology," Jacqueline said, "you might like to see a book on Alaskan animals that I brought along." Tempest gave her a look people normally reserved for psychopaths. Jacqueline felt the corners of her mouth twitch up. "It's old, but the information is still accurate." Jacqueline rummaged in her duffel bag, feeling for the book, which she'd packed in the bottom.

"Didn't you hear what I said?" Tempest demanded

"Sure." She found it near the top, just under her notebook. Grandma must have repacked. "Here, Midnight Wilderness." She thrust it toward Tempest. "It's about the Arctic National Wildlife Refuge." Tempest looked as if she was being offered rotten fish.

"Afraid you'll enjoy it?"

Tempest snarled, "I don't want anything of yours. And like I told you, don't take anything of mine."

"Fine. Realize one thing, the five of us are alone here. If we don't start getting along, we're all going to be miserable. Worse, if disaster strikes, the situation could become life threatening. We all need to put aside our differences and get along." She put the book down in front of the brat.

Tempest's expression proclaimed that she'd rather commit murder than practice peace. "You're such a bitch." She grabbed the book and threw it across the small space, barely missing her face, then stormed out of the tent. The book hit the canvas wall with a dull thud, ricocheted and grazed her shoulder before collapsing on top of her sleeping bag.

"I don't know why I try," Jacqueline told the fluttering tent flap. She wiped her damp palms on her thighs, then picked up Midnight Wilderness. As she smoothed the abused pages, a folded yellow paper fell out. Jacqueline's heart stopped. Her joints gave out and she dropped the volume in a haphazard heap just as Link pushed the green nylon aside and peered into the tent.

"Jacqueline, are you any good at cleaning fish?" His presence seemed to fill the shelter. Engulf it. Devour the air.

Jacqueline could only stare at the paper whale lying next to Midnight Wilderness. "What?" Jacqueline fought for breath. Wildly, she told herself that there was plenty of room. But, there wasn't.

"You're white as a ghost." Link hunkered down next to her and put his palm to her forehead. "You're chilled. Did she hurt you? Are you sick?"

She tore her gaze from the paper, looked at Link and shook her head. The concern in his warm eyes sent a spark of heat to her frozen core. "I'm fine," she lied.

"I saw Tempest come out of here. She looked ready to murder something. Are you sure you're okay?" As if he was unwilling to sever his contract with her, Link's hand dropped to her shoulder. Link's thumb traced her jawbone. Heat radiated through her, like the sun melting ice. His other hand brushed her hair away from her face. "Tell me what's wrong."

Jacqueline gestured toward the origami orca. Link frowned, then picked up Midnight Wilderness and leafed through it until he came to a photo of a seal swimming under an iceberg.

She couldn't believe that Link hadn't noticed the horrible yellow threat, which meant that her stalker could contact her anywhere. Jacqueline stared at it and perspired as if suffocating heat filled the tent.

"I read this a few years ago," Link said. "It's good."

"Not the book. That." She pointed to the whale, certain it was emitting invisible tongues of flame and heating the tent. Link picked it up and examined it. The paper looked fragile in his powerful hand. Jacqueline realized how ridiculous her behavior must appear.

Link cleared his throat. "You're into origami?"

"No." Her voice cracked. Surprise evident, his attention riveted on her. Jacqueline wished she knew how to make him understand what finding the note meant to her. "Someone keeps leaving me notes like this." Her throat felt dry.

"It's cute." Link looked from her face to the little leviathan on his palm. He frowned. "Mind if I read it?" Jacqueline nodded. Carefully, Link opened the folds.

9

Link's bewilderment intensified as he scanned the childish scrawl:

Scorching strand. Inferno of
infatuation,
inferno of endearment, inferno of
desire,
inferno of love, inferno of passion,
inferno of ardor, inferno of delight,
Passion's Fire...
you know they are mine. ALL MINE.
This is the last time I will ask.
Return what is mine—
you can't hide from me...
you can't hide from God.

Link looked up from the pleated page, hoping Jacqueline would explain the odd poem, but she was rocking back and forth, arms across her stomach as if in mortal pain. He wanted to scoop her up and hug away the problem, but experience had taught him that hugging kids was more dangerous than canoeing a class five wild river.

Since he didn't want this crazy attraction to go

anywhere, he reread the note. The strange tone made him want to crumple the paper in his fist. Who had given her the note? Why had she brought it along if it upset her? And was she as ill as she appeared? Was it a sordid love poem, as he'd initially thought, or a threat? Though he was certain he'd been the first to unfold the thing, she acted like she knew what it said. "You've gotten more of these?" She managed a rigid nod, but continued rocking and wheezing for air. The tent undulated. Outside, Tempest's tone was shrill as she chatted with Carmen.

Link settled into a more comfortable position and held the note toward her. Jacqueline shrank back as if the paper were contaminated with the plague. He moved the paper away and her terror faded to agitation. Fascinating how the paper frightened her. "How many have you gotten?"

"I never kept count."

That sounded like a lot. "Can you guess?"

Jacqueline blanched and took several deep breaths. "They started about three years ago."

She looked ready to either pass out or throw up. Link wished he knew how to help. Link realized he'd unconsciously been drumming his fingers on the paper and he felt like a heartless heel. "Sorry."

"Don't apologize. I know I'm overreacting." Jacqueline swallowed. "Every time I see one of those notes, I turn into a blithering idiot." She took a deep breath, exhaled slowly and stopped rocking. "The notes started about a year after I started working for Envirohab." She cleared her throat. "At first, I thought Adam was sending them to me."

The warmth in her tone when she said Adam's name made Link's teeth clench. Did she still love the guy? He told himself he didn't care.

"They were different at first." Jacqueline pushed her hair out of her eyes with a trembling hand. "Childish, but nicer."

"When did they change?"

Jacqueline's lips quivered. He remembered feeling her words spoken against his lips. Down, boy, keep it cool. "About a year ago, whoever is writing these, started using red ink." She wiped away perspiration. "Until then, it was mainly blue, sometimes black." She looked him square in the eye. "I never thought about it before, but I think that when the color of the ink changed to blood red, the message's tone changed from lousy poetry to something sinister." She bit her lip, then continued, "This may sound naïve, but I overlooked them until—" Her voice broke. She took a breath. "Until after the fire."

"And?" Link asked.

"I thought Adam was writing them. He denied it, but..." She shrugged, as if it didn't matter, but anger coupled with fear sparkled deep in her shimmering blue eyes. "I don't know who is sending me the rubbish. I wish he or she had the guts to face me instead of creep around leaving those things."

"What's this inferno stuff about?"

"I don't have a clue." Her fists clenched. "I want to wad those notes up, ram them down his throat and watch him choke. At least I assume it's a he."

Link believed she'd do it, too, at least she would if she could ever bring herself to touch the paper.

"Of course, if I killed the jerk, I'd never know why he had kept sending them." Scarlet spots appeared on her pale cheeks. "When they started to scare me, I called the police." Jacqueline glared at the note, then looked him in the eye. "Cops are supposed to be able to figure these things out. Right? That's what they're trained for.

Right?"

He nodded.

"The neo-Nazi officer I spoke to made me feel like an idiot. For all I know, he's the one who keeps sending me this trash." Her fist hit her other palm with a resounding smack.

"Why do you suspect him?"

The knuckles on Jacqueline's fist turned white. "His attitude for one plus the fact that I discovered that he'd thrown the report out."

Link frowned. "Did you get the feeling he knew about the notes, and was mainly interested in your reaction?"

"Maybe, but at the time, I had the impression he thought I was trying to get attention and making up a story to exonerate Adam."

Link gritted his teeth as he tried to follow her explanation. "Exonerate him from what?"

"The week before I received that note, the Fire Marshal had declared that Envirohab's fire was arson and Adam's death was a suicide, which meant that his life insurance was void and I was broke. The officer seemed to believe that I was trying to find a way to change the cause of death so I could collect the insurance." She took a deep breath as she shook her head. "Not that I couldn't use the money." She cleared her throat. "Assuming it was arson, I'm positive Adam didn't set it." Her trembling finger pointed at the wrinkled paper. "If it really was arson, I think whoever keeps writing these notes, with their fire themes, did it." She swallowed hard. "That means my husband was murdered." Jacqueline took three deep breaths. "But, like that neo-Nazi officer pointed out, I could have made up the damned note or Adam could have written it before he died and I only found it later." She blinked away tears. "All I know for certain is that after the officer left, I found his report crumpled up in the prickly pear patch near the front door."

Link touched her hand.

"I'd hoped the crane was the last, and I'd run far enough away, but it wasn't." She shook her head, apparently unable to finish the thought.

"Crane?"

She nodded. "It came the same day Envirohab's grant was canceled. Can you believe the timing?" She gave a strangled laugh.

"When was that?"

"Sixteen days ago." She looked small, defenseless, fragile and cold. Link wanted to hold her. Warm her. Protect her. But he knew she'd never let him. "I came home from one of the worst days of my life, stepped into my kitchen and there it was on my table, under a sprig of plumeria and in the center of a sunbeam.

"Obviously, whoever had left it had been in my house.

"I was desperate to get away and I started thinking about Grandma and how good it would be to see her. So, I packed up my car and ran. Then, halfway here-" She fought to control her breathing. "I found a note in my car. If all that wasn't bad enough, no sooner did I arrive, then Grandma sent me off with you." Jacqueline rubbed her temples, as if she had a headache.

"And you pack a book, which just happens to have another message in it. Rotten luck."

Jacqueline shook her head. "I borrowed that book from Grandma. For the note to get inside it, either Grandma has been sending them or the psychopath somehow found a way to put it there. And I'm positive

Grandma hasn't been sending them."

"Shit."

"Oh, yeah, you got that right," Jacqueline said. "Several times on the way up, I felt like someone was watching me and I thought he was driving the same old blue pickup I caught a glimpse of, but I never got close enough to be certain."

"That's why you kept looking out the back window. I thought my driving gave you the heebie jeebies."

Suddenly, her eyes began to glisten with tears. "Oh, Link, thank you."

"For what?"

"For believing me. For understanding. For listening."

"What else did you— " A tear rolled down her cheek. It took everything he had not to touch her, cradle her in his arms, and kiss away her pain.

Link grabbed the paper and held, in the hope it would be a shield between himself and temptation. Her gaze fixed on his hands, her expression brooding. "What are you thinking?"

"That whoever leaves me these notes must have some sort of sick fantasy about me." Link frowned. "See how obsessive his images are?" Her trembling finger pointed at the sloppy writing. "Scorching strand. All kinds of in-in-infernos: endearment, desire, love, passion, ardor, delight." Her index finger jabbed the air inches above each word as she spat it. "It's sick the way he combines images of love with hell." The little hairs on the back of Link's neck quivered. "One note said something about feelings going up in flames. I burned it." A tear rolled down her cheek. She wiped it away with the back of her hand. "I felt so smug when I set that note on fire, like I'd beaten the pervert at his own game. Two weeks later, Adam burned to death." Jacqueline's breathing sounded like she'd jogged up a mountain.

Link took her hand in his. Seeing her tan fingers against his palm intensified his impression of how small yet tough she was. He gently squeezed. "Do you think you caused his death?"

"Yes." The admission was barely discernible.

He shook his head. "More likely, it was a coincidence."

Her entire body trembled. "I thought three thousand miles would be safe. It isn't. I thought the middle of the wilderness would be safe, but it isn't, either."

Link put his arm around her shoulder and half-hugged her while he studied the childish script scrawled over the crumpled paper. "You can't be sure he followed you." Jacqueline made a disagreeing sound. "He couldn't have followed us this far north from Valdez. So, we have all vacation to figure a way to permanently free you from this lunatic."

"Two weeks. I'd forgotten." Jacqueline kissed his cheek, then shook off his arm and sat back on her heels. "I've never been able to figure out what could obsess a guy enough to follow a woman from Tempe, Arizona to Fairbanks, Alaska. You're a guy, why would you do something like that?"

Great, now she was lumping his motives in with some psycho's, who obviously had a fire fetish. "What makes you think he followed you to Fairbanks?"

"Midnight wasn't where I remember packing it this morning." She rubbed warmth into her upper arms.

"Or Tempest snooped, while your bag was in her room." Though possible, it didn't explain the orca's presence. Tempest wouldn't have known that Jacqueline considered origami a threat, so if it was already there and she was snooping, she would have left it. Which meant the only thig for certain was that someone had placed it there after she had borrowed Mavis' book.

Jacqueline swallowed, then took a deep breath. "I am certain I put it on the bottom. Someone went through my things after we left Stone and Ariel's and tempting as it is to blame Tempest, she hasn't had an opportunity to snoop."

This was worse than Link had expected. How could someone follow him when he'd used the company plane? Anyone who knew about private aircraft; anyone who could read tail numbers; anyone willing to check the flight plan.

Link massaged his own temples.

When he'd met Ariel and Tempest, a killer had been after them, but they'd known who wanted them dead and why. If a hunter pursued his prey for days, weeks or years, as the kid was suggesting, shouldn't intelligent prey know who and why? Jacqueline's innocent bafflement had to be the best acting he'd ever seen.

What was she hiding? Why lie to him? Did her stalker want her dead? When Peter had caught up with Ariel and Tempest, he'd lashed out with such fury that no one had been safe. Would Jacqueline's stalker become a threat for the rest of them? Unwilling to follow that line of thought, he focused on the note's odd message. Why the allusions to a combination of love and hell? Had her husband really died, as she'd said? Had she been married? If so, how old had she been? Twelve? Thirteen? Younger? What sort of creep had the man been?

Too many questions, not enough answers.

Link stood up so quickly he bumped his head on

the tent's low ceiling. "I need to clean the fish."

"I'll help."

Later, when Link settled into his sleeping bag, his thoughts were still a chaos of unanswered questions. Falling asleep, he dreamed about menacing shadows chasing Jacqueline. As a dark wisp wrapped around her, a voice shouted, "Link."

Heart hammering, Link sat bolt upright. Pale green light filtered through tent. Phillip made a soft chuffing t-t-t-t-t-t-t sound in his sleep.

As his heart slowed, from the nightmare and accepted reality, Link recalled a forgotten incident the previous year. He'd come home to find Tempest sitting on the back yard picnic bench, sobbing her heart out. Not knowing what else to do, he sat down, put his arm around her shoulders and listened to her pour out her woes, much as he'd done with Jacqueline earlier that day.

Tempest's problem had been simple: she hated school because, as the new kid; she felt like no one liked her. He'd told her he liked her. She sobbed that she'd never have a boyfriend because she was too stupid and ugly. He told her she could say he was her boyfriend. He had meant to boost Tempest's ego, and he'd thought his comment were harmless.

If only he'd realized she was taking him literally. No wonder she'd gotten the idea that he belonged to her! He'd made the problem, now he had to find a way to fix it.

But Tempest's attitude was a mere annoyance while Jacqueline's could be life and death. What could have happened in Jacqueline's past to motivate anyone to pursue her over so many years and miles? He frowned. Her tale of woe and pursuit seemed too farfetched to be true. Yet he'd learned that fact was often stranger than fiction. Still, why would anyone follow another person so damned far? He frowned. While Jacqueline seemed competent and intelligent, the cop hadn't believed her. But what would she gain by folding that whale and writing the note?

Attention?

Sympathy?

If she was as manipulative as Tempest could be, he'd fallen into her trap. Worse, he liked Jacqueline's company so much that the snare felt good. Sitting there in the softly undulating tent, Link admitted that he was attracted to Jacqueline even though she was only a kid.

Liked her way too much for a kid.

Link punched his pillow.

Phillip grunted and rolled over.

Had she really been married? If so, Mavis had never mentioned the guy.

What if she'd murdered her husband, assuming there had been a husband, and used the notes as a deception, like the cop had figured? That scenario seemed more likely than the officer tossing away a report. The sheen of perspiration chilled him. If she'd been married, why was her name still Cardew?

None of it seemed logical, yet she didn't seem like a liar. How could he feel so close, so attracted, to a possible murderess and probable liar? Link punched his pillow again and tried to clear his mind of all frustrating thoughts.

The following morning, Link ignored Tempest's glares as she sullenly settled into the middle of Carmen and Phillip's canoe. Jacqueline perched in the front of Link's canoe, which floated low in the water, heavy with its burden of equipment, her paddle poised, as she waited for him to push them off the sandbar.

Link heaved the equipment-laden canoe into the water, then leapt into the stern. A moment later Jacqueline dipped her paddle into the frigid water and expertly sent them across the current to a calm section. With another deft stroke, the canoe stopped.

Paddle poised, again, Jacqueline waited and watched the other canoe.

Link settled onto his seat, gripped his paddle and watched Phillip stand in the stern and try to push the craft off the sandbar with his paddle. The other canoe rocked violently. Carmen grabbed the gunwales as she pitched sideways, then, she held on for dear life. Tempest fell forward and seized Carmen's shoulder. Carmen yelped. The canoe tilted toward the icy flow. Tempest squealed. Phillip tripped backward and landed on top of them.

The boat lurched into the current.

It was going to be a long two weeks.

"Amazing," Jacqueline muttered.

Link wished Jacqueline's bulky sweatshirt didn't camouflage her figure, then he chastised himself for having such thoughts about a mere kid.

With much splashing and minimal headway, Carmen, Phillip and Tempest pointed their boat downstream. Link positioned his paddle for a stroke. Though Jacqueline didn't turn around, their paddles dipped into the freezing water at the same moment and their canoe effortlessly joined the flow.

As the air warmed and the glare increased, Link discovered that every stroke was as unified as the first. He'd never had such a compatible partner. Such a confusing partner. Or such a captivating one.

Link's thoughts kept returning to Jacqueline. He had the sensation that he had known her for years. That strange sense of familiarity made it easy to talk with her.

This was defiantly going to be the longest two weeks of his life.

Ahead the sunlight glinted off Carmen's blond curls, momentarily giving her a halo. Carmen could be the worst hellion he knew, yet she possessed more good qualities than bad. The fact was that, for the last few years, he'd missed her like crazy, so much so, that he'd adopted Ariel as a substitute sister and Tempest as his niece.

His mind traveled from the golden aura around Carmen to a different shade of yellow … the folded sheet of legal paper.

If someone was actually stalking Jacqueline, how had they managed to get the note in her bag? Furthermore, how much did Mavis know about Jacqueline's stalker? Assuming she believed the story, could that be why she'd insisted on him bringing Jacqueline here?

Possibly, but it was difficult to imagine Mavis favoring running away from a problem, when she had always preferred to confront unpleasant situations. In truth, it was a miracle she'd never shot someone dumb enough to mess with her or her own.

None of it made sense.

Tempest and Ariel had endured a similar situation, but they'd known why Peter wanted them dead. Was Jacqueline lying about her ignorance? Lying about everything? Despite how his thoughts circled, they always seemed to come back to that question.

Link swallowed hard, but the lump in his throat remained.

Hours later, Carmen's voice rippled upstream. "Bear to the right."

When the other canoe rocked instead of changing

course, Link shaded his eyes. Phillip threw down his paddle, grabbed his can of pepper spray and looked frantically to the west. Link helplessly watched Carmen flail away with her paddle while Phillip looked for the danger and their canoe plowed straight into a sandbar.

Carmen fell forward into the prow and Tempest shrieked as she tumbled into Carmen's now vacant seat. Can of pepper spray clenched in one hand, oar gripped in the other, Phillip pitched to the right and landed headfirst in the numbing water. For a moment, time stood still and Phillip stayed in a rigid headstand, his ankles and sneakers above the frigid water, then the angle changed and his feet disappeared beneath the water.

Jacqueline's paddle dug into the water and their canoe shot forward.

The aerosol can bobbed to the surface. For a heart-stopping moment the can and a few bubbles were the only sign of him. When he resurfaced, Jacqueline expertly maneuvered their canoe alongside. Link grabbed the back of Phillip's shirt and Jacqueline immediately drove their vessel into the sandbar.

As he hauled Phillip out, he thought he'd never known another woman who could steer a canoe better from the front than most people could from the back. Even though the rescue had been efficient, by the time they beached the canoe, Phillip's lips were blue. "We need a fire." Jacqueline heaved their canoe ashore. "Link, help Phillip get out. Phillip, take off those wet clothes. Carmen, pull your canoe up and secure it. Tempest, get a fire started – now."

Tempest looked ready to scream. "You heard her," Link snapped, "do it." He grabbed a sleeping roll in one hand, Phillip's waist in the other and waded onto the sandbar.

When Carmen didn't move, Jacqueline secured both canoes, then knelt in front of Carmen, who was holding her face and crying. Her tears were mixing with blood. Link shoved Phillip toward a large rock, threw a blanket around his shoulders, then rushed to Carmen. "Are you all right?"

Carmen stared mutely at him though a veil of tears and blood and shook her head. "She needs her nose reset." Jacqueline's confident tone amazed him. "I'll see to it. Get Phillip stripped before hypothermia sets in."

"But— "

"Now." Link didn't move. Jacqueline turned to him. "I'll take care of Carmen. Phillip has to get warm."

Link knew she was right. As he went to Phillip, he heard a sharp snicking sound accompanied by a gasp from his sister. "Oh," Carmen said, "that feels better."

While Link helped Phillip out of his sodden clothes, he watched Jacqueline skillfully bandage Carmen's nose.

Tempest returned with an armload of dried grass and glared at Carmen. "Next time say steer. No, that won't work, he'd look for a damned cow. Say turn." She pivoted to Phillip. "And you, dump the worthless can and keep your damned paddle in your hand."

Link said, "Since you know so much, perhaps you should show him how to paddle a canoe."

Her chin went up a notch. "I couldn't do worse."

10

As Jacqueline squinted against the glare from the rippling water, a cool breeze brushed her singed cheeks and burnt nose. Unfortunately, they were the least of her aches and pains. With every breath and stroke of the paddle, her shoulders throbbed from the activity she was no longer accustomed to. When the current caught their canoe, guiding it straight and true, she settled her paddle across her lap and began kneading the tense flesh at her nape while she told herself that blistered hands and painful muscles were a small price to pay for the sense of safety she felt. She inhaled deeply realizing the air even smelled fresher - freer.

Life was good.

Aches and pains aside, Jacqueline hadn't felt this wonderful in months. Coming to Alaska had been the right choice. Abruptly, the rear of Phillip, Carmen and Tempest's canoe swerved in front of them. Jacqueline grabbed her paddle and backstroked to avoid a collision. Phillip, oblivious to everything except the view through his binoculars, continued studying the surrounding landscape. With three more backstrokes, Jacqueline created a buffer zone between their bow and the other canoe's stern.

Their canoe rocked slightly as Link leaned forward. "Good save," he whispered, his breath brushing her ear.

"Thanks." When she felt the canoe adjust for his weight moving away, Jacqueline turned to look back at him.

"Good idea letting them get ahead." Link glanced at the other canoe, his expression tense. "It's safer for everyone."

As she gave him a thumbs up, she saw a flash of movement upstream. She squinted and looked over Link's shoulder, but couldn't see what had caused it. "Must have been my imagination," she muttered.

"What?"

"I thought I saw something come round the bend."

"A bear?" Link stowed him paddle and reached for his rifle.

"More like a swan." He raised a brow, so she explained, "It was white and seemed to be floating before it darted back out of sight."

"You're sure it wasn't a grizz or a polar bear?"

Jacqueline nodded. Link visibly relaxed. "Good, Tempest loves bears ... I might have been tempted to ask Phillip if he had more pepper spray then send her back there." The corners of his mouth tilted up.

"You're bad."

Link pantomimed firing a gun and clicked his tongue. "Yesterday, when you reset Carmen's nose, how'd you know what to do?"

"Nursing school." His expression proclaimed her statement a joke, so she added, "I am a licensed nurse."

"Are you serious?"

"Of course I am." As if responding to some unspoken cue, they each placed their paddles across their laps and allowed their canoe to drop farther behind Carmen's. As the distance lengthened, Jacqueline began to imagine all sorts of trouble Phillip and Tempest could create. She bit her lower lip as she calculated how much time it would take them to catch up. "Should we get a bit closer?"

"Let's hang back this distance for a while."

"Are you sure?" She frowned as the other canoe disappeared around a bend. "What if they need to be fished out?"

"That's what it might take to get Tempest to stop rocking the boat and if they all get a good dunking, Phillip might even start paying attention to the job at hand instead of act like a tourist with nothing better to do that gawk."

Downstream, boulders were sprinkled in the water like a child's toys after a rowdy day of play. "This is a rough place to learn that lesson."

"But relatively shallow and slow. In a word, survivable." Link pulled a cooler out from under his seat and tossed her a can of ginger ale. He knew her preferred drink, Jacqueline was impressed. He popped the tab off a Pepsi for himself. "Have you spoken to Carmen, or anyone else, about that note?"

"No."

His smug expression made her think he'd guessed the answer. "I've been thinking about when it got into your book." He took a swallow.

"You have?"

"Someone could have put it in your bag at the hangar." If she hadn't come up with the identical conclusion, she'd never have gotten any sleep the previous night. "I take it my deduction doesn't surprise you."

When it became obvious he wasn't going to let the matter drop, Jacqueline sighed in resignation then she looked him in the eye and shook her head. "I don't want to talk about my stalker. I want to savor the untouched beauty of this wild land and relax."

"I bet the new guy put it there."

Jacqueline straightened. There had been over a dozen people in and around the hangar, all of whom had been strangers to her, but of course Link would have known them. "Which one was he?" She unconsciously held her breath, hoping he could describe her nemesis, so she could finally put a face on her elusive shadow.

Link's expression took on a look of concentration. "He helped Drew load the bags."

Jacqueline studied the tiny beads of condensation that formed an abstract pattern on her ginger ale can. "Which one was Drew?"

"The blond with the greasy rag in his back pocket. The new guy had one bushy eyebrow." He laid his paddle across his lap. "It went from here to here." Link tapped each temple.

"Sounds attractive." But it didn't ring any bells. "What else?"

"Navy coveralls. Long beard," Link indicated a hand span above his belt. "Brown hair below his shoulders." He shrugged. "I don't remember anything else." Link gulped his Pepsi.

"It's more than I've ever had to go on before." But she still couldn't be certain if she'd noticed him in the chaos Tempest had created when she'd realized she wouldn't be allowed to sit next to Link. "Unfortunately, I have a mental image of a musk ox." Link choked and began thumping his chest. "Are you all right? You look flushed."

"I'm fine." Link picked up his paddle and made a minor adjustment.

How like him to take care of little things without

expecting the fanfare Adam had always seemed to need for the least little thing. "I'm not used to a guy being concerned about my problems." The admission escaped before she even realized it was a thought.

Link stared at her for a long moment. "I thought you were a widow."

Something in Link's face told her that he wouldn't let the subject go unless she explained. "Adam was absorbed in his own ambitions. He didn't have much time for anyone else's issues or problems."

"And you call that a relationship?" He stared at her. She glared back at the nosy man. He blinked, then as if he'd suddenly realized how incredibly rude he'd been, he asked, "Do you know how to handle that handgun of yours?"

"Do you think I'd be stupid enough to have it with me if I didn't?" A smile smoothed his lips and summoned the memory of the way they'd molded to her own. Jacqueline abruptly faced forward and looked at the dramatic, untamed landscape, but even the boundless beauty couldn't make her forget the feelings he'd aroused.

"How are you with rifles?"

"That depends on the rifle," Jacqueline said. "When I was eleven or twelve, I had an old Mauser eight-millimeter-aught-six Acklie improved. I can hit a snake's eye with that at one-hundred-yards, but with anything else..." She shrugged.

"Your parents let you have a bear killer?" Doubt dominated his tone.

Jacqueline swiveled around so quickly the canoe rocked. "My father modified its caliber and shortened the stock two inches so I could handle it, then he gave it to me for Christmas." His eyes widen with surprise. She grinned. "My mother gave me a scope for it." Let him choke on those facts.

"What the hell for?"

"Weren't you listening?" she asked innocently, "Christmas."

"Why did you need so much firepower?"

Jacqueline laughed. "Probably because I wouldn't stay close to home, and my folks didn't want me eaten." Link's confused expression looked comical. "Didn't Grandma ever tell you anything about her past?" Link shook his head. "I grew up in a cabin just a mile or so up the mountain from Grandma." Surprise crossed his features. She frowned, wondering why her grandmother would set her up with this man when it was obvious that in the decade she'd worked with him she hadn't told him anything about her own life. "My father and my grandfather were lumberjacks. We lived in the wilds of British Columbia. Our closest neighbors were a family of black bears. Rory and I thought they made great neighbors, but Mom never trusted them." Knowing that she was making a mishmash of it and needing time to decide what she should tell him, she fell silent.

"Did you shoot them?"

"Never."

He nearly laughed at her outrage. "So why'd you leave the mountain?"

Tears filled her eyes at the bitter memory. "A tree fell wrong and Grandpa was killed. We stayed a few months after that, but it was never the same. Grandma hated the reminders. She even stopped chasing Cin out of her kitchen."

"I beg your pardon?"

"One of the black bears was cinnamon colored. Really beautiful. Unfortunately, he had a fondness for fresh baked pies." Jacqueline smiled. "Cin was also good at opening doors. He got his first pie when he was about half a year old. Grandma chased him out of her kitchen with her broom. She whacked him all the way across the yard, raising great clouds of dust; he bawled like she was killing him." Jacqueline chuckled at the memory. "He mustn't have been as upset as he acted because he kept coming back and Grandma kept beating him. It became a ritual with them." Jacqueline snickered. "Grandma only stopped when she broke her broom on him." She chuckled at the memory. "When she stopped and stared at her broom, Cin stopped and stared at her. I've never seen such a confused and disappointed look on a bear's face."

"She lit out after a bear with just a broom?" Jacqueline nodded. "Was it orphaned or something?" She shook her head. "No wonder Mavis doesn't think twice about locking horns with riggers."

"Those were happy times."

"But they ended," Link said.

Jacqueline nodded. "After Grandpa died, Grandma moved to Valdez. Eventually, we moved to Washington State. I hated it there. There were so many people, and they seemed so superficial." She shrugged and grinned at the naïve child she'd been. "At least that's how they seemed to me. The girls were more interested in going steady with someone cool and being in style than learning." Memories of trying to fit in when she felt like a square peg in a community of round holes overwhelmed her. Why was she telling her personal thoughts and feelings to Link? Jacqueline turned her back to him, and tried not to dwell on the past.

In the ensuing silence, the grandeur of the landscape and the solitude began seeping into her soul.

A tiny seed of confidence, which had lain dormant since her marriage, sprouted. As the frigid current swept them past boulders and gravel beds, Jacqueline admired the massive mountains and wondered how soon the dramatic heights would give way to the forested foothills.

Link often laid the paddle across his lap, so eventually their canoe fell back so far that they occasionally lost sight of the other canoe, but they never got so far behind that they couldn't hear Tempest.

Jacqueline adapted to the rhythm, but wondered if he wanted to stay so far behind because of Tempest, who had thrown a tantrum when he'd tried to fulfill the threat of making her steer or if he wanted the safety margin to compensate for Phillip's erratic course.

"Have you ever killed anything?"

Link's question startled her.

"Yes." Her spine stiffened at the shameful memory. Slowly, she turned to look him in the eye. "Seven years ago."

"Are you going to tell me about it?"

"It was a rattlesnake." Jacqueline hoped her answer would satisfy him.

"Tell me about it."

She sighed. "My father got a job offer he couldn't refuse. So, when I was seventeen, we moved to New Mexico. The first week there, a snake decided to take a nap on our front porch. Mom screamed bloody murder. Since no one else was there, I grabbed the shotgun and shot it." She shrugged.

"Bet that left quite a hole in the porch," Link said.

"While I went to get my rifle, it took off across the yard. I shot it about fifty yards from the porch." She shook her head. "Rory got pissed off when he heard about it and said I'd shredded a perfectly good potential belt."

Link burst into laughter.

Over his shoulder, Jacqueline saw the distinct silhouette of another canoe against the gleaming gray water. A second later, it vanished behind a boulder. A chill rushed over her and gooseflesh broke out over her body, as something deep inside told her that her stalker was still on her trail.

11

Link woke with a pounding heart. He rolled to his right, then to his left, and back again until the soothing reality of the tent assured him that it had only been a dream.

A clank resonated through the still night.

Link told himself the breeze had tipped something over, but the tent's nylon hung limp in mocking contempt. Stealthily, he slipped from his sleeping bag. The chill air chased waves of gooseflesh across his bare chest, unheeding of the discomfort, he grabbed his rifle then grabbed the tent flap. The zipper sounded loud as a siren in the still night. Any chance of stealth lost, Link whipped aside the flap.

For a moment, there was tense silence, followed by a soft grating sound, then a rock splashing into the water. The pounding thuds of running feet brought his attention to a bulky silhouette dashing upstream, into the cold light of dawn.

He sprinted out of the tent, after the person, but the contents of one cooler were strewn in an arc, as if the looter had fled in the middle of sorting through it. He paused, torn between securing the food and tracking the perpetrator. Food, which equaled survival, won.

"What happened?" a voice demanded.

Link whirled and leveled his rifle. Jacqueline jumped aside. His heart slammed against his ribs. "Christ!" Link swore, shocked that he'd drawn on her.

"Don't sneak up on me like that." He secured the safety.

"Sorry." She squatted to study the ground and studied the mess. Her T-shirt hiked up to reveal perfect thighs. "A bear didn't do this." His gaze fastened on the shirt's hem, and his breath caught in anticipation of the fabric inching higher. Jacqueline looked up at him, tilting her head as she studied him, then in a smooth move, she ejected the clip from her gun. Link wondered why he hadn't noticed the weapon. "I heard someone running away."

He nodded.

She scanned shadows, then began repacking the chest. Link squatted down to help, but paid more attention to her hemline than fitting the food inside the cooler. She said, "We're missing some powdered eggs and coffee." She wrinkled her nose. He'd never seen her consume either item, so was surprised she'd notice their absence.

He stood and looked upriver. "Must have been someone trying to get breakfast."

Jacqueline made a derisive sound. "If people have to steal food, they don't belong here."

"I agree," Carmen said. Carmen had jeans on under a thick flannel nightgown, but she was rubbing her arms as if she was freezing. Dressed only in sweat pants, he was cold, too. "What's going on?"

"Nothing." Link moved from foot to foot.

"Now." Jacqueline amended, then continued packing the cooler, as if totally unaffected by the chill.

Carmen squinted first at Jacqueline, then at him. "Did I interrupt something?"

"Someone vandalized our camp." If the zipper had been quieter, he'd have caught the thief.

Carmen frowned. "I didn't know anyone else was

around."

"It's easy to believe that." Jacqueline stood up. "Do you think it was another river runner, or a local?"

"Natives never bothered me before," he said.

Carmen stared, shivering, into the darkness. "I hope they don't come back."

Jacqueline got an odd expression on her face, then visibly paled. "Think it might be your phantom?" Link asked.

"If it was, I wish we'd caught him." She cradled her gun. "I'd love to get that jerk face to face and give him a piece of my mind." Her tone said thrash the living daylights out of him.

"Who are you talking about?" Carmen asked.

"A spineless fool. And a rotten poet." Jacqueline turned and stalked back toward her tent. Link liked the way her hips swayed beneath the thin cotton.

"What's wrong with her?"

Link gestured toward the campfire. As they squatted next to its residual heat, he quietly related the story Jacqueline had told him. Carmen frowned. "Either Jacqueline didn't tell you everything, or, like she said, the guy is a spineless fool." He nodded. "How much do you know about her?"

"Only what I've found out in the last couple days." He looked around the peaceful campsite and pursed his lips. The tents looked serene, but appearances could mislead.

Carmen massaged her temple. "I like her."

"So do I." More than he wanted to. "If someone were writing you letters, the anonymous kind, do you think you'd have an idea who was doing it and why?"

"Probably." She thought a moment. "Yes," she said, decisively. "I got some when I was in junior high. They were the secret admirer sort." She shook her head. "I knew who sent them."

"Who?"

"J.T. Henry. His handwriting was as lousy as his spelling." She gave a short laugh. "I wished they'd been from Mitch Wallace."

"Wasn't he captain of the junior varsity basketball team?" She nodded. Link scratched his head. "I don't remember J. T."

"He wasn't someone people remembered. He sort of blended in with the surroundings."

He looked upriver. "Do you think this stalker of Jacqueline's could be someone like that?"

Carmen shrugged. "We don't know enough to guess."

He inclined his head in agreement. They fell into a companionable silence. Link gazed into the shadows around their campsite. This far North, there were shadows all the time because the sun never seemed to totally set and the earth never rotated far enough for it to be overhead.

Regardless of who had gone through their things, Link didn't like the invasion of privacy. His attention fastened on the cooler and he thought about the glimpses he'd gotten of the kayak, which had seemed intent upon keeping out of sight upstream. The sneak-thief had run toward the sun, was his purpose in doing that to head back to the kayak or so others could only see his silhouette against the bright light?

Carmen rubbed her shoulders and flexed her neck. "Stiff?" he asked.

"Oh, yeah. I haven't had such a tough workout in ages."

"Want to swap partners tomorrow?"

"I'd like that a lot," she admitted with a guilty glance at the tents.

"Phillip's lack of skill is getting to you, huh?"

"No." Her tone was defensive. "In fact, for a person that's never been outside a city before, he's doing very well." She wet her lips as she faced him. "I've been hoping you'd get to know him, and tell me what you think."

Link didn't need to share a canoe with the guy to do that. Plain and simple, Phillip was a nerd. But if Carmen couldn't see that herself, he wasn't about to point it out. "What exactly do you expect me to learn?"

"I love him and I'm certain he loves me." Carmen clamped her mouth shut, as if she'd said too much.

"Hasn't he told you?"

She shook her head. "We talk about a shared future all the time, but he's never actually proposed."

"You told me you were engaged." That was the only reason he'd made an attempt to find something likable about the guy.

"I think we are. I hope we are," She bit her lower lip and looked ready to cry. "But then again, I can't be certain." Link poked the dying embers with a twig. "I want to know if you think I'm wasting my time." Carmen's tone was dejected. "I don't want to wait forever for a kiss or a word of confirmation."

She couldn't seriously mean what she'd just said – surly, if she considered herself engaged, they'd at least kissed. "You don't need to be married." Her defensive expression, made him change the direction of his topic. "It's not like it was for Mom, when being a wife and mother was the main goal for a woman. There's nothing wrong with being single."

"I know that," Carmen snapped.

"Sure doesn't sound like it to me."

"I want a home, a husband, and a family. I want them for me, not because of what society accepts or rejects. Yes, I'm a complete person without them, but for the last year or so, the desire for that kind of stability has grown. Can you understand?" She studied his face.

"Your biological clock is ticking."

Carmen looked ready to strangle him. After a long pause, she sighed. "Maybe it is as simple as that. Regardless, those things are missing in my life." She looked lost and forlorn.

He hugged her. "Carmen, I'd do anything for you. You know that."

"I know." They sat in companionable silence, each loath to leave the warmth.

Link looked around the campsite. There were definite similarities between Jacqueline's stalker's stealthy way of doing things and whoever had methodically dumped their food, but it was ridiculous to think someone had trailed her all the way from Arizona into the wilderness. Still, the plane that had landed shortly after they arrived had brought someone, and if that someone had been a stalker, who had not had time to pack necessities, like food...

Carmen rose to her feet. "I need to get some sleep. If we're going to trade partners, does that mean you get Tempest and we get the cargo?"

"You really expect me to take her?"

"Her eyes still follow you everywhere and the looks she gives Jacqueline ... ouch." Carmen shook her head. "I don't think it's a good idea to have them in the same canoe."

"Yet they manage to sleep in the same tent." He sighed. "Sorry. I do understand what you mean, but I don't know what to do about it. Got any suggestions?"

"Hold fast. Eventually, she'll outgrow her infatuation."

And in the meantime, she'd make his life miserable. "We can still get a couple of hours sleep." Link took a last look upstream, where shadows bisected by the glimmering band of frigid water could hide an army of determined stalkers.

12

Morning mist swirled over the water as Jacqueline, Tempest, and Carmen eased the rain shield off their tent. Then, while Carmen wrapped the thin nylon into a tight roll, Jacqueline removed the ribbing from the main tent shell.

"Today, I'll take Phillip. You go with Carmen," Link barked the unexpected mandate. Jacqueline pivoted, mouth agape. Though he was looking at Tempest, Link's grim expression filled her with such a sense of rejection that her heart constricted.

Carmen stood up. Jacqueline expected her to protest the separation from her boyfriend, but Carmen cheerfully gave her brother a mock salute and clicked her heels together.

Tempest's mouth twisted into a vicious smile, then she stuck out her tongue at Jacqueline.

Phillip, who was reading something on his ever-present iPad, appeared oblivious to the ramifications of Link's order.

Jacqueline turned back to her work and blinked away tears as she tried to concentrate on packing the tent. As she rolled the fabric, she wondered why she had expected to be Link's permanent partner.

She wished she didn't care.

Was she as bad as Tempest?

No, she was not some lovesick teen looking for her

first love.

Was she a desperate woman ready to leap into the next man's arms with Adam only eight months dead?

Hardly.

Was she a wilting violet, heart aflutter as a sinister shadow terrorized her?

Only when she found plumeria blossoms or origami.

She did not need a man to fight her battles, she had fought them for herself so far, and she would continue to do so. Jacqueline gritted her teeth and yanked the last pole free. She tested its weight and feel. In a pinch, it would make an effective weapon.

While loading their gear, Tempest sidled up to her and sniffed loudly. "You stink. No wonder Uncle Link didn't want you close to him."

Jacqueline tried not to laugh. "I'm so sorry if I offend your refined sensibilities. Perhaps you should take the front." Jacqueline held out Carmen's paddle. Tempest's mouth flattened. "You'll be farther away of me, there."

Fury replaced the triumphant smirk. "You expect me to give you a free ride? No way!"

Jacqueline looked Tempest up and down. The girl looked physically fit and was taller than she. "I've been paddling canoes since I was half your size. You've gotten a 'free ride' so far."

"I hate you."

"Get rid of your chimera."

"Do what?"

"Chimera, fantasy. You think you love Link and for some mysterious reason, you want a villain, which will give you a tangible reason why he isn't returning your affection. Carmen won't do because she's Link's sister.

Phillip?" Jacqueline shook her head. "That leaves me to be the great foe - the threat to your great romance. Guess what, kid, I'm not your competition. I do not want him or any other man. I want to resolve my problems by myself."

Tempest glanced at Link, who was packing the cooking gear, and lowered her voice. "I don't think I love him. I know I love him. I'll marry him someday."

"Send me an invitation, I'll send you a gift."

Tempest looked startled. "You really don't want him?"

Jacqueline shook her head. "I want a peaceful life. I want a fulfilling job. I think I'd like a kitten. I've tried marriage. Single is better." She wished her still-throbbing feeling of rejection wasn't at such odds with what she knew was best for her.

Tempest blinked. "I know you're lying to me. I watch you together. You like being together."

"So? I enjoy being with Carmen and Phillip, too."

"Then why'd you come if it wasn't to grab Link?"

"I was set up by my grandmother... Do you know Mavis?" Tempest nodded. "Then you must know how controlling she can be and how hard it is to avoid getting sucked into her plans."

"Mavis is trying to set you up with Link? Why?"

"Good question". Jacqueline shrugged. "Perhaps my visit came at an inconvenient time and she had other plans she didn't want to admit to." But the thought of her grandmother trying to hide a blazing affair, or something seemed totally unlikely. "Perhaps she would like me to fall in love with Link, but it won't happen."

"Why not?"

"Would you like it if your grandmother set you up with a stranger on a two week long blind date?"

Tempest's nose wrinkled as if she smelled a hundred skunks. "Ugh."

Jacqueline nodded. "Finally, you get my point."

Tempest's brow furrowed. "Then why'd you come?"

"It's complicated." Jacqueline gestured toward the encompassing mountains. "For one thing, I needed time to decide what I want to do with the rest of my life."

"And for another your grandmother made you?"

"She can be domineering."

"Uncle Link is scared to death of her." The image of big, muscular Link Gavallan quailing in front of tiny Mavis Maureen Knowlton Cardew made Jacqueline laugh. "What's so funny?" Tempest demanded. "It's true."

Jacqueline wiped her eyes with the back of her hand and looked at Tempest's serious face. She took a deep breath. "Grandma adores both Link and Stone, it's hard to imagine her taking anything out on them." Tempest gave her a dubious look. "Think about it. You'll see I'm right."

"I'll try." Tempest walked away. The sound of her footfalls seemed identical to the intruder's gait. Could Tempest have been their midnight marauder? Had she been in her sleeping bag when the stealthy sounds woke her? Jacqueline frowned, unable to recall. Believing Tempest had vandalized the supplies seemed more probable than believing her nemesis had followed her this far north.

Moments later, Carmen claimed the bow and Tempest secured the center of their canoe. Jacqueline pushed off. As she vaulted into the stern, she glanced upriver. For a fleeting moment, she thought she saw the hairy face that she'd seen at the Trading Post peering around a boulder. A chill of apprehension skittered down her back and she blinked. The face disappeared. She dipped her paddle into the water, and propelled the canoe downstream. Their canoe zipped past gravel bars and boulders, as she tried to tell herself that her imagination was getting away from her.

"Slow up," Carmen said. "Give Phillip and Link a chance to catch up."

Jacqueline looked upstream. Phillip was adjusting the small solar panel in other canoe and LInk was looking heavenward, but there was no hint of any other craft.

Carmen rubbed her right shoulder. "I feel eighty years older than I did last week."

"Paddle some and you'll work the kinks out," Jacqueline suggested.

"I did not want to hear that." Carmen's chuckle was infectious. "Even if it is true."

Jacqueline shaded her eyes. "Phillip is finally holding the paddle right."

"Why didn't you say something yesterday?" Carmen asked.

Jacqueline shrugged. "I'm here to have fun. Enjoy the scenery. Get away from things. Not to criticize."

"In other words you were thinking about your stalker." Tempest's body wrenched, as if an electric current had gone through her.

"Link told you?"

Carmen nodded.

Tempest nearly upset them as she whirled to face the stern. "You're being stalked?" Her voice squeaked.

Jacqueline nodded. "It's aggravating as all get out."

Tempest's pupils looked dilated. "Aggravating?" She shuddered as if she'd fallen into the Sheenjek's glacial waters. "Aggravating!" She screeched the word as they floated past a large boulder. "You call being stalked aggravating?" Quack-quack-quack-quack. A pair of ducks exploded into the air spraying droplets over the canoe. Tempest yelped and threw herself onto the floor. Jacqueline looked from the girl, hunched into a fetal position, to the escaping birds.

"Wonder who got scared worse?" Carmen giggled. "Us or the ducks."

Tempest tentatively sat up, her mouth flat and her eyes blazing, as she glared back at Jacqueline. "You're a raving lunatic," Tempest's voice rose until it was loud enough to hurt the ears, "if you think being stalked is 'just a little aggravating'."

"Real life stalking isn't like the movies," Jacqueline said. "This guy leaves me notes and sometimes flowers where I'm not expecting them, so they startle me. I don't like the situation, but things could be worse." Were worse, if her suspicions about the mystery kayak were accurate.

The child's face turned white as the snowcaps. "Yeah, you could meet him face to face," Tempest scoffed.

"Tempest," Jacqueline began, "I know everything seems dramatic when you're a teenager, but— "

"Don't patronize me," Tempest snarled. "Ariel and I were stalked for over five years. Peter Baldwyn was a mercenary and he tried to kill us. He almost succeeded, too. Don't you dare tell me about being stalked, I know all about it."

The fierce words hung over their boat like an ominous cloud. Jacqueline cleared her throat. "How did you know he wanted to kill you?"

"He said so." Tempest glared at her. "What'd ya' think? That I'm making this up?" She lunged to her feet. Oblivious to the violently rocking canoe, Tempest clenched her fists. "I'm not." She leaned closer. "Stone almost got killed, trying to save us. Ask Uncle Link."

Gooseflesh erupted from Jacqueline's scalp to her toes and she remembered how inconsolable her grandmother had been a couple of years earlier.

Tempest apparently realized how precarious standing in a canoe was and sat down, red spots of color blooming in her cheeks. She held onto the gunwales, her knuckles white as Carmen's face. Jacqueline stared at Tempest's fiery cheeks and thought of blood red ink. Was she ignoring a real threat? She'd seen the color dozens of times, but had never associated it with death. What if she was being naïve and murder was his purpose? Blood red ink. How many times had she thought of the shade red in those terms, yet ignored the connotations? Jacqueline wet her lips. "Tempest?" She cleared her throat. "Was your stalker ever caught?"

"No. But it's ok now."

That statement begged for more questions, but the closed expression on Tempest's countenance told Jacqueline to save them. "Well, that gives me hope." She adopted a cheerful tone. "Maybe in a couple more years, I'll meet the fool and be able to say the same thing."

Tempest shook her head. "Don't ever wish to m-m-meet him f-f-face to f-face. Don't ever w-w-wish that."

A ball of fear constricted Jacqueline's throat.

"Why not?" Carmen asked.

"B-because s-sometimes you get what you w-wish for, and p-people you love," she swallowed, "d-die." Her expression darkened with bitter memories. "And you get c-c-covered with their b-blood." Tempest's voice cracked. "It never w-washes off, no matter what you d-do."

Mouth half open, Carmen stared at Jacqueline over Tempest's rigid shoulder.

The silence lengthened until Link and Phillip pulled

up parallel to them. Link raised a brow. "Having problems?"

"No," all three said.

Two horizontal ridges appeared above Link's eyebrows. His attention settled on Tempest. Finally, without uttering another sound, Tempest faced forward, her shoulders rigid.

Once free of the girl's mesmerizing gaze, Jacqueline heard the babble of running water and caught the scent of fish, but as the day wore on, silence prevailed. Held hostage by her thoughts, Jacqueline's memory replayed Tempest's outburst. With each repetition, tentacles of doubt grew about the security of her own situation, until Jacqueline peered into every shadow twice and her ears strained to decipher every sound.

That evening they camped on a mammoth gravel bar, which looked as if it had been dry for centuries. As she secured the canoe, Jacqueline felt physically and emotionally exhausted. Tempest gathered grasses and other bits of combustible material, then Link built a small bonfire near the lapping water. While the others toasted marshmallows and laughed over jokes, Jacqueline turned her back to the fire and stared into the night. She still felt the heat of the blaze, so she got up and walked along the pewter ribbon of water.

"Hey, Jacqueline," Carmen hollered, "come toast a marshmallow."

"No thanks." The wind shifted and she smelled smoke. The stench always reminded her of the reek of burning flesh. Once she was far enough away, Jacqueline ducked into the shadow or a boulder, then sank to her knees, arms tight around her stomach. Eyes shut, she rocked back and forth. The others' laughter drifted away and the memory of another night strengthened.

That night had been cool and cloud covered, too. Adam's step was carefree as he approached the lab's office door, while Jacqueline lurched toward the kitchen door, her crutch catching on a crack in the uneven sidewalk. She'd started falling and only regained her equilibrium after putting weight on her swollen ankle. To keep from crying out and distracting Adam, who was already angry at her for wasting so much of his precious time, she bit the insides of her cheeks. By the time the lab door had slowly drifted shut, she'd negotiated the rest of the walkway, with Adam none the wiser about how clumsy she'd been. An owl had hooted as she fitted her key into the lock.

As the tumblers fell into place, there was a loud muffled boom behind her. She swiveled so fast, she tripped herself with her crutches, her shoulder hit the doorframe so hard she cried out in pain. Then the lab's windows exploded in fiery arcs. Jacqueline could never remember falling face forward and dislocating her nose on the porch floor; she could never forget how her body trembled when she smelled burning flesh and knew it was Adam's.

"Want one?"

Jacqueline jerked out of her reverie. Link was standing next to her, holding a golden brown orb that sagged precariously from the end of the long fork in his hand.

Unsteadily, she scrambled to her feet. "No." How long had he been there? Had she said anything out loud?

With a flick of his wrist, he tossed the goo into the dark swirling water. "Are you all right?"

"I'm fine."

"Uh huh. Are you cold?"

"I'm fine."

Link took her chin in his palm and raised it until she was looking at his face. "What's wrong?"

"Nothing."

His thumb caressed her cheek. "Tell me." Sparks from the distant fire were reflected in his eyes.

Jacqueline jerked her head away and turned her back on him. "Nothing is wrong. I just don't like marshmallows. The smell makes me ill."

Link towered over her and simply stared. For several long minutes, she felt like a specimen in a bottle. He glanced from her face to her hands and she realized she'd been unconsciously rubbing her upper arms. "You're cold, come nearer the fire," he said softly.

"No." The word came out sounding panic-stricken, but she was past caring what impression she made. "I like it here."

After several thudding heartbeats, he nodded. "So that's it."

"What is?"

"You're afraid of fire."

"What kind of person do you think I am? Some weak little mouse that's afraid to confront her own stupid fears?"

"That never occurred to me." Link draped his arm around her shoulders in a companionable gesture. "Why don't we take a walk? You can tell me why." Jacqueline shook her head. "Fine. Then let's just take a walk. If you feel like talking, you can."

Jacqueline tried to wrench free of Link, but only succeeded in stumbling closer to him. "Okay, I'll walk, but I don't want to talk about fire."

"It might help." She didn't believe that for a

moment. "Was it a bad fire?"

"Yes."

"Thought so. It would have taken a blaze from hell to make someone as strong as you so upset. It was the one that killed Adam, wasn't it?" The matter-of-fact tone of his voice shocked her.

"How did you know?"

"Mavis mentioned a scientist burning to death last year." Link's tone sounded accepting. Jacqueline gagged. "Did you watch him die?"

"I couldn't see him."

"And you couldn't help."

"I'd sprained my ankle and the f-flames. Oh, God, the flames." Tears poured down her cheeks. "Flames were everywhere and they were so hot. So unbelievably hot. Even the doorknob to the house felt hot. Even while I dialed 911, I knew no one could have survived that blast." Jacqueline shivered. Link's arm tightened. "I felt so helpless. All I could do was stand there and watch everything I'd worked for go up in flames." She took a shuddering breath. "It seemed like Adam screamed forever, but I know it wasn't really him, he had to have died instantly, but there was this sound." She wet her lips. "Probably heat expanding oxygen particles." She swallowed. "And the stench." She could still smell the singed hair and burned flesh. Bile rose in her stomach. Jacqueline took several deep breaths. Link hugged her tight. The steady beat of his heart against her cheek calmed her. "Adam wasn't even supposed to be in the lab," Jacqueline added in a choked whisper. "I always did the final check, but I'd sprained my ankle, so he checked the fax machine." It was hard to talk around the lump in her throat. "My job killed him. I killed him because of a stupid soccer game."

Link stroked her spine in a reassuring way. "You couldn't have known." Her tears spilled, drenching his shirt. Instead of pushing her away, his arms seemed like a protective cocoon.

"If I hadn't played that game, I wouldn't have torn those ligaments, and I'd have been able to do my job."

"Then, you'd be the one dead."

She shook her head. "The Fire Marshal said his cigarette ignited a gas leak. I don't smoke."

"Are you blaming yourself for living?"

"I— " She struggled for breath. "I blame myself for not getting to the phone fast enough and for not dialing 911 right the first time."

He hugged her tighter and made soothing sounds. All the while, his hand caressed her spine. A lump blocked her throat. Jacqueline swallowed hard. "Adam won't blame you." She shook her head. "Did you force the cigarette on him?

Jacqueline shook her head, again. "He wanted to quit, but couldn't."

"There's a reason for everything, a destiny. Obviously that was his."

Could Link be right?

13

The lemony scent of Jacqueline's perfume saturated Link's dreams, so by the next morning he couldn't look her in the eye. While his discomfort scored smiles from Tempest, Carmen looked perplexed. Jacqueline merely shrugged. Phillip stayed mercifully oblivious to personal interactions, so Link could relax as their kayak drifted down the river. He was so pleased not to be asked questions that he told Phillip their route for the day was easy to single-hand and he encouraged Phillip to read his iPad or just watch the scenery.

The next night, Link again dreamed that Jacqueline shared his sleeping bag, fulfilling wild fantasies he refused to admit to when awake. When he emerged from his tent the following morning, an unexpected glimpse of her swinging ponytail made his knees weak. Furious with his unruly subconscious, Link kept his canoe so far back, that when they did catch sight of the other one, it looked the size of a rubber ducky.

At dinner, Carmen bubbled with happiness, apparently believing he was fulfilling her hopes of getting to know Phillip, better. He was trying to find a polite way to mention that Phillip seemed happier after spending a day reading, when the tilt of Jacqueline's chin made him forget to swallow. As he coughed, Link decided that since evasion had only intensified whatever his problem, he should confront his obsession. Thus, after the dishes were cleaned, Link approached Jacqueline. "Let's go for a walk."

Jacqueline glanced around the campsite, then back at him. "Me?" He nodded. "Where to?"

"Pick a direction."

She scrutinized his face. "What's wrong?"

"What makes you think something is wrong?"

Jacqueline crossed her arms over her chest in an exaggerated imitation of his stance. "Your body language."

He stuffed his hands into the back pockets of his jeans. "Better?"

She hesitated then asked, "We can't talk about it here?" Link inclined his head toward Tempest, then shook his head. Jacqueline glanced at the pouting teen, before she nodded in agreement. They were soon picking their way over a narrow trail. She tripped, then chuckled.

"What's so funny?"

"I was just wondering if this was a mountain goat super highway or an obstacle course."

"It's an expressway for Dahl sheep."

When they could no longer hear Tempest's high-pitched whine, Jacqueline stopped and looked at the rugged scenery. The steep slopes were gradually giving way to foothills and scraggly pines. Link peered into the shadows. If her stalker was upstream, he preferred a more open vista.

Jacqueline faced him. "What do you want to talk about?"

"Maybe I just wanted to get away from Tempest's woebegone looks and the way she yowls so loud to bring attention to herself."

Her eyes narrowed. "That's probably part of your motive, but I think you're worried about that kayak, and wondering if I know more than I've said."

Not even his mother read him as easily as Jacqueline. The more he got to know her, the more he believed that she really was twenty-five instead of the fifteen he'd suspected. Did her height make her seem younger? "Well, what's the answer?"

"I don't know who is upriver, but I keep wondering why they are trying not to be noticed." Her mouth flattened. "I keep telling myself this land is so beautiful that it must be safe." She made a helpless gesture with her hands. "No matter how often I repeat it, I know it's easy to die anywhere. And the real truth is that out here, no one would ever be able to figure out what happened." She paused for breath. "So if that kayaker is my stalker, he's got a golden opportunity." Jacqueline took a deep breath.

"But he hasn't made any openly hostile moves."

"Except the note."

"True, but it could have other meanings." She straightened her back and stared at him. "Don't get me wrong, I can't think of a civil meaning, especially in light of losing your husband, but I'm open to the possibility."

"Every day, I imagine I'm going to be shot by a sniper."

"You always seem calm."

"I can't win by having an emotional breakdown. Besides, I'm certain that if I have a destiny, hysterics won't change it."

"I've always believed that myself, but I don't know if I could be as composed as you in your circumstances." Which explained why he wondered how truthful she was.

"I've been stalked by this creep for three years."

Jacqueline closed her eyes and messaged her temples. Then, she straightened and looked at him. "Link, I'm embarrassed that I overreact so badly to that note. The truth is, I think they're worse than any face to face confrontation could be." She might have a point. Jacqueline crossed her arms and stared into the distance. "Logic tells me I should be able to figure out who is stalking me and why they're doing so." She shook her head. "But I didn't know anyone could be so persistent. Since those notes started arriving, I've learned to fear fire, the scent of plumeria, red ink and yellow paper. Isn't that ridiculous? I know it's stupid to be afraid of colors, but I am. And I despise myself for being so weak." As she turned her face away, he saw a tear roll down her cheek. "I'm not calm, I'm pathetic."

Link did something he'd wanted to do for days. He gathered Jacqueline into his arms and hugged her close. Her arms wrapped around him, as if she was trying to soothe and protect him in return.

Defending Jacqueline felt right. "You aren't weak," he assured the top of her head.

Her face buried deeper against his chest, and he felt her lips move, "Yes, I am. This fear of the unknown is horrible."

Not knowing what to say, Link buried his face in her hair. A gentle breeze picked up a lock of her hair. It tickled his nose. It smelled of lemon and Jacqueline. The fragrance had such an erotic effect that keeping his mind on the conversation was a struggle. "You'll get through this. I'll help you."

"I want to confront my stalker."

"You can't do that."

She pushed away from him so roughly, she would have butted his nose if she'd been an inch taller. "Why not?"

"Think about where we are," Link said.

She frowned up at him. Petite though she was, nothing about her appeared defenseless.

"I come from Texas," he said. "The badlands aren't far away from where I grew up. They're rugged and beautiful, just like it is here, but every year people disappear." Link took a deep breath. "Since we know there's danger, we're not sitting ducks. Or at least I hope we aren't." He smiled. "Except, now you have me wondering if the kayaker is your stalker and if he has a good high powered rifle."

"If I'd had any idea he followed me to Fairbanks, I'd never have agreed to come with you. My presence puts you and the others in danger."

"Accidents happen everywhere. Just because someone is stalking you doesn't make him all-powerful. The fact that you know he is there gives you an edge you wouldn't have against a random act of nature."

"Like what happen to your father?"

"How'd you know about that?"

"Carmen told me that when you were growing up, he had an accident. She said he's a paraplegic."

"I'm surprised she mentioned it."

"She seems to take your father's paralysis for granted. What happened to him?" Jacqueline asked the question with genuine interest. Instead of brushing her off, his arms tightened around her, pulling her cheek against his chest. She snuggled against him. For the first time in his life, Link felt ready to face the past.

"Dad and I used to go fishing and camping together. Just me and him; since I was the oldest. By the time Carmen came along, and then a couple years later, the twins, dad and I had a pattern of spending Saturday mornings together doing guy things." Jacqueline raised a brow. He grinned. "We built birdhouses, tied flies for fishing. Played catch. Shot baskets. Hiked." He shrugged. "Guy things."

"So, you think males are the only gender that like that sort of stuff?"

"Not any more." Remembering was easier than he expected. "Dad was an industrial engineer. He started his own consulting business when I was seven. Money was tight at first, but he was building a good reputation and every month he and Mom had fewer fights about money. And no matter what, he always made time for me."

"My philosophy is that we're spirits having a human experience." She grinned up at him. "I doubt if money is a heavenly factor."

"Interesting idea." Link smiled back. "You could be right."

"Go on with your story."

"On the weekends, when rodeos were nearby, Dad rode bulls. It was his hobby."

"That's how he got hurt? Getting thrown from a bull?" She tensed. "Did it stomp him?"

"No." Link's throat felt tight and dry. It took him three tries to swallow. "I only told you that so you'd get an idea of the physical type of man he was before the accident."

She nodded. "Go on."

"He'd flown up to Lubbock to see a factory they wanted to expand. The company plane hit wind shear." Link couldn't go on.

Jacqueline's comforting arms tightened and her hands caressed his spine. "I'm sorry for him, for you and for the rest of your family. It must have been terrible."

"The worst part was when we brought Dad home. I

hadn't been able to visit him in the hospital because I was too young and mom had only said he'd need help. I didn't understand or accept his limitations."

"Like I said, the unknown is usually worse."

"I guess I built up unrealistic expectations, and I sure didn't expect a paraplegic." The lump was so large Link could barely breath. "When Dad came home, he was depressed and suicidal. I don't know if he was like that in the hospital or if our reactions to him triggered it." Link held onto Jacqueline as if she was his lifeline in a sea of misery. "I kept telling myself that he'd get better, but every day, he seemed worse."

"When Grandpa died, Grandma said that if God loves you, he tests your strength and keeps testing you until you're tungsten."

"She is that."

"But we were talking about your father. He was a very active man, and his world got turned upside down. How is he now?"

"Better." Link felt a heavy weight leave his shoulders. Suddenly breathing was easier. "It took Dad a year to realize he could roll his wheelchair up to his drafting board. The worst part was that by that time, the clients he'd built up had abandoned him."

"They couldn't wait?"

He shook his head. "They had timetables. As a business owner, I understand, but I didn't back then." He cleared his throat. "Medical bills soaked up everything. Dad filed for bankruptcy. And Mom got food stamps. I hated being the welfare kid."

"No insurance?"

"The premiums cost too much."

"Do you blame your father?"

He shrugged.

"How are your parents doing now?"

"Fine. Dad rebuilt his business, but it took him ten years. He's riding again." Link smiled at the bittersweet memory. Jacqueline blinked up at him. "Horses, not bulls. It's a type of physical therapy."

"Thank goodness for that," she said. Link felt tears scald his eyes, but he laughed instead of crying. "What?"

"The horse he rides has ambitions of being a steeplechaser."

"So, despite everything that happened and the rough years, your dad is still a macho man, huh?"

"I guess so," Link agreed. "As far as paraplegics go, Dad is still a bull rider." Still the man he'd worshiped as a boy and mourned as an adult.

"Link, I appreciate you telling me about him, but you didn't bring me up here to talk about your family, did you?"

He shook his head. "What do you know about this stalker-guy?" She shrugged, her look blank. "Do you really think he'd try the sniper approach?"

"I hope not."

"After all this time, you must know something about him."

"He always uses yellow legal paper."

"That's something."

"And then there's his handwriting; he always presses down hard on the paper. And he always very precise, like he wants every letter to be perfect."

"So he's specific," Link mused.

Jacqueline blinked, then nodded. "He always mixes images of fire and love."

"Odd choices."

"He folds the letters into a different shape each time, but if he leaves a flower, it's always plumeria." She frowned. "I've never been able to figure out any hidden meaning for the shapes or flower, but recently I've started to worry that the red ink could be a threat." Jacqueline pushed away from him and began pacing.

Link's arms felt empty. "Origami takes some of the menace away, doesn't it?" Link said. "It reminds me of the way we sent notes in grade school."

She stopped pacing and whirled to face him. "Could he be a juvenile?"

He shrugged. "Everything about this guy's notes seems childlike. The heavy pressure, the shapes, even the anonymity." A gust of wind blew Jacqueline's hair into her eyes. With a quick, fluid movement, she shoved it away. While Link knew Jacqueline wasn't trying to entice him, never the less she was succeeding.

"Assuming he's the man you saw, he's old enough to have grown a long beard."

Link gave himself a mental shake. "If the person I saw was him. It could have been a new hire. We won't know for sure until we get back."

"You're right, but something about your description feels right. Do you think he's some sort of simpleton? A child in a man's body?"

"That could explain a lot."

"But what made him fixate on me?"

He didn't have an answer.

"Since you described the new guy, I've tried to form a mental picture of every person I met about the time or just before I received the first note. I even tried recalling your description without the beard, but didn't get anywhere. I tried to remember meeting anyone I even suspected of plucking one big shaggy eyebrow." She sighed and sadly shook her head. "I haven't been able to think of a single soul. You'd think someone like that would have been memorable, but I don't even remember seeing the hairy guy in the hangar."

Link laughed. "He was mostly hair." Trust Jacqueline to pick up on that. "He looked downtrodden. Sad." As if anyone who didn't take care of their appearance could look any other way.

Jacqueline rubbed her temple. "For now, I'll assume that was him. In the past, I tried to picture both men and women."

"What were you doing when you originally started getting the notes?" Link asked.

"I'd just graduated from grad school and had started working at Envirohab." She made an odd expression. "Adam finally proposed, but he insisted on keeping our marriage a secret, because he'd recommended me for the job as his assistant and he figured his superiors wouldn't understand that he really did value me as a research assistant." She snorted. "I kept my maiden name." Her mouth flattened.

"Yet you lived together openly."

"Separate bedrooms, same house, which was a couple miles away from neighbors. Like we were putting one over on anyone. Dumb, huh?" She shook her head. "The first note arrived the morning after our first real argument, which I won't go into." She made a dismissive gesture. "Even though he denied it, I always thought Adam sent it, at least that's what I thought up until one arrived after he'd died. Kinda hard to send them from the grave." She looked heavenward. "Remembering back, I realize it was silly to believe someone as domineering as Adam would ever send whiny notes, plus Adam had tiny, precise handwriting."

Cold bands tightened around Link's chest, and he wished Jacqueline hadn't moved away from him, not only did she feel good against him, he could think better with her in his arms. "So they only started to bother you after he died?"

She nodded. "Yeah. Mainly, they pissed off Adam. If I'd known he really hadn't sent them, I'm sure they'd have disturbed me." She began slowly walking back toward their camp. "Envirohab was located at the intersection of nowhere and Timbuktu. We had to drive for an hour just to get groceries, so it isn't as if there were hundreds of new faces in my life about the time the notes started."

"How many others worked there?"

"None. That's why he didn't mind us sharing a roof, but insisted on keeping a separation on any paperwork his bosses could see. That included filing separate income taxes." She frowned. "That's another odd thing that started after I got married – every year, the IRS came after me claiming I hadn't filed my tax forms correctly, even though I had a CPA do them after the first fine." She looked ready to kick something.

Link studied their two distant tents, which were illuminated by a waning moon, and decided she should have been able to figure out the stalker's identity with such limited possibilities. "Your husband must have had a playful streak if you figured it was him."

"Adam was brilliant, but he didn't have a sense of humor."

"I've met the type." Phillip could read by lantern light or while drifting past incredible scenery. "Smart at book learning, but socially inept." Their marriage sounded more like a convenience than a love match.

"That was Adam." She sighed, then rubbed her arms as if chilled.

"Want to head back?" She nodded with apparent

relief. In silence, he walked her as far as his own tent, where he retrieved his fishing pole, then he headed toward the river, settled onto a boulder, and prepared to cast his lure. Something plopped into the water. Link looked upriver for the source of the sound, but only saw a brief movement in his peripheral vision. The kayaker was either antisocial as a grizzly, or tracking them with the skill of a master predator.

Link didn't like feeling like prey. If he'd been alone, he would have forced a meeting. But four other people were relying on him, so his options were limited.

14

During the following days, Jacqueline frequently caught glimpses of the mystery kayak. One day, she, again, borrowed Phillip's binoculars and confirmed that a large bearded man was the kayak's sole occupant. Why hadn't he ever approached her to explain himself and settle whatever his problem was once and for all?

Did he enjoy terrorizing her?

While no more notes appeared, that didn't mean it was a coincidence that the kayaker looked shaggy and Link thought he might be the same stranger that had helped load the baggage. If he was actually her stalker, and was not communicating, it could be as simple as not having more paper. Or perhaps he was afraid to come into their camp after Link chased him off. This assumed he was the one who had invaded, which she admitted might be a stretch.

Or was he plotting something horrible?

Previously, he'd contacted her when only she and Adam were around. Did that mean something or was that simply due to their isolation?

Thursday evening, while they went through what had become a pattern: Carmen dealt with the dishes and Phillip read by the fire, Link tied more flies and Tempest continued to mope over not being Link's center of attention. Jacqueline sat with her back to the dying embers staring through the shadows and wondered if anyone was watching them.

Link stretched his back, then stood looking at the surrounding terrain, then said, "We should reach Fort Yukon tomorrow." She felt a mild jolt of optimism surge through her. Link stretched his long legs, then finished tying the fly.

Jacqueline bit her lower lip and looked from face to face, then cleared her throat and said. "When we get to Fort Yukon, I think it would be best if the rest of you returned to Fairbanks."

"Why?" Link demanded.

"Because." She glanced upstream. "I need to get this resolved, or at least find out if my worst suspicions are fact or fiction." She swallowed. "If that kayacker actually is my stalker, he might be shy, so as long as the four of you are here, he'll never come close and I'll never find out what he wants."

"Are you insane?" Tempest demanded. Jacqueline shook her head. Tempest snorted. "Then your stupid."

"Maybe, so, but I just want to understand what this is about and I don't think anything will get resolved when it's five to one."

Carmen looked from her to Phillip and back again. "I'm okay with spending extra in Fairbanks." Phillip smiled and nodded in agreement.

"When we get there, I'll call Stone," Link said. Tempest smiled from ear to ear. "But I don't like the idea of leaving you alone." Tempest's smile faltered and her eyes narrowed.

The following day, as they neared Fort Yukon, the kayak following them frequently popped into view, then ducked out of sight. By the time they arrived at the main dock, everyone acted as tense as Link felt.

As soon as the canoes were secured, everyone except Jacqueline headed toward the store. "Aren't you coming?" Carmen asked.

"I think I'll wait here and see if he shows. If he does, I can get it over instead of go through all this silly subterfuge."

"If you're staying, so am I," Link said. He cupped her elbow in his palm and guided her into the dappled shadow beneath a thin, twisted pine.

"Won't you please reconsider and leave with the others?"

And face her grandmother's wrath? "No."

"Even if you're being with me makes him too shy to contact me?"

"No."

"How about if I say please?"

"No. Don't you understand the word?" He glared down at her. "You stay; I stay. You want me to leave, you come with me. Period, end of discussion."

They alternately watched the dock and stared upstream until their eyes watered, but the kayak never arrived.

"It's been two hours," Jacqueline whispered.

The hair on the back of Link's neck quivered. The kayaker's failure to show neutralized all previous doubts. "He's not coming." Tempest's voice came from behind the trunk.

"You were supposed to stay with Carmen," Link said.

Tempest's head and torso appeared. The anxiety in her expression was as obvious as the pinesap on the shoulder of her crimson shirt. Link stared at the fabric and knew why they'd waited in vain. He wished he'd never brought Tempest. Not just because of the time she'd just wasted, but because she seemed to be reliving the nightmare time of her life.

Jacqueline tore her gaze from the soiled blouse and said, "I'm hungry, what about you?"

"At breakfast I couldn't eat." Tempest completely emerged from behind the tree.

"That's because you were busy trying to convince me to run away," Jacqueline said.

Tempest snorted.

Jacqueline's face displayed raw determination, but no fear. No worry. No second thoughts. Though part of him thought Jacqueline's decision was reckless, Link admired her spunk.

"For all the good it did," Tempest said. "You're nuts to want a confrontation." She glanced up at Link and her mouth flattened. "And you call me a raving lunatic."

"Tempest, you need to apologize to Jacqueline," Link said.

Jacqueline shook her head. "She's probably right and since you refuse to listen to reason, you could qualify, too." She winked at him.

She might be correct. Link had tried to analyze his feelings, but they simply didn't make sense. Yes, she was Mavis' granddaughter, and deserved to be looked after. But to the point of possibly risking his life? Logic said no.

Link's heart disagreed.

Jacqueline looked at Tempest. "Come on, let's see if there's any ice cream for sale." Link drifted after them.

Carmen looked up as he walked into the mercantile. "You're frowning. What's wrong?" He sighed. "Is it the stalker?" Link shook his head. "Tempest? Jacqueline?"

Twice more he indicated negative. "I was thinking about Phillip."

Carmen wet her lips. "I know you don't like him. He's different from anyone I've ever dated. I'm sorry I brought him." Once Carmen was nervous enough to babble, it was difficult to stop her. "He's been miserable and it's contagious. I know you're using this supposed phantom as an excuse." He took her arm and steered her outside.

He led her away from potential eavesdroppers, before he cut in, "The stalker is real." Carmen's mouth sagged. "And do not apologize for Phillip," Link said. "He's a fish out of water, but I doubt if I'd do half as well as he's done if I had to survive the urban jungle."

"You like him?"

Link nodded. "Do you love him?"

"I can't imagine my life without him."

"In that case, when I get back, I'll find my shotgun."

Carmen shaded her eyes and studied his face. "You want our relationship to be permanent?"

"Only if you do. You are the one that would have to live with him. Not me."

"But he doesn't fit in."

"At least not here. If we ever take another joint vacation, we'll find a destination where everyone feels comfortable," Link said. "In the wilderness, Phillip gives the impression of being a wimp, but I'll wager that if you gave us each a keyboard, he'd trounce me within the first five minutes." Carmen's face looked as if she didn't know whether to laugh or cry, but was perilously close to weeping. Link spotted Tempest coming toward them. Her head kept turning as if she wanted to watch every direction at the same time. "Thank God, we're getting her out of here," Link muttered.

"She really got to you with her crush, huh?"

"I wouldn't want to endure another one, but that's

not what I meant." Tempest was almost within earshot. "Ask Ariel about their stalker. No, cancel that. You'd better ask Stone, but make it private." Carmen gave him a perplexed look.

"Uncle Link, do you love Jacqueline enough to die for her?" Tempest demanded.

"I like her." A lot, his mind added. She's feisty. Brave. And smart. "But I don't think the circumstances are deadly."

"All stalkers are out for blood," Tempest said. "There's nothing I don't know about them."

Carmen cleared her throat. "Tempest, is every single person the same?"

"What do you mean?" A raven flew overhead and cawed. Tempest cringed.

"Does everyone who hunts enjoy killing?" Carmen asked.

She thought about the question for a long time then shook her head. "Some people kill for the sake of killing." Tempest's trembling hands moved to her stomach and perspiration beaded her forehead. Link wanted to hug her, but in light of her recent misunderstanding, knew he couldn't.

Carmen gave him a penetrating look, then wrapped her arm around Tempest's quaking form. It gave the child enough security to continue. "Peter liked to hunt so he could kill." Her voice squeaked. "Uncle Link and Stone hunt if there's an animal that's hurting people; like that grizzly that killed two people last winter." She squinted up at him. "You said that you felt like you were stooping to the animal's level by hunting for the simple sake of slaughter. You really don't like hunting, do you?"

"Sometimes terminating a life can't be helped. Do you remember the first time you saw me touch a gun?"

Tempest nodded then began chewing her upper lip. "I'll bet your first thought was that I was a murderer and enjoyed it."

Her eyes widened. "How did you know?"

"Because it's natural. You would have been basing that belief on what you'd learned in the past. We all do it. It's human nature. But the truth is that our evaluations aren't always fair or accurate because we normally don't take the other's motives into account."

Tempest gestured toward the river. "So you really, truly don't think he wants to kill her." Her voice faltered. Carmen's arm tightened, drawing the quaking form solidly against her side.

Link shook his head.

"But— "

"Tempest, think about it," Link cut in. "Assuming the guy in the kayak is the stalker, he's followed us through more than a hundred miles of wilderness. If he wanted to harm Jacqueline, he's had plenty of opportunity. Can you think of a better place to dispose of a body or even bodies?"

A red spot appeared on each chalky cheek. "No. But why bother following her if killing her isn't what he wants? It doesn't make sense."

"Not to us, but it must to him. That's one question I intend to ask him if I ever get the chance. I'm sure the guy's reasons make perfect sense to him. And I'm sure the list of stuff that he keeps telling Jacqueline makes sense to him, too, and if she understood what he wanted, this might have been settled a long time ago."

Tempest nodded solemnly. He was relieved to see healthy color begin creeping back into her complexion. "I've been so worried for you and Jacqueline."

"Her, too?"

"I hated her at first, but I don't any more. I wish I could be like she is. She's about the bravest person I've ever known."

Or foolhardy.

Impulsively, Tempest grasped his arm, stood on tiptoe and kissed his chin. "That's for luck." Red began creeping up her neck. Whirling, she broke free of Carmen and sprinted toward what passed as the general store.

"You did great," Carmen said quietly.

"Thanks, I think." He frowned. "What did I do?"

"Treated her as if her fears were worth considering and helped her put them to rest."

"They were honest fears." Link wished he believed what he'd told her. Whenever human nature got involved, logic wasn't always dependable.

What if the man was a killer? Had he made plans to murder them all? Was he waiting for the right opportunity?

It was a possibility.

Link knew he must be nuts to stick his neck out. Tempest had a valid point; there was no logical explanation for the man's actions, which only left an illogical one. Link's thoughts led to another unsettling idea. Did he love Jacqueline? He tried to laugh off the idea, but couldn't. Suddenly, the question of love took on a broader significance. What if the stalker was acting the way he was because of some misplaced idea of love?

15

Tempest and Jacqueline stood shoulder to shoulder on the porch of the log cabin that passed for Fort Yukon's terminal and watched Linkstone's small company plane taxi across the gravel and worn weeds, which covered the rustic runway. When the plane stopped, her attention riveted on the Cessna's door and when it swung open, Tempest walked stiff as a robot toward Stone. Shaking his gentle touch off, she crawled into the rear seat, then pressed her face against the window. If Jacqueline had thought it would do any good, she'd have boarded the plane, too, but that would only have put off facing the unknown and she'd already done that far too long. Jacqueline doubted if the child understood why she had to do this and knew that if Link suffered so much as a hangnail, the kid would make her life a living hell of retribution.

Carmen's features were a caricature of woe as she gave Link a tearful, clinging hug.

Stone closed the baggage compartment, then grabbed Link's shoulder and pulled him out of sight of the Cessna's passengers. Jacqueline watched Link's face. Though she was too far away to hear, it didn't take much to guess the topic of conversation's content as Stone motioned toward the river, then pointed toward the plane. Link's shoulders were rigid as Tempest's had been, though his casual stance and the thumbs he had stuck in his pockets seemed relaxed. Stone made a forceful gesture toward her.

Jacqueline took a backward step. Her bottom whacked against the solid wall of the log structure. "Talk, Stone, talk," she whispered softly. "Get Link out of here. Make him change his mind. Save him." If Link gets hurt or worse, dies, while helping me, I'll never forgive myself. Link threw up his hands. Jacqueline's eyes watered.

Link shook his head.

Stone punched Link in the shoulder. A lesser man would have been knocked on his backside, but Link didn't budge. Jacqueline massaged her collarbone, certain that she'd be black and blue from head to toe if anyone ever gave her such a companionable blow. Link gave Stone a matching cuff. Then the two men gave each other a back-thumping hug. Finally, Stone got in the plane and the propeller started to turn.

Link waved a final farewell.

Jacqueline bit her lower lip and blinked away tears.

If her stalker wanted her dead, she'd have died long ago. Since she was alive, it stood to reason that Link was correct about him wanting something tangible from her. If her stalker had devised a trap, which Adam's cigarette would trip, it meant he had meant to kill him, not her. But had the cigarette ignited the blaze as the fire marshall claimed, or had it been something else? Had she been the target? Or had Adam? Or had it all been some sort of scam, so he only appeared to die? Acid indigestion ate at her stomach. Her stalker had hinted at his hatred of Adam with every scrap of origami— until the fire. By staying, Link could be making himself appear to be new competition and be in serious danger.

Jacqueline wished she knew what the phantom

wanted, and if her or Link's lives would be expendable after he got it. One of her father's favorite phrases circled like a broken record in her mind: 'Better the enemy you know than the one you don't.' She finally understood his philosophy.

As the Cessna accelerated, prop wash whipped Link's hair and clothes. He turned and jogged toward her. Upon reaching her, he threw a companionable arm around her shoulders. "You're a lot like your grandmother, and I know her pretty well. In fact, the only mystery about her is why Mavis hates phones so much."

"That was meant as a compliment, wasn't it?"

"Yep. Mavis is one great lady."

"She likes you a lot, too." He grinned, but shook his head, as if humoring a kid's idealistic belief. "Are you aware that Grandma is hard of hearing? At home, her phone has a volume control. She keeps it on high. I answered it once and thought my ear was going to disintegrate from the shock."

"That's the problem?" Link rolled his eyes heavenward. "She should have said something!" He looked at the Cessna, as if seriously sprinting after it, but it's engine was revving for take off, so he pulled his cellphone out of his shirt pocket. "I'm texting Ariel and telling her to get one for the office." Slowly, the plane began to roll. It gathered speed then lifted into the air.

Jacqueline and Link stepped out into the thin sunlight and waved. As she followed the flight path, she saw a movement out of the corner of her eye. Jacqueline turned toward it. For a brief moment, a man's head and shoulders were outlined beside the log cabin. In the fleeting instant before he moved out of sight, Jacqueline noticed long scraggly hair, a beard halfway to his navel and what might be one thick eyebrow. Her entire body tensed as she leaped toward the corner.

But hands grabbed her, holding her back. "What's wrong?" Link asked.

"I just saw the guy."

His fingers grasping her shoulder tightened. "Where?"

She pointed. "By the northeast corner."

"Stay here." His determined look forestalled objections. "I'll go check it out." He sprinted toward the corner. Finally free, Jacqueline dashed toward the opposite one, hoping she'd catch the man or at least get a second look.

She skidded around the corner. Something jumped in front of her. Jacqueline stopped too fast and stumbled. The terrified arctic hare loped off to safety. Jacqueline landed hard on her backside, but quickly scrambled to her feet.

"I thought I told you to stay there," Link said. She whirled around. He pointed toward the front and gave her a glaring look.

Jacqueline tilted her head and glowered back at him. "You do not have the right to tell me where to stay."

Link closed his eyes and rubbed his neck. Then, he took a deep breath. "You don't use miniature swords for letter openers, do you?"

"No. Why?" To her astonishment, after asking such a bizarre question, he turned his back on her and walked away. Jacqueline wanted to turn and stomp away in the opposite direction.

Instead, she stood still.

Link was being a better friend than Adam had ever been and she'd thrown his concern back in his face. She owed him. Resolved to do the right thing, she went in search of Link. She wandered into the gift shop, which was filled with furs and Athabascan beadwork. One leather shirt caught her attention. Its soft golden tan background was covered with bright, iridescent turquoise flowers and emerald leaves. It was garish, yet somehow simple.

"You like it?"

"I like the colors." She turned to Link. "I shouldn't have snapped at you like that. Please accept my apology." The heavy emotional burden lifted from her shoulders.

"I'm not your boss, nor am I in any way superior to you." His tone sounded formal. "I was out of line." She smiled. He leaned forward and kissed her forehead.

Rising on tiptoe, she kissed his chin. "Link, why didn't you listen to Stone and go back with him?"

Link frowned. "Stone never suggested that."

"I thought that's what he was talking about when he took you aside."

Link guffawed and shook his head. "He wanted to come with us. I reminded him that he had a wife and family to think about, but he claimed that didn't matter, so I reminded him that he was supposed to be on his second honeymoon." He shook his head. She raised a brow. "He only gave in when I told him we shouldn't give Mavis the idea that she could run the company by herself."

"To hear Grandma tell it, she already does." By the look on his face, he'd taken her literally. "Link, I was joking." She took his hand. "Seriously, she doesn't know what she'd do without you two. She loves it when one of you has an office day, but if you haven't figured that out, I guess she must still be having a problem hiding her emotions." She paused. "Hungry?" He nodded.

Entering the restaurant, Jacqueline sniffed in

appreciation. She scanned the menu, rejecting anything she'd eaten during the past few days. A small section listed breakfast entrees. Those powdered eggs had been inedible. Thank goodness the midnight marauder had taken them. The menu crumpled under her grip.

"What are you thinking about?" Link asked.

"Powdered eggs and coffee. Groceries. I am so stupid. I should have staked out the store instead of the dock." He frowned. "The food burglar took basics." She explained. "Since we're almost certain the kayaker is my stalker, he must be the one who— " She clamped her jaws shut tight in fury.

"Stole the stuff and he'd head straight for food," he finished.

"I don't know what's wrong with my mind," she seethed. "Food and water attract all wildlife. That's what makes watering holes ideal locations for observation blinds."

"If it makes you feel any better, I didn't think about it until a couple hours ago. Sammy said the guy was in earlier and bought dried beans. Twenty pounds of them."

"You've got to be kidding."

"Sammy figured he wanted jet propulsion."

"Well, we wanted to learn more about him, but I'd hoped for something more significant than knowing he's a walking methane factory."

"Sammy said one side of his face was badly scarred. She thought it looked like an old burn and he'd grown the beard to hide it."

Just when she'd thought it couldn't get worse. "What if he burned the lab and Adam? What if he was actually there? What if he was Adam?"

"I don't think anyone could grow a beard that long in the time since your lab burned," Link said. Obviously, she had asked the question aloud. It was kind of him not to suggest her husband might be her stalker or point out that anyone could purchase a false beard.

"Let's assume he got injured in another fire." Link twirled the thick glass saltshaker. "Disfigurement might indicate a history of pyromania. Do you know anyone with a fire fetish?"

She swallowed. "Adam always flicked his lighter while he waited for things."

"And you're certain he's dead?"

"The body was identified by dental records."

"Is there any possibility that he switched the records?" She'd wanted to know the answer to that question for a while, but had no clue how to verify the data. Link's expression indicated that he noticed her uncertainty. "Just for the sake of argument, let's assume the stalker is your ex, do you have anything he'd need? Is there any reason for him to keep following you?" Her stomach rolled as she shook her head. "Was he the jealous type?" She nodded. "You think there's any possibility the dental records could have been faked?" Link's hand covered hers as she shook her head.

"The firemen weren't able to get to Adam until the next morning because it was too hot." Assuming the body was his. "I saw him go into the building and there was only one corpse. He has to be dead." The smell of cooking beef no longer tantalized. Her stomach heaved. She thrust back the chair so hard it tipped backward.

Jacqueline barely made it to the bathroom in time.

After emptying her stomach, Jacqueline wrapped her arms around the porcelain as if it was a long lost lover and held on tight. But nothing could purge the awful memory of Adam's death. Eventually, she found the strength to stand and bathe her face in cold water. The reflection seemed to waver and change into a disfigured face. The distorted image mocked her with the fact that a memory could render her helpless.

Would she ever be able to think of Adam's fiery death unemotionally?

Be able to look into flames and not have her stomach turn?

Before the fire, she'd loved watching flames atop slender tapers flicker. Looking deeply into them, her imagination had wandered. They'd been like watching a beautiful sunset, which had yellow, orange and purple rays of dancing light.

Shakily, she wiped her face.

As she opened the door, the first thing she saw was Link leaning against the wall. He glowed with relief when he saw her. "Are you all right?" She nodded. "Come here." He gathered her into his strong, protective arms and held her close. "Everything is going to be fine." Every cell in her body ached to believe him. Link kissed her forehead. "Don't worry, we'll get through this together."

"I don't want anything to happen to you."

He hugged her. She snuggled into Link's arms, relishing the feeling of security. For a passing moment, she thought she could spend the rest of her life trusting his calm reassurance. But friendly hugs were only Band-Aids; they protected a hurt while it was raw, but you couldn't wear them forever.

"I don't feel very well," Jacqueline said. "Would you be upset if I went back to the hotel and got some sleep?"

"I'll come."

"Eat your meal. I'll be fine." He took a step toward the door. She stopped. "Please?" Reluctantly, he nodded.

That night, she dreamed she was hobbling through velvet darkness on rubbery crutches while shadow demons swirled around her. Suddenly, her universe exploded and in one heart-pounding moment, her body blistered. Jacqueline woke drenched with sweat.

16

Early the next morning, while they loaded their gear into the remaining canoe, Link studied Jacqueline. Circles under her eyes and lethargic movements made him suspect he wasn't the only one who had awakened at every nighttime sound and there certainly had been plenty. The old creaky building had groaned like the soundtrack of the vampire movies his brothers loved. It would be good to get back to the soothing sounds of nature and fresh fish for meals. It would be even better if he knew Jacqueline's stalker wasn't hiding around the next bend.

Link's gaze traveled around the rustic dock area, but he didn't see their shaggy shadow. He didn't know whether he felt relieved or disappointed.

Why would anyone follow a person for thousands of miles - all the way from the Lower Forty-eight, then through the wilderness - and never speak to them?

Who communicated with vague messages, twisted into silly shapes, wrote with child-like penmanship, or used an angry tone coupled with threats? Odd as his list was, he made them sound like actual items. What kind of person demanded that things be returned, but refused to meet face to face so that whatever he wanted could be exchanged?

Of course, that assumed the odd list was tangible things.

What if the person had used fire as a weapon,

before? If so, that would make the fire images more sinister, especially to Jacqueline.

Rational people had their own agendas. And sometimes that agenda was to act irrational, which generally unbalanced the opposition, thus allowing them to dominate the meeting.

Except this fellow didn't seem to want a face-to-face.

Link massaged his temples for a moment, as his thoughts circled the problem and kept coming back to the same illogical thoughts. He shook his head, then got back to securing their gear in the canoe.

In business, money was generally the primary motivator. While finances remained a strong personal goal, the objectives could get more complex than the bottom line. Jacqueline's goal was obvious: she wanted a confrontation so she could give her fears a face; and she could get a step farther away from the terrifying unknown.

The stalker's strategy eluded him, unless he was serious about wanting the weird list, but they'd need a rosetta stone to figure out what the odd descriptions actually meant. Did the stalker even have an agenda? Link paused after he knotted the rope and rubbed his temples.

"Don't you feel well?" Jacqueline asked.

"What do you mean?" Link tugged the line tight.

"You keep clenching your teeth, scowling and rubbing your head."

"Just thinking."

She glanced around. "I guess I don't need to ask what you were thinking about."

"Pancakes or waffles. Sausage or bacon." She blinked. "Breakfast," he said. "I was trying to decide what sounded best."

"Sure you were."

"You don't believe me? Food choice is a major factor, after all, this is the last meal we'll eat in civilization for another week."

"In that case, order one thing for me, the other for you. We'll share."

He grinned. "Deal."

She handed him their water container and he secured it in the canoe. "I'd like to make another deal."

"What kind?" He glanced at her out of the corner of his eye. She looked harmless enough, but Mavis did most of the time, too and he knew just how dangerous she really was.

"Call Stone and tell him you've changed your mind. Have him pick you up."

His glance flicked to her empty hands. "Only if you come with me."

She shook her head. "This is my problem."

"And I'm making it mine."

"You're trying to, but it's not working."

"What do you mean?" Link straightened.

"Exactly what I said. You aren't being honest with me. You weren't thinking about food. You were thinking about the stalker. If you insist on coming with me, you've got to be truthful."

Link rose to his full height and put his hands on his hips. "That goes both ways."

"I agree." She spoke too quickly to have realized what he meant.

"I'll admit that this situation worries me," Link admitted. "Will you acknowledge your fears? Stop trying to hide your phobias?" Her eyes widened as she looked up at him. "You constantly try to conceal the things that bother you. If I hadn't seen your face and read that note, would you have told me about your problem?" Would she admit to the other things he'd guessed at?

She shifted from one foot to the other. "Probably not."

"That's what I thought. To succeed, a partnership needs trust and acceptance. I'll tell you my inner thoughts, but you need to be more open about yours, too." Link paused for a moment, realized what he'd said and wished he could rephrase it, but if they were to do this, it was exactly what they both needed to do. Her brow wrinkled as if his pronouncement was no more welcome to her than him. "The situation could arise when our lives depend on each other. We need to know what to expect. For instance, it makes me feel better knowing you can back me up with your handgun."

"If you're talking about self-defense, I studied Tai Chi."

"That's good to know, but I was thinking that we need to find out each other's strengths and weaknesses, be honest about what we think and feel. I'll try not to judge you, because I know you must have a good reason for what you do. Heaven knows that I'm not perfect."

"You're right." The words sounded as if they were dragged from the depths of her soul.

"In that case, let's get those waffles and pancakes."

"Bacon and sausage, too."

Link held out his hand. Unhesitatingly, she took it. Together, they walked toward the source of the intoxicating smells. He glanced down at her and saw a hint of a smile playing around the corners of her mouth. He was tempted to lean down and kiss it. Link satisfied himself with squeezing her hand and felt a responding pressure.

"That bacon smells wonderful. I haven't had any in

ages," she said.

"Me either."

She looked up at him. "Really? You eat fish for breakfast, even at home?"

"Actually, yes."

She wet her lips with the tip of her tongue. It was a habit he'd noticed before, and always found sensual. "I figured it was simply a camping thing. Living off the land, eating what was available."

"Back home, we've got a freezer full of fish."

She blinked and her brow furrowed. "Why?"

"For the past three or four years, I've been trying to catch a trophy fish. We eat all the losers."

"So, you have a freezer full of small fry."

"Not exactly. The state has minimum weights for each species. For instance, King Salmon must be sixty pounds. If I catch a fifty-nine-pounder, it gets set free."

"But keep the little ole sixty-one-pounder?"

"Yep." He held the restaurant's door open for her.

"Do you go fishing often?"

"Not as much as I'd like to, but if I went more frequently, we'd either have to open a fish market or buy another freezer."

"Modest, aren't you?" Her eyes twinkled with mischief.

"I'd call it honest."

"I'm sure you would." She slid into a chair.

The waitress brought them both huge white mugs of steaming coffee. Jacqueline inhaled its aroma. "Mmm. This smells almost as good as what you make." She put it down, though her fingertips maintained the contact. Jacqueline sighed. "I wish the stuff didn't upset my stomach." She pushed the cup toward the middle of the table, where it joined the salt, pepper and sugar dispenser. "Do you think Phillip will be able to find out anything?"

"Probably." Though if he did, bad as cellphone reception was on the next leg of their trip, there was no way Phillip could tell them what he discovered. "Stone is going to hook him up with Windy. Phillip may be good with computers, but if anyone can track a felon, it's Windy." Tiny furrows indented across Jacqueline's forehead. "Windy is Gaelic's nickname." She looked even more confused. "Stone's sister. The one with the FBI." Light dawned.

"I think Grandma mentioned her. Doesn't she investigate plane crashes?"

He nodded. "Not all crashes are pilot error or mechanical failures. Some are murder." Link sipped his coffee. Jacqueline's expressive eyes widened. She bit her lower lip and he wondered what it would be like to nibble that lip himself.

A small tremor of desire shook him as the waitress slid a heaping plate of food in front of him. "Thanks," he said. "It looks good." For several minutes, Link ate and watched Jacqueline chew as thoughts played across her face. After several minutes, curiosity won and he asked what she was thinking about.

"About the crazies in the world." Her fork shoved a bite of egg around her plate. "People blow things up simply to get their names in headlines or because they think they can improve lives by destroying them. It's really senseless. Know what I mean?" She sipped her water.

"Do you have something specific in mind?" Like her husband's death. "Or are you being as general as the IRA or Taliban terror tactics?"

"I was wondering if my stalker belonged to some

weird faction." She pushed a strand of hair out of her eyes. "The way he handles issues seems senseless or something a weird cult would do to improve things."

"He must have a reason."

"What do you think it is?" Jacqueline asked.

As Link settled back, the chair creaked. "I'm pretty sure this guy is a solo act." She nodded in agreement. "Everyone does things for a reason. Maybe they don't make sense to anyone else, but they are reasonable to at least one person; for this stalker-guy, it's writing notes."

"I guess I should be grateful that he isn't some demented terrorist bomber with dozens of like-minded brethren, ready to launch a jihad," she said.

Link nodded in agreement.

"Sometimes I feel like Frodo, with Gollum sneaking around behind me." He wondered what she meant. "I guess you haven't read Tolkien or seen the movies."

"No," he admitted.

"Frodo was a hobbit who became the ring bearer. Gollum had been the ring's previous keeper. Unfortunately, he became psychotic about not having it. Anyway, when Frodo became the new ring bearer, Gollum stalked him all over Middle Earth."

"Hobbit?" She nodded. "I saw some ads."

She sighed. "My problem is that I haven't got any rings." She held up her hands. The ring finger on her left hand didn't even have a shadow from where a wedding band would have been.

Link gazed at Jacqueline's serious expression. "Do you think that some event or object drew this guy's attention to you?"

She shrugged. "Whoever he is, something motivated him to start writing." She moved the fork's tines through the golden goo that had once been an egg. "It must be something big since he's kept writing for three years. Despite the fact that I can't figure the situation out, he's consistent, so it can't be a random pattern."

"Didn't you say each shape was different? That the color of the ink had changed?" She nodded. "Doesn't exactly sound consistent to me."

She rubbed her forehead. "But the stuff he lists has stayed the same. Maybe he seems methodical because of that and because he's always used the same familiar tone in his notes, no matter what color ink."

"By lists, you mean the love analogies?"

Jacqueline nodded. "I keep feeling I should know him. Yet he's a mystery to me." She rubbed her upper arms as if chilled. "I don't like the eerie feeling that he knows me, but I don't have a clue who he is."

"I imagine celebrities feel the same way. People watch them doing their jobs: singing, acting, whatever, and feel they know the individual. Then, if their silver screen idol crosses their path in real life, they act accordingly."

"I can definitely identify with that," Jacqueline said, then quickly added. "if I ever tried to sing, every wolf within ten miles would howl an accompaniment. As for acting," she grimaced, "I believe playing mind games is a total waste of time."

Remembering the letters she'd admitted writing to the actor, Link understood why she seemed uncomfortable with the topic. He preferred dealing with real issues, too. That was one of the things that he admired about Mavis. The more he got to know Jacqueline, the better he liked her. Yes, she had her flaws, just like everyone else, but she was a good person.

As Link finished eating, he wondered what the

stalker's plans were and he hoped the man didn't plan an ambush.

17

Jacqueline's fingers tightened on the paddle as she dug into the water and resisted looking back to see if her stalker was following. To release frustration, she dipped the paddle into the glacial water again and again.

The canoe surged forward faster and faster.

"I thought the idea was to contact the guy, not race him," Link said.

"True, but he doesn't have to know that." With every mile that separated them from humanity, her feeling of unease intensified. Had she made the right choice? While she tried to understand this unprecedented sensation, they passed driftwood, boulders, and tiny gnarled trees. Half the time, she wished she'd escaped on Linkstone's plane; the other half the time she wished she'd insisted that Link leave.

"If that's what you want." The power of Link's paddle joined hers and soon they were far away from the settlement.

Intuition told her that if she'd fled the river at Fort Yukon, this sense of uncertainty would have haunted her for her for another four thousand miles or three years, whichever came first. Whatever else she might think about the 'ghost', the man was tenacious. It was too bad he didn't use that quality for a more civilized enterprise.

She took a deep calming breath and exhaled

slowly. No matter how much she might want to retreat, there was no going back. The Yukon River flowed one way, and they were destined to follow it as far as the North Slope Haul Road, where Stone would meet them.

Jacqueline hoped a week would be enough time to accomplish her goal. She glanced back at Link, who was rubbing the back of his ear. She turned around and chewed her lower lip. Link rubbed his ear when something bothered him. It was an odd, endearing habit. Only now, knowing he was worried increased her tension.

"You about ready to stop for lunch?" he asked.

"Sure." Jacqueline gestured to a large gravel beach about a quarter mile downstream. "How about there?"

With a twist of his wrists, Link sent them hurtling toward it.

Once there, they made sandwiches while staring up river. After about ten minutes, the kayak hove into sight, but it quickly reversed direction.

Link rubbed the back of his ear several more times. Finally, Jacqueline couldn't take the silence any more. "What do you think he's doing?"

He took a bite. "If he's smart, he's eating lunch."

"That's not what you think. You're worried."

"No more than I have been for the past several days." He rubbed the back of his ear.

"Yes, you are. You always try to calm yourself by doing that. It's the same thing my brother does to settle his dog's nerves."

"What?" Link stared at her as if she'd sprouted two heads.

She mimicked him. "Rory does that to Konica to calm her when she's bouncing around." Belatedly, Jacqueline realized she might have offended Link and clamped her lips together.

His full, rich laughter rippled across the sandbar. "You're right, it's a bad habit. But in this case, I've got a mosquito bite."

She leaned toward him. "Let me look at it." She pushed aside his golden hair. "Mmm. Not a mosquito. I think this is a no-see-em bite. I'll get a tea bag."

"I'm fine," he protested. Link acted like her brother, Rory, who could have a compound fracture and still vehemently deny that he needed medical care. Jacqueline had a pretty good idea where Rory had gotten his hatred of the medical profession, though she doubted that Link had gotten his attitude from her grandmother.

"Sure you are. But if we don't get this taken care of, you'll be in misery." She got to her feet and went to the dry goods container. Moments later, she came back with a tea bag, which she soaked in hot water, then let it cool. Carefully, she positioned it over the swollen red skin. "There, that should do it. Can you hold it there for a minute?"

"I'm fine. Really."

"Sure you are. Just hold it in place while I find something to secure it, and you'll feel better. Trust me on this. I don't know what it is about tea, but this is the best way I know to deal with this sort of problem."

Link sighed. He looked so much like a petulant little boy that Jacqueline was tempted to kiss him. Her heart did a flip at the thought. She moved away before she could follow through on her wayward idea. What was wrong with her? Did she have to fall for every guy she got isolated with? Was there some Adam and Eve syndrome at work? They were alone in the middle of a wilderness, so she felt the need to do something. But what? Not mother him. This was nothing like her relationship with

Adam. Jacqueline dug in her duffel bag and found a clean bandana at the bottom. She folded the fabric and returned to Link.

"You know, this remedy of yours actually seems to be working." Link looked surprised.

"Of course it is. I've used it for years, but it needs to remain in place for several hours to be totally effective." Kneeling next to him, she secured the tea poultice. She sat back on her heels and surveyed her work. A smile played at the corners of her mouth. The off-center wrap made Link look like a rakish blond buccaneer. At the thought of a pirate piloting such an insignificant vessel, she coughed to cover a chuckle.

"I wondered why you packed all those generic tea bags and only drank herbal tea."

"Now you know."

"From the look on your face, I look ridiculous."

"The red looks nice with your coloring."

He rolled his eyes heavenward, but seemed pleased with the comment. "Do you want to put up the sign asking for the meeting now or later?"

"Maybe we should do it now. If he's willing to face me and talk, we might get this thing resolved by nightfall."

"That's what I was thinking."

Jacqueline got to her feet, dusted off the knees of her jeans and wished it were as easy to sweep away her dread. "I'll get the poster board and marker."

"What will you write?" Link asked.

She stared at him. "What would you suggest?"

"Beats me. What do you want to say?"

Jacqueline glared upstream. "Forget chit chat and friendly invitations. I want to chew him up into itty-bitty pieces and spit him out, but if I write something hostile, he'll never meet me face to face."

"Animosity attracts animosity?"

She nodded. "That's why it must be a friendly invitation." Her fingers tightened around the marker and her arm rose as if to stab the paper.

"How about simply inviting him to join us for dinner?"

"That might work." Her tense muscles relaxed. "I can write, 'Stalker, join us for dinner and an explanation'."

"Stalker is the way you think of him. He probably has some sort of virtuous view of his actions." Link shifted and stretched. As always, he was right. Jacqueline sighed. "Why don't you simply write, 'yellow kayak, please join us for dinner this evening.' It's plain and to the point."

"I like it." With bold strokes and large block letters, Jacqueline printed out the words, then held up the sign for his inspection.

"What do you think?"

He gave her a thumb up. "Prop it up so he can read it as he comes downstream, then let's get packed and go."

Fifteen minutes later, as the current carried them downstream, Jacqueline calculated the odds of having the answers to her questions before the day was over and her anticipation mixed with dread. Her tension increased until her hand trembled.

Two hours later, as they rounded a bend, she spotted a grizzly bear on the far bank. It stood on three legs, its fourth paw raised and ready. The bruin focused on the frigid water flowing beneath its belly.

Link guided their canoe into a still stretch near the opposite bank. Jacqueline placed her paddle across her lap and studied the bear's posture. This was either an intelligent animal that knew they posed no threat, or man hadn't hunted it. Standing, it probably would only be about seven feet tall. Still, it was big enough to make Jacqueline glad they were watching from a safe distance.

With lightning speed, the paw dipped into the water. A fish flew out of the water in a glistening silver arc and landed high on the bank. Immediately, the scraggly shrubbery quivered. Two cubs burst into view and pounced on the flopping fish. Uttering vicious growls and grunts, the cubs each grabbed an end of the fish.

Abruptly, one of the cubs lost its grip on the slippery tail. He somersaulted down the bank and splash-landed near his mother. As she dipped out a second fish, she growled at her cub.

Link abruptly pushed them back into the current. Jacqueline felt mildly disappointed. After a mile, she turned around to comment on the flight of an eagle, and saw the furious expression on Link's face. "What's wrong?"

"Did you see the size of that dolly?"

"Dolly-what?"

"Dolly varden. The second fish," he snapped.

She tried to remember the streak of flapping life the bear had tossed up the bank. It hadn't been as large as the first, but the color had been different. Jacqueline wished she'd spent as many hours studying fish as she had mammals. "I was watching the cubs," she admitted.

"Did you see the way they were mauling that she-fish?" he asked in disgust. She nodded. Why was he so upset? "You can bet anything that they'll make a mess of the dolly, too."

"Why does it matter?" Fish were merely food, weren't they?

"That dolly was trophy size. Do you know how long I've been trying to catch one that big?"

"Years?"

"That's right. And the bear simply flicks one out of the water for her cubs to use as a toy." His paddle dug into the water.

"What technique have you been using?"

"Spinners and a baited hook," he snapped.

"Well, there's where you went wrong. Obviously, you need insulated hip boots and a spear, or something."

Link looked at her as if she was daft. Jacqueline tried to stare innocently back, but his outraged expression seemed at such odds with the crimson bandana, she felt her lips twitch. His expression took on a sheepish cast. "You must think I take fishing too seriously."

"If you enjoy it, why shouldn't you treat it any way that makes you happy?" Now that he seemed to be past the worst of his temper, she asked, "How come you were upset about the second, not the first? The first was bigger."

"Yep, but it was only a she-fish."

"Not so valuable, huh?"

He nodded. "It was a plain old whitefish, while the dolly is a trout, and good eating. It tastes like lobster when you cook it right."

Jacqueline rubbed her chin. "Do you primarily fish for a dinner or to win a trophy?"

Link stared at her, then grinned. "You know, you may have a point. I've lived off what I've caught for so long that I'm not sure why I'm fishing. I'll have to think about that."

"Well, if you're in it for the prize, maybe we can get you a cub disguise, sneak back upstream. When mama bear catches the next gold cup winner, you can win it through tug-of-war."

His eyebrows arched. "Jacqueline, you have a very strange sense of humor."

"Sorry."

"Don't be, I like it."

His sincerity sent warm fuzzies through her. Adam had never liked her jokes, so she often found herself swallowing teasing remarks unsaid. "You know, I'm surprised that you haven't wet your line. If there's one trophy fish around here, it stands to reason there will be more."

Link reached for his tackle. "I definitely like the way your mind works. At the very least, I'll catch something for dinner. A dolly would taste good, especially for company."

She nodded, but her smile ebbed at the reminder of her stalker. Plus, she wasn't sure she thought of him as company. A half-hour later, Link caught a nice dolly varden. Though it wasn't as large as the bear's, it was still big enough to feed three and he was pleased.

They picked out a broad gravel bar, with a steady breeze to keep the mosquitoes away, and set up camp. Then they waited.

18

Though they took their time setting up camp for the night, the bright yellow kayak didn't appear. Holding onto a thin thread of hope that the invitation would work, they spent another hour casting furtive glances up river instead of starting dinner. Link's stomach growled. "Still no sign of him. Think we should wait longer?"

Instead of answering him, Jacqueline started mixing the ingredients for biscuits, so Link heated the pan to fry the fish. "Do you think he found the sign?" she asked.

"Yep."

"Then why hasn't he responded to the invitation?"

Didn't she realize that not showing up was an answer? Granted, it wasn't the one she wanted, but it was a possibility that he'd warned her about. "Same reason you've never seen his face, but I don't know what that is." Link put the Dolly Varden in the hot grease. The oil spat, two droplets hit his hand, though he'd yanked it back quickly. He licked the tiny burns.

Jacqueline placed the biscuits on aluminum foil, folded it, then heaped embers around the package. "You don't think the bear got him, do you?"

Link shook his head, his tongue still pulling the heat away.

"How can you be sure?"

"We would have heard something. Perhaps a

gunshot or at least a scream – he's not that far behind."

She sighed. "I hoped this evening over dinner, things would get resolved. Now, I'm beginning to wonder if he intends to follow me for the next fifty or sixty years." The pure dejection in her voice tore at his heart.

"That's not going to happen." Link gently stroked her cheek. "Since the forward approach didn't work, we'll simply have to figure out a different strategy. Don't worry, by the time Stone meets us at the bridge, you'll have had your encounter."

Her large black pupils dominated her eyes as she studied him. "I believe you."

"Good. Now, let's relax and think about something else."

"Such as?"

"Anything. My mother always swore that things happened when you least expected them. It's part of the watched pot theory."

"That it never boils?" she asked. He nodded. Jacqueline grinned. "What do you want to talk about?"

That was a good question. He could think of a dozen topics he'd like to quiz the kayaker on, but if he'd had his choice, he and Jacqueline would have a conversation that didn't require words. But if he gave into that temptation, when they were trying to lure a possibly homicidal stranger into their camp, it could be the stupidest thing he'd ever considered.

Link shifted away until she was out of reach. Unfortunately, his fingers still yearned to touch her. Worse, the extra distance allowed him to notice that her skin not only felt soft, it looked silky as a ripe nectarine. Amazing how the woman could be soft and rock-solid at the same time. Thinking about her skin made his fingers began to itch, and Link wished he hadn't sent the second tent back with Stone. When they'd pared things down to a bare minimum in case they needed to escape, sending it back had seemed logical, now, he wondered how he'd expected to control his impulses while temptation slept in the same tent.

How long he could go without sleep?

"I think the fish is done," she said.

"You're right." Carefully, he removed the pan from the fire and placed the fillets on the blue enameled plates.

Jacqueline delicately sniffed. "It smells wonderful."

"Let's hope it tastes as good as it smells."

"It will." She added biscuits and vegetables to the plates. "There we go, a feast fit for royalty." She took a bite of the fish and a look of rapture spread across her face. "This tastes wonderful. Aside from Rory, you're the only man I know that can cook a decent meal on an open fire."

"Practice." He eyed the perfect, golden biscuits. "It looks like I'm not the only one that's had it."

She chuckled. "Embers from open fires are where I learned to cook. I had a terrible time learning how to cook on an actual stove."

Link tried to decide whether to laugh or not. Though her expression looked serious, who in their right mind learned to cook on a campfire? "You are kidding."

She shook her head. "When I was growing up, we lived in an old cabin with mud chinking. We were out in the middle of nowhere and only had trees, a river and wildlife." It sounded as if she'd been raised on another planet or hundreds of years in the past. "Basically, our cabin had three rooms. The south end was the main area and had a huge fieldstone fireplace, which Mama used for cooking. The other end was my parent's room. Rory and I each had a loft."

"No bathroom?"

"An outhouse. It was spooky if you needed to use it at night, and wasps liked to live in it in the summer." Jacqueline's nose wrinkled. "Rory's loft was over the folk's room, mine was over the kitchen."

"What'd you do, take baths in town?"

She laughed as she shook her head. "There wasn't a town." As her mirth subsided, she reminisced, "We had a big antique tub and heated water by the fireplace. I loved it. When the ice melted, we used the river, but that was really cold." She sighed. "Then we moved to the city, I thought it was the noisiest, smelliest place I'd ever seen. And the urban tubs." Her nose wrinkled. "Sorry, I'm babbling. Guess I'm more nervous than I thought."

"So, you went from the middle of the wilderness to the middle of civilization."

"Not exactly." She gave him a dazzling smile. He swallowed a bite of biscuit without chewing it, then had a coughing fit. "Are you all right?"

Link nodded. He coughed a few more times, then drank some water and motioned for her to go on.

"We moved to the outskirts of a small town, but I thought it was a booming metropolis and that we lived in the suburbs." Jacqueline toyed with her biscuit. "I'd have died of culture shock if we'd moved somewhere like New York City, or L. A."

"Did you like having radio, television, phones and all the things I took for granted growing up?"

"For the first couple years, I hated everything about the city," she admitted. "But, by the time I turned into an adolescent, I'd gotten hooked on a couple shows and I was really into music." She shrugged. "I never really learned to like cities. Who knows, maybe that's why I chose the profession I did. Generally, when you contract for the type of research I do, you're a good distance from humanity."

"Interesting."

"You must think the way I was raised sounds odd."

"Different," he said. "I'm trying to decide if I'm envious or not."

"Living in tune with nature was a great way to grow up. I sometimes think social problems come from people getting too far from the natural order of things." She made a frustrated gesture. "It's like they've lost their identity and are lashing out."

The image of the kayaker came to Link's mind. Was her stalker someone that had lost touch with reality? If so, the man was getting a good dose of it.

She tried to hide a yawn. "It's late. I guess we should give up on my stalker."

He nodded in agreement. "I'll bank the fire." As Link proceeded to put his words into action, he singed a finger and wondered if they should have kept the camp stove. It had been necessary when they began their trip, because firewood had been nearly nonexistent, but once there were some trees, it had seemed like excess baggage.

Involuntarily, his eyes focused on Jacqueline. With quick, practiced movements, she took care of the dishes and secured the food. She was a great wilderness companion. He suspected that she did things his way to create a sense of compatibility, not because she lacked knowledge of the wilderness. Everything she did seemed like a product of effortless harmony. Paddling. Setting up camp. Cooking. Conversation.

Link didn't think he'd ever met anyone who was so open and honest. At times, he knew Jacqueline didn't actually want to talk about a given subject, but she didn't back off from it, either. She faced life head on, just as she wanted to face her stalker. In her own unobtrusive way, she was one of the most courageous people he'd ever met.

Once their campsite was secured, Link crawled into his sleeping bag. Moments later, Jacqueline settled into hers. Rolling onto her side, she faced him across the two feet of plastic flooring.

"Good night, Link. Sweet dreams."

"Thanks. Sleep well." Though with her so close, he'd have to fight to relax, much less sleep.

Listening to the soft rhythm of her breathing, his body proved him wrong. He dreamed of being a boy who lived in the wilderness. Assorted animals followed him wherever he went. Birds perched on his shoulder. Grizzly bears tossed prizewinning fish in his lap.

Abruptly, he jerked awake. Tensely, he lay as he'd been, ears straining for the sound in the night that had roused him. There was no sound in the tent except Jacqueline's low, soft breathing.

In the distance, a wolf howled. Closer, an owl hooted, and water lapped against something.

His eyes opened into slits. A lock of hair had fallen across Jacqueline's cheek. His fingers itched to reach out and move it, but he forced himself to remain still.

Finally, convinced that whatever had woken him was only part of the strange dream, he drifted back into sleep.

Hours later, the harsh screech of a raven woke him. Link opened his eyes and found himself looking into Jacqueline's sleepy blue ones. She gave him a drowsy smile that melted his entire body. "Morning," he whispered.

She brushed her hair out of her face. "Want me to fix breakfast?"

"I'd never turn down an opportunity like that." It wasn't every day that a desirable woman offered to cook for him. In fact, other than Ariel's dinners and his mother's, he couldn't remember any woman cooking for him.

Jacqueline eased out of her sleeping bag. For a moment, her hand touched his shoulder; a second later, the contact was gone. She applied insect repellent, then unzipped the tent and slid out.

Contentedly, Link settled back down. It wouldn't take much effort to get used to living like this or sharing his life with someone like Jacqueline. She was great company, and willing to share the load fifty-fifty. Plus, she looked fabulous in a rumpled sweat suit.

With her gone, the tent didn't seem as pleasant. He couldn't watch her sleep. And smelling her lemony scent frustrated him. Link knew it was foolish to dwell on what he couldn't have, particularly when he needed to focus on the task at hand. He decided to get up and start packing the camping supplies.

Link kicked aside his sleeping bag and reached for the insect repellent.

Jacqueline screamed.

He lunged for the opening. Jerking it aside, he almost tore the tent flap's zipper. "What's wrong?"

19

"You rotten coward." Jacqueline shook her fist at the river. "You spineless yellow-belly. You – you – you -" She took a great gulp of air. "How dare you do this to me?" She wanted to kick the darned cardboard, but knew that would be childish and only confirm to Link that he was treating her correctly.

"What's wrong?" Link stumbled from the tent, his foot caught in a sleeping bag and he fell through the flap. He scrambled upright, the fabric still clinging to his left foot.

Jacqueline pointed a shaking finger at the filthy poster lying next to her toes. "That."

Link took a moment to pull the sleeping bag free then hunkered down next to the grimy mess that might have been poster board in a previous life. Gingerly, he tipped the cardboard up and, as expected, saw writing on the other side. The poster board floated back to the ground. The tip of his finger came away black. "What'd he use to write this with?"

"Charcoal would be my best guess."

He rubbed his fingers together and nodded. "That'd smear like this." They silently studied the scrawled response.

Trick me once with your smiles and temptations.

Shame on you.
Trick me twice, shame on me.
You know what I want:
BURNING DESIRE,
HEAT OF THE NIGHT,
And, and, and
all the INFERNOS.

She read it a fourth time, but it didn't make any more sense than when she'd first read it. Her fingernails dug into the palms of her hands. "I'd like to make him explain what this sign means." She laughed, but it sounded shrill instead of jolly. "And after I knew why he wrote this stuff, I'd rip the cardboard into itty-bitty pieces then ram them one by one down the damned kayaker's throat." There, the infantile truth was out.

"This still sounds like some sort of list." Link began buttoning his shirt. Too frustrated to talk, she threw her hands up. Link looked up from his crouched position. His brown eyes studied her. "At least we know a couple things."

"What?"

"One, that poster board can't be folded into origami and two that the kayaker is definitely Stalker-guy." Hearing his assessment, her knees gave out. Jacqueline sat down with a plop of dust.

Silently, Link shifted closer, then put his arm around her shoulders, pulled her against his side and held her. Peace radiated from Link and calmed the frantic beating of her heart. As his warmth enveloped her, Jacqueline realized how chilled she felt.

The melancholy bellow of a lonesome moose echoed down the river. At least she had Link. Adam would have put her down for her fear of fire, and for attracting a stalker; he'd have made her deal with the man on her own.

How had she ever gotten lucky enough to find Link?

In some ways she felt more intimate with Link than she'd ever been with Adam. Jacqueline frowned as she considered that fact. How could a few days of Link's pleasant friendship seem closer than years of marriage?

It didn't make sense.

Link cleared his throat. "Can you think of anyone that you've tricked?"

"What do you mean?" she mumbled.

With his free hand, he gestured to the first phrase. "'Trick me once with your smiles and temptations. Shame on you.' It's the same thing he's been writing since he started the notes. The only differences are that he obviously ran out of space, so closed with a generalization and that he's using charcoal and poster board instead of ink and legal paper.

"Who had you been dating prior to marrying Adam?"

"No one." Jacqueline exhaled her breath in a long sigh. "I was in college, carrying a full class load and working thirty hours a week at the Humane Society. I barely had time to eat and sleep."

"I can relate. I worked to put myself through school, too."

"Then you know how it was. The only people I saw were either in class or applying to adopt a stray." She rubbed her aching temples. "I've tried to picture everyone, but it's impossible."

"You ever get a chance to know anyone from work?"

She shook her head. "I remember a couple of coworkers, but no one had the potential to look like a musk ox." His arm tightened around her. "Obviously, whoever wrote this was focusing on you instead of either learning or his work.

"That's assuming you knew him from your college days." Link frowned. "What worries me is that he seems like some sort of mental case." Jacqueline bit her lip at hearing the same conclusion she'd come up with. Link pointed to the last line. "I can't understand why he says, 'all the infernos'. How many fires have there been?"

"Just the one that killed Adam." Jacqueline blinked away tears of frustration. "What sort of mental case is he? A psycho? Is he dangerous? Harmless? What on earth did I do to him to make him want to place blame on me for some sort of shame that he thinks I deserve?" Thoughts and words she'd kept bottled up for months poured out. "I can't remember anyone with his description and that scares me." She clenched her fists. "It makes me wonder if I have some sort of memory problem I'm unaware of."

He shook his head.

"For him to know me as well as the tone indicates, he must at least have met me. Don't you think?"

Link grunted.

"So, I have to wonder if I sleepwalk, or have a split personality, which means I'm just as insane as he is."

"Jacqueline."

"Wouldn't you remember someone with one big shaggy eyebrow?" Link picked up the poster board with his free hand and studied it. "'*Trick me once with your smiles and temptations.*' It sounds like your previous invitation was some sort of flirting, like you were offering yourself up as dessert instead of serving a main course."

Link chuckled.

"Never in a million years." He laughed harder. "It's not funny," she said.

"You're right." He swallowed. "It isn't."

"I have never flirted with anyone. Yes, I've tried to be pleasant." She paused for breath. "What am I supposed to do when I meet someone? Frown? Glare?"

He tried to look serious as he shook his head.

"This is no laughing matter. Especially if I'm crazy or some lunatic thinks I've been flirting with him when I was only being myself."

"I doubt if you know how to flirt."

"So, you think I'm crazy." Jacqueline's body ached with the effort of maintaining a calm appearance.

"Don't put words in my mouth." Link's tone sounded far too jovial.

"If you ask me, flirting is a waste of time. Board games and cards just fritter away time, too."

A smile tugged at the corners of Link's mouth. "Just like your grandmother."

"Probably," she admitted. "And don't expect me to apologize. I happen to think Grandma is great."

"I agree," Link said. "And she isn't senile enough to believe she might have a split personality, either."

The intensity of his gaze unnerved her. Glancing down, Jacqueline noticed the sooty scrawls. "The straightforward approach didn't work. Why is he willing to follow me for thousands of miles but not to face me?"

"That's definitely a question I'd like the answer to."

She jabbed at the phrase 'Shame on you'. "I resent the guilt he's trying to heap on me. What did I do?" Jacqueline lunged to her feet and began to pace.

"Beats me."

"It's got to have something to do with some sort of

meal. Why else would he reject a dinner invitation?" She stared at the river. "Link, I want to talk to him face to face. Now more than ever."

"That basically leaves us with one option."

"What?"

"Confront the lion in its den," he said.

Jacqueline rubbed her upper arms, but the bone-deep chill persisted. "That sounds ominous."

"Can you think of another way?"

She rubbed the gooseflesh harder. "At least the invitation got a reply. Maybe it was a step in the right direction. This is the first time I've been able to establish a dialogue."

"So, what do you want to do?" His gaze was unflinching. "Leave another message? Become pen-pals?" He arched a brow.

"That's better than all communications going one direction." Jacqueline blew out a deep breath so hard that her bangs fluttered. "But I still want to see his face. Ask him to explain." She kicked a clump of grass. "I hate all these unanswered questions."

"We have six days before Stone picks us up." Link grinned. "If we keep leaving notes, the next couple days he'll get used to it, and probably figure we don't want to see him any more than he wants to be seen. He might get a sense of security."

"He'll relax," she said.

Link nodded. "Then, in four days, we'll go to plan B, and hope his camp isn't too hard to find."

Four days seemed like forever, yet no time at all. "Okay, we'll go with your plan."

"You aren't so upset, now," he observed.

Link was right, she felt calmer, but he didn't need to know how well he'd read her. "I'm hungry." She picked up the blue enameled coffeepot.

"So am I."

"Tell you what, you pack the gear and I'll cook."

Link looked at her and arched his brow. "Sick of my cooking?"

For a terrible moment, she wondered if she'd offended him. "What girl wouldn't be thrilled to find a man who was willing to cook for her?"

"So it isn't my cooking?"

She shook her head. "But when I was a kid, we each prepared part of the meal. Dad cleaned fish and game, Rory chopped vegetables, Mom manned the fire and made sure nothing burned." For a moment, Jacqueline felt overwhelmed by the poignant memories. Especially of a time when fire had been the center of family life instead of shrouded in fear. She took a cleansing breath. "I baked biscuits. Sometimes, we took turns."

"No wonder your biscuits are so good. You've had years of practice."

She laughed. "You wouldn't say that if you tasted the ones I bake in an oven. Rory's dog buries them like they're a bone."

"I don't believe that."

"You should." Jacqueline measured the coffee into the basket then added water, and finally put the pot on a bed of embers she'd reclaimed from the previous night's fire. "Go on. I'll have breakfast ready in no time."

Now that she'd made the commitment to do it, Jacqueline was determined to see it through. Flames and heat or not, she was going to ignore her panic long enough to make breakfast.

Link gave her a jaunty salute before he ambled off to pack the tent and its contents.

As she prepared the food, Jacqueline focused on what to write to her stalker. Another dinner invitation was out. Should she write him a long letter that bared her soul and the frustration he'd caused her? It was tempting, but something like that could also give him more power.

Maybe a blunt, logical approach would be best.

What to write?

21

As Link rolled Jacqueline's sleeping bag into a tight coil, he smelled … something. He tied the laces then brought the dark green nylon to his face, pressed his nose against the material and inhaled deeply. Lemons and sunshine. Jacqueline. If anyone was watching, they would probably think he looked like one of Stone's huskies. Link tossed her bag out the tent flap, before he could do something ridiculous, like slobber.

Quickly, he secured his own bag, then began stowing their gear in watertight sacks. Before he'd completed his task, the intoxicating aroma of breakfast cooking invaded the tent. It almost smelled as good as Jacqueline. He whipped off the rain cover, then removed the support poles.

The thought made him pause in the middle of folding the tent. What was wrong with him? He had never felt like this in his entire life. What was so special about Jacqueline Cardew? He shook the tent's pouch open with excessive force. Why did so many of his thoughts center on her and her situation?

Link rammed the tent into its nylon bag.

Though attractive, Jacqueline was not the most beautiful woman he'd ever seen.

But, she might be the smartest.

Plus, there was an earthiness about her. On the rare occasions when women had been included on his camping trips, they had either been intimidated by living in the wild or expected him to wait on them hand and foot. Jacqueline acted as if she were at home and cooking barbecue in her own back yard. In fact, she probably thought she was. He chuckled as he flipped the tent on top of the pile of things to pack in the canoe.

"Breakfast in five minutes," Jacqueline called.

"Coming." She had a nice voice, too, Link reflected. Enticing aromas grew stronger until his mouth began to water and his stomach growled. Whatever she was making, it wasn't his standard fare: fried fish and grits.

He quickly loaded everything, then approached the banked embers, sniffing as he tried to figure out the sweet, oddly familiar, aroma. "Smells good." His stomach voiced its agreement.

"Thanks." Jacqueline glanced up and gave him a dazzling smile. "I was getting tired of the same thing every day."

"You should have said something."

"I did." She winked at him. "I volunteered to cook. Hope you like it."

She pushed embers aside and pulled out a pot. When she began dishing up the food, he squinted in disbelief.

"Blueberry muffins?" He rubbed his eyes, but the vision remained.

She nonchalantly gestured toward a boggy area. "There are some bushes over there." Her forehead furrowed as she poked at the contents of a second pan. "I'm not sure how this will taste. I used the leftover dolly varden to make fish croquettes." She sniffed. "They smell all right." Jacqueline filled the empty space on the plates with a small heap of fresh strawberries than handed him a plate. "Enjoy."

The first bite of croquette melted in his mouth "I think I'm in love." He stiffed a big bite into his mouth. She laughed. After eating six croquettes, he nibbled the corner of a muffin; heaven melted over his tongue. Groaning with delight, he stuffed half into his mouth.

"I guess you like the food." Her musical laughter echoed across the sandbar.

"You should sign on as a cook on guided backpacking trips." Much to his dismay, Jacqueline seemed to give the idea serious thought. Link wasn't sure why that bothered him, but it did. To his vast relief, she shook her head.

"It might be fun for a summer, but it would get old in a hurry."

"Well, whenever I go camping, you've got a standing invitation to come along."

She shook a finger at him. "Don't say things like that. I might take you up on it."

"I wish you would. You're good company, Jacqueline Cardew." He heaped the leftovers onto his plate.

"So are you, Link Gavallan."

For several minutes, they ate in silence until he was down to two bites. The hint of onion in the croquettes was perfect. But how could there be onion, when he'd forgotten to pack the spices? He held up his fork to examine the next bite and noticed bits of green. "Did you buy chives at Fort Yukon?"

"They're wild onion tops." Jacqueline gestured toward another portion of the bank. Link looked from the bank to his fork and back again. Jacqueline's eyes begin to twinkle with amusement. "Humans have lived off the land for millennia. It's just the last few generations who lost touch with nature. Link, I hate to tell you this, but other foods besides fish come from nature. And best of all, you don't have to deal with bait and nasty hooks to get most of it. Of course, the fish cakes wouldn't have been very good without your fish."

"Guess I'd be one of billions who couldn't survive if I was forced them to live off the land."

Jacqueline chuckled, then turned sober. "If there was a global disaster, most people would probably poison themselves within the first couple of days. After that, the fights for dominance would kill off most of the rest."

"I take it that you don't think mankind is all that civilized," Link said.

She shook her head. "Scratch the surface and you find a predator. Take my stalker for an example: I've never seen anyone better at pestering prey. I just wish he'd jump and give me an opportunity to even the odds."

"Pretty confident, aren't you?"

"Not really. But I'll be switched if I'm going to take a defeatist attitude. Mind over matter and all that Zenish stuff. Strange as it sounds, it works."

"If you believe you are or will become a victim, you increase your chances of it happening?"

She nodded. "I prefer to concentrate on winning."

Link couldn't argue with the logic of her statement. Over the years he'd seen too many people with true talent and potential waste it on a pessimistic disposition. His own father had been a prime example of that for over a year. He still didn't know what had turned his father around; he didn't even know if the transformation had been one cataclysmic event or simply a gradual change in outlook.

Now that Link thought about it, he realized he used a similar philosophy when he decided what he wanted, then gave his all to get it. It had worked well in both school and business. Why shouldn't Jacqueline employ it to achieve her personal goal?

"You're awfully quiet," Jacqueline said.

"Just enjoying your cooking, the morning and thinking about what you said. By the way, I agree with you."

"But I suspect you never thought about it in those terms."

"Can't say that I did." Link grinned. Switching the topic to a more pressing issue, he asked, "What are you going to do? Leave another message?"

"Since he's obviously been here, I don't know whether he's upstream of down." She gnawed her lower lip. "What do you think is best?"

Link rubbed his chin. There was always the possibility that Stalker-guy had gotten in front for an ambush or something. "If you intend to write again, I'd wait. Hopefully by lunch, we'll have caught a glimpse of him. If we have, and he's behind us, leave it then."

She nodded in agreement. "That'll give us time to decide how to phrase the next message. I'm tempted to air my frustrations and leave a note that says, 'Who are you? Why are you following me? How did I trick you?' But without knowing his personality, I can't determine how he'd react." She frowned. "This not knowing who or what I'm dealing with is exasperating as all get out."

"It'd certainly make things easier if we knew whether he's sane or not." Link stared at his canoe. "Trust your gut instinct. If you leave that message, maybe it'll get him to show himself."

"How?"

"Everybody wants to be understood. Even babies. If you sound confused, he might come out of the woods long enough to explain himself and his motives."

"Then that is what I'll do."

He hadn't realized she was tense until she made up her mind. Suddenly, Jacqueline smiled. It felt like the sun had burned away a cloud.

Hours later, as the current carried them past magnificent vistas and rugged rocks, Link focused on the fluid motion of Jacqueline's muscles beneath her faded green T-shirt as she negotiated the prow around a fallen tree. Suddenly, a branch slapped him in the face. "Crap," he muttered to himself. "I must look like some ridiculous lovesick cow."

Jacqueline glanced back. "Did you say something?"

"Thinking out loud." Link felt foolish. "Have you caught sight of Stalker-guy yet?"

She shook her head. "This may sound crazy, but that worries me. Until now, I thought the worst thing that could occur would be for something dreadful to happen to us. Now I'm thinking that if we go to all this trouble and still don't come up with answers, that would be worse."

Link was momentarily speechless at the reminder that Jacqueline put lack of confrontation higher on her list of hazards than facing her adversary. Most women, and several men that he knew, avoided facing unpleasant situations at all costs.

Not Mavis or her granddaughter.

In some ways, her boldness was intimidating. It was also one of the things that he admired most about her. "One way or the other, we'll get you your answers," he promised.

She bestowed a smile on him. He suddenly felt hotter than a campfire. Link unexpectedly recalled something he'd barely noticed at breakfast: fire terrified

Jacqueline almost to the point of hyperventilation, yet she used it to cook. At least she used the embers. He'd noticed that she tried to avoid looking directly at the flames when she used a stick to move them into their own small, protected area. Yes, she had fears, but she only acknowledged them enough to work around them. She didn't let them dominate her. He wondered if anything could make her succumb to blind terror.

He hoped neither of them would ever find out the answer to that particular question.

21

Though they still hadn't gotten a glimpse of her stalker by lunchtime, Jacqueline wrote: *Who are you? Why are you following me? How did I trick you*? on a new poster board and propped it up against the twisted branches of a bush.

That night, she dreamed of shadow images and ashen words scrawled in the sand. The next morning, she woke to a reality that mirrored her nightmare. His latest message written in cramped, charcoal letters on the back of the poster board:

You know as well as me,
I'm the man you claimed to love
but used, instead.
You know what I desire, a confession
of your
guile and the return of my life.
How did you trick me?
We both know I lost
months of my physical life and my
entire professional existence.
I want:
burning desire,
heat of the night,
passion's fire,

absence of lies,
scorching strand.

I KNOW the infernos were for you, but
I want
them back.
All of them.

"*I lost months of my physical life and my entire professional existence,*" Jacqueline whispered the words. "Adam?" She shook her head; people only survived infernos like that in fiction. And why did he list all the love/hell images he'd written they were some sort of list? Tears of frustration stung her eyes as she read the message aloud, "*I want: burning desire, heat of the night, passion's fire, absence of lies, scorching strand. I KNOW the infernos were for you, but I want them back All of them.*" A cold chill moved through her soul. "Who in Hades is he, and why is he talking about loving me?"

"How many men have you rejected?"

Link's tone cut her to the quick. "You make me sound like some two-bit lady of the evening who had so many customers she couldn't keep them straight." He held up his hands in surrender. Jacqueline immediately regretted her outburst, but wasn't about to apologize. She and Link didn't speak to each other for the next twenty-four hours and Jacqueline's stomach remained clenched during their silent feud.

"At least he's consistent. Confusing, but consistent."

The next day, the round of notes followed the same pattern.

Jacqueline was so upset that she only managed to

doze. She didn't know which was worse, trying to hide her exhaustion or face the nightmare images of her dreams.

Link spent every spare moment fishing.

Jacqueline woke with a jerk from a doze that hadn't refreshed and lay watching the nylon undulate. They had two and half days left until Stone picked them up, one and a half before they tried to corner him in his camp, assuming they could find it. At this rate, she'd never get any resolution. She turned her head to look at Link, wishing she could relax like he did; wishing she had his faith that there would be a confrontation and that she'd finally understand what the phantom was talking about. The worst thing that could happen was if they did corner the guy and he spoke as strangely as he wrote, so she'd never know. She laid in the shadowed tent; eyes burning with unshed tears, wondering if the tension would ever end.

Maybe she'd simply have to accept that not every situation was logical or had a logical explanation other than that the guy was certifiable.

Link's deep, even breathing made her wish she could find peace in sleep. She knew his doubts increased with every note and Jacqueline understood why. The persistent way the stalker insinuated that he knew her made her doubt herself and her memory.

Finally giving up on sleep, she shoved aside her sleeping bag and let the cool air bathe her. Her stalker's laundry list of demands circled in her mind. Did the blazing lunatic know about the fire phobia Adam's death had created? If so, was he trying to disconcert her with his choice of the words, or did he love fire? She frowned, recalling that he'd used the same phrases from the beginning. There must be another explanation.

She should have told Link the truth. Even knowing it was the right thing to do, Jacqueline still didn't want to admit that her first serious date had come on her twenty-second birthday, when Adam had taken her to dinner. She pinched her eyes shut and shook her head at the thought that she still considered that bucket of chicken as being taken out to eat.

Yet, it had been her first date, but confessing that meant Link might perceive her as undesirable, as other males had. And that idea made her feel ill.

Link made a soft snoring sound.

This situation was so familiar. It was the same old colleague pattern. The only difference was that this time, the man was Link. When a tear slid down her face, she rolled to her side and faced away from Link.

Jacqueline didn't want Link as another pal. She wanted more, but going after what she wanted would be the dumbest thing she had ever considered. Tears burned the insides of her eyelids. Did she truly care about him or was she merely responding to the close proximity of his endorphins? Jacqueline quietly cried herself to sleep, then she dreamed she was back in high school, crying to her brother because boys always treated her like a comrade. Rory chuckled deep within the swirling mist. "Talk less and smile more."

The haze thinned as she looked out a window into a familiar back yard. It was prom night, but no one had asked her. The fog twisted around her. "Sweety, you're just a late bloomer," her mother said. "Things will be different in college." The campus solidified out of the swirling cloud. Jacqueline stood in her dorm room, facing her new roommate, Nora, a girl who was bubbly and stylish, everything Jacqueline wanted to be. A huge sprig of mistletoe dropped in front of her. The white berries jeered at her. "No one wants to kiss you." Then the berries liquefied. The goo reformed into Adam's sneering smile.

She awoke. Heart racing, she listened to the stillness. A contented snore proclaimed that her nightmare hadn't invaded Link's dreams.

Adam. The notes had started the morning after their first argument, and granted, he'd denied writing but she had always thought he was so embarrassed by the whimsy that he'd lied. She'd seen a body, which had been identified as his. Logic told her that Adam could not be the writer, yet he was the only possibility. He was also the only man who had looked at her twice. Too bad that what had initially attracted him had been her professional sounding research papers.

Which months was he referring to? What guile? Did Adam mean he thought she'd caused the fire or was he referring to something she'd written for him?

She had not set the fire. Despite her twisted ankle, she'd wanted to check the machines; he had insisted on going, so she could go put her foot up and get back to work on the paper he needed her to finish to get approval to extend their grant.

And he'd died for his efforts.

If her stalker was indeed her husband, and he'd miraculously survived the explosion, it was far more likely that he'd faked his own death.

But why?

And if Adam hadn't died, who had? There certainly weren't many people around to toast as a decoy, so if it had been someone besides her husband, it had probably been planned.

She hadn't planned to wreck her ankle, so how could he have planned the timing? Jacqueline frowned with the effort of holding in her frustration.

Granted, their marriage had its low points, but they'd worked well together. She'd accepted the lack of romance in their relationship, and Adam had appeared to appreciate her contributions to the success of their project.

What did he want? The life insurance? He could have it all, if he'd just leave her alone and figure out a way to prove that it hadn't been suicide, so he could claim it. If that wasn't an oxymoron! Jacqueline raised her right hand and looked at her palm. The shadows hid the circular scar where the heat from the lab's doorknob had seared her flesh.

She closed her eyes and tried to remember. Was there any chance Adam could have gotten out of the lab or taken someone else inside? There might have been time. But why hadn't he come forward before now? And who had died? Where had they come from and how had they gotten into the lab and why? Had Adam needed to hide from someone? Had he really faked his own death, or was her imagination going wild?

Had someone already been in the lab and attacked him?

She'd been focused on getting to the house without falling and her back had been turned to the lab, could someone have followed him in?

The Coroner had identified Adam by his dental records. If Adam had switched the records, then he must have planned the fire and killed someone else in some twisted, evil plot. She shuddered. That did not sound like something her unimaginative husband would have done. But it could certainly be the foul deed of whoever left her the messages.

If her stalker wasn't Adam, who was he?

Coffee would taste good.

Jacqueline frowned at the thought and wondered why she should crave something that upset her stomach. She tried to ignore the idea, but the lure was so strong that she could taste the coffee.

Her nose quivered. She could smell it.

Jacqueline glanced at Link. Though his eyelashes fluttered, it appeared more of a response to a dream than playing 'possum.

Quietly, Jacqueline wiped away her tears, then she eased out of her sleeping bag. She bit her lower lip with the effort of keeping slow and quiet as she unzipped the flap.

As she moved the fabric aside, she glanced back to see if she'd disturbed Link. He gave a soft snore through his wrinkled nose. Cautiously, Jacqueline crawled out the opening.

The early morning sun made her squint while her eyes adjusted from the tent's dim light. The sandbar they were camped on looked the same as it had the previous evening, with one exception: someone had unbanked the fire.

At the sight of the small flickering flames Jacqueline's stomach lurched. Then she noticed the coffeepot perking contentedly at its edge. Link must have gotten up earlier, prepared it, than gone back to sleep.

Though it was a great explanation, she didn't believe a word of it.

She scanned the surrounding area, but nothing stirred. Steeling her nerves, she stood up, straightened her back and walked toward the fire.

"Slept in, did you?" The deep, gruff voice from behind her made it feel as if her heart had leapt into her throat and formed a quivering, solid mass. Praying that she wouldn't disgrace herself, Jacqueline slowly turned. A shaggy man was sitting on a bank roughly fifty feet away. The bough of a stunted diamond willow shadowed his face and untamed beard. She felt more than saw his eyes peering at her from beneath the wide brim of his grimy hat.

Unless it was artificial, Adam couldn't have grown so much hair since the fire — could he? "Who are you?" she demanded.

"You know me."

Jacqueline clamped her teeth together and counted. One, her left foot took a step toward him. Two, the other foot took a step. Three, she was sick and tired of this game of his. Four, she did a double pace. When she hit ten, she was halfway to where he had been, but with every step she'd taken, he'd slid backward into the grove of twisted trees. Planting her feet, Jacqueline put her hands on her hips and glared at the shadow figure. "If I knew who you were, I wouldn't ask."

"Better back up. You know the rules." He eased to his feet and looked ready to run.

"Don't you dare leave." He stopped moving. "I've wanted to meet you face to face for three years."

Shadows hid his entire upper body. "If you take this to court, I'll make sure they know you were the one that broke the rules."

"Fine. So be it." She paused. "What rules?"

"The restraining order."

"What restraining order? Who are you?"

"Jacqueline, who are you talking to?" Link demanded.

She was afraid if she took her eyes off him, her stalker would use the opportunity to disappear. "My stalker; and guess what, he says there are rules for this."

"Are you referring to me?" the deep bass voice in the shadow asked.

"Until you give me a name, I don't know anything better to call you." He backed away until he came up against an impenetrable wall of trunks.

"You don't move like Adam." Jacqueline took a deep breath and tried to regain her composure. Link came up behind her and placed his left hand on her shoulder. It helped regulate her breathing. "Look, whoever you are, I'm sorry for shouting at you. Thank you for fixing the coffee. Won't you please join us? You and I need to talk to each other, not shout."

"What is this about a restraining order?" Link asked.

"I've never heard of one." The shaggy man stood up uncertainly and took a step toward them, so she felt safe in turning away. "How about it? Will you join us and explain about these supposed rules and this retraining order and this list of – stuff – that you keep asking for? I have a lot of things I would like to speak to you about."

The shadow stood quietly for so long Jacqueline thought he'd turned to stone. When he finally spoke, his voice was much gentler. "You sound different than I remember."

"How?"

"You look shorter and skinnier, too. Maybe it's because of the angle."

"Please come down," she said. "I like to see people's faces when I talk to them. Please? We won't hurt you." Slowly, the shadow began to move forward. Link's hand tightened on her shoulder. By the time her stalker came to a stumbling stop halfway to them, Link's fingers dug into her flesh so hard that she knew there would be a row of circular bruises if he didn't relax.

Jacqueline placed her hand on top of Link's.

"You said you hated my face after the fire." The bass voice sounded confused. "You couldn't stand looking at the scars."

"I don't remember ever saying that to anyone."

"You know better than that."

"Are you Adam?"

"You took up with him after you dumped me. It wasn't until he incinerated that I realized you'd burned me, too."

"Adam is the only man I ever dated and I certainly did not burn him or anyone else," Jacqueline protested.

"Is that your story? Is that why you told the police all those lies?"

"Who are you?"

"Ray Capolucho."

"Well, Mr. Capolucho, it's nice to finally meet you."

"Where did you meet Jacqueline?" Link asked.

"Hawaii. Watching Kilauea erupt."

"Kilauea?" She shook her head.

"Don't you remember? At first, I couldn't tell if you were wrought up with love of lava or just too upset to live." His voice faltered as he stared at her with his odd, unblinking eyes.

Jacqueline's skin crawled. "I've never been near a volcano. At least not an erupting one. And I've never been in Hawaii." Her hands balled into fists and she took a step toward him. Her stalker took a step backward. Jamming her clenched hands into her pockets, she began a slow, silent, calming count. With each number, she took a deliberate step toward him.

One. Half the buttons from his shirt were missing.

Two. One huge, bushy eyebrow nearly covered his forehead.

Three. His eyes were an odd shade of green.

Four. The breeze gusted and her nose wrinkled at the pungent, unwashed smell.

Five. His scraggly beard didn't hide his grimy skin.

Six. He had burns on his face; that must be why the whiskers didn't grow evenly.

Seven. His right hand was badly scarred, too.

Eight. Wow, did he need a bath!

Nine. The scars reminded Jacqueline of the ones she had on her own palm.

Ten. His body language bespoke terror.

Jacqueline came to a halt and watched him for a sign that he might attack her; instead, his unblinking eyes began to register blank confusion. "You aren't Jacqueline. What have you done with her?"

"I am Jacqueline. If you doubt my word, I'll introduce you to my grandmother."

The man began to shake. "Is she a small white haired spitfire?"

"Yes." Jacqueline raised her voice over Link's belly laugh. "That would describe her."

The stranger studied her intently. "Did you hurt her?"

"I would never hurt my grandmother."

"My Jackie."

"Oh. Of course not." She massaged her temples and breathed in the scent of coffee, hoping something would help her figure out who the man was jabbering about. She sighed. "How could I hurt your Jackie? I don't know who you're talking about." Jacqueline leaned closer as she tried to see past the matted hair and grime to see if she could identify anyone familiar. Another gust of wind brought his stench. Stronger this time. Involuntarily, she wrinkled her nose.

"Mr. Cap— " She frowned. "What did you say your name was?"

"Cap O lew cho."

"Right, Capolucho. Would you like some coffee?" Had he doctored it when he made it? Poisoned it? Even if he hadn't, her stomach rebelled at the idea. How could something smell so good and taste so terrible? But if drinking the crud was what it took to figure out what was going on, she'd drink a gallon of it.

Slowly, Capolucho edged around her and shuffled to the tiny fire. Reaching into a baggy pocket, he brought out a grimy metal mug and filled it. Jacqueline crossed her eyes and pinched her nose. Then, before he saw her reaction, she pasted a smile on her face.

After getting her own mug, she poured herself some coffee and sat upwind. It didn't help much, but it was better than downwind.

Link went to their food chest and got the makings for breakfast. He approached the fire. "You two have a lot to talk over. I'll start breakfast."

Capolucho looked at the food in Link's hands. A tiny rivulet of drool trickled through his unkempt beard. How long it had been since the man had eaten a decent meal? Had he been surviving on beans? She shifted another inch upwind. "We can wait to talk until after we've eaten."

Capolucho tore his gaze away from the food and shook his head. "No, I need to know where I lost my Jackie. Was it Valdez? How'd I end up following you?"

"I have no idea." She asked a question of her own. "Why did you start sending me those notes after I started working at Envirohab?"

His eyes widened. "That was you?" She nodded. "You mean I've been— " Unable to finish the thought, he put his hand to his forehead and his sleeve shifted to reveal a forearm covered with horrible scars that could only have been made by fire.

Her stomach turned.

22

Link poured himself a cup of coffee, then raised it to his lips as he watched Jacqueline treat Capolucho like an honored guest, instead of a guy who acted like a basket case and looked worse. Just as he was about to sip, a malevolent odor nearly asphyxiated him. What had the man put in the pot? Ten-year-old gym socks?

Jacqueline lifted her cup, sipped, then quickly set the cup aside, her face looked chalk white. "It's a bit hot for me." Link put his untasted brew down and hoping to appear casual, he moved behind Jacqueline, placed his hands on her shoulders to help support her, then began to knead the knotted muscles in her neck. Her color slowly returned.

Glancing at the direction of her gaze he saw the horrible scarring that covered Capolucho's hands and arms and wondered if the coffee or disfigurement had turned her stomach.

Link patted her back. "Can I talk you into making a batch of your muffins?" She leaned back against his hands and he massaged the knotted muscles some more. He turned to Capolucho.

"Jacqueline is a gourmet cook when it comes to wilderness survival."

"My Jackie couldn't cook," he mumbled.

Link nodded. "Not too many women can. They've become too reliant on prepackaged dinners." The tense flesh slowly relaxed. She placed her left hand on top of his right one, stilling the motion, then turned her head and kissed his finger.

He felt the gentle touch of her lips all they way up his arm. With his left thumb, he stroked her neck.

She trembled.

He inhaled.

"I'll go see if I can find some berries." She hurried away, tripping over her mug and spilling half the contents in the process. "Ooops!" She bent down to grab the mug, but in an uncharacteristically clumsy movement spilled all the contents. "Oh, no." She made a frantic gesture; her elbow hit the pot; it tipped alarmingly, but Capolucho grabbed the handle before a second spill occurred. "I'm so sorry. I must be nervous about finally meeting you. I'm really not this clumsy normally."

"It's only coffee," Capolucho said. "You didn't burn yourself, did you?" She shook her head.

Link glanced from the mug to Jacqueline to Capolucho to the steaming pot. He doubted that Capolucho realized her 'accident' hadn't been a mistake. Link went back to his breakfast preparations, finished slicing the leftover baked potatoes for hash browns, then took the coffeepot off the embers and put the frying pan in its place. Capolucho studied him intently, so he didn't dare a second 'accidental spill'. Link added bacon to the heated pan.

"How long have you known her?" Capolucho jerked his shaggy head toward the clump of blueberry bushes.

"I've known members of the family about ten or eleven years," Link said.

Capolucho grunted. "Think it's odd there being two Jacqueline Cardews?" Before Link could answer, Capolucho cupped his hands to his mouth and shouted at Jacqueline, who was hunkered down next to a knee-high bush, "You are Jacqueline Cardew, aren't you?" Mouth outlined in blue, she merely nodded. "Don't know how I connected with the wrong one," Capolucho muttered.

Was the man making up his tale as some sort of cover up for his actions? Nothing else made sense. "How do you think you came to follow the wrong one so long?" Link asked. Capolucho shrugged. Dirt fell from his beard and landed in his mug, but the man drank it, dirt and all. Link gave the bacon much more attention than it actually required and tried to figure out a way to accidentally tip the coffeepot.

After several minutes of awkward silence, Jacqueline returned and began mixing batter. The scent of cooking bacon began to permeate the air. Capolucho leaned toward the aroma. Link wished it were strong enough to mask the guy's stench. Between the BO and foul coffee, the day didn't look promising. Link hoped the man wasn't trying to lull them into a false sense of security, because no matter how pitiful Capolucho seemed, Link refused to take the man or his motives at face value until he was presented with proof.

Jacqueline used a stick to tuck embers around the Dutch oven, then, still using several superfluous motions, she sat back on her heels. Her knee connected with the coffeepot. It tipped, the lid fell off and the contents spewed onto the ground. "Oh, no. Not again!" She landed on her bottom with a thump, then scrambled to her feet, the picture of abject guilt.

"Smooth move." Link gave her a surreptitious thumb up and a smile.

"Why am I always so clumsy?" Capolucho started to rise. She made shooing motions. "I made the horrible mess, and after you were so kind to brew the coffee, too." She looked downright miserable about the spill. "I'll clean off the dirt and brew a new pot. It's the least I can do." Spewing a string of apologies for her awkwardness, she hurried away with the coffeepot and both their mugs.

Silence descended around the fire as both men focused their attention on the bacon sizzling in the frying pan.

Jacqueline bustled back, just as he finished adding the last strip of bacon to the spitting grease. She added coffee to the pot, placed it next to the Dutch oven, sniffed the air above it, then turned to Capolucho. "Why did you think I was someone else?" He shrugged. "Do I look like this other person?"

"From a distance, you appear about the right size. Same type hair. Didn't think two women would have the same name less it was Jane Smith or som'thin'." The mangy whiskers covering his lower face drooped. "Course I always wondered why you kept your hair brown. My Jackie was always dying hers."

"I see." Jacqueline chewed her lower lip. It was a trait that Link found endearing. "Why didn't you ever approach me before? This could have been cleared up years ago, if you had."

"The restraining order."

"I don't know what you're referring to. Could you please explain?"

Capolucho downed the contents of his mug. Link pretended to concentrate on cooking, but most of his attention was on the conversation. His nerves tingled, as he kept his body and mind ready to counter any hostile move.

"Told you that I met you...." His eyes widened. "Er, my Jackie, at Kilauea." Jacqueline nodded. "She was a mess. Said she'd been partying for a week. Looked to me like she'd been living off booze and popping pills for longer un that."

Jacqueline wrinkled her nose.

"Don't know what she was doing by that volcano. Always thought she'd had a mind to jump in, like some ancient Hawaiian sacrifice or something."

Link straightened. "You thought she wanted to commit suicide?"

"Yeah. Probably." His eyebrow wrinkled in concentration. "She was a mess. Old looking and real pitiful, sorta like a stray dog I once took in. A'course, once she was off the crap, it was like decades dropped away."

"You took her in, didn't you?" Jacqueline asked softly.

Capolucho nodded. The action sent bits of dirt drifting, forming a halo around him. Link yanked the frying pan out of danger and was about to tell him to bathe, but one look at Jacqueline's face made him hold the thought.

"How long did she stay with you?" Jacqueline asked.

"About two years."

"And then she left?" Capolucho inclined his head. She bit her lower lip. "You lived in Hawaii all that time?"

Again, his vigorous nodding filled the air with dust. "Had a shack near the beach. And scraped by selling my paintings."

Capolucho was the most unlikely looking artist Link had ever seen and if he didn't stop agreeing so enthusiastically he'd never finish frying. The coffee began perking, adding it's rich aroma to the building scent of blueberry muffin-cake.

"Why did you leave?" Jacqueline asked.

"It burnt."

The comment stopped conversation long enough for the bacon to finish cooking. Link distributed it onto three dishes, then threw the potato slices into the grease and checked the coffee. "Coffee's ready. Want a refill?" Jacqueline shook her head, while Capolucho enthusiastically thrust his mug forward.

"The fire was when my Jackie and I split. I was angry at her cause she told the coppers that I'd torched my place. I didn't do that. I would never have done somt'hin' like that."

"Of course you didn't."

Capolucho thrust out his hand, palm upward, upon which was a crazy-quilt of scars. "I tried to save my paintings and stuff."

"Were you able to?" Jacqueline asked.

"No," Capolucho said. "The fire bankrupted me."

"Fires are terrible things," Jacqueline agreed. Link added the potatoes to the plates while Jacqueline added big chucks of blueberry-muffin-cake.

Link handed a loaded plate to Capolucho. For a moment, he thought the man was going to lap the food off the blue enamel like a dog, then Capolucho's disfigured fingers wrapped clumsily around the fork, and he began stuffing food into his mouth as if his life depended on it. Link exchanged a look with Jacqueline and saw sympathy in her eyes. Judging by her compassionate expression, she was buying the guy's story hook, line and sinker.

Link wondered how much of it could be corroborated. One thing was certain, the moment they got a cellphone signal, he was going to give Windy a call and have her check out this crazy story. Two people by the name of Jacqueline Cardew were unlikely. Furthermore, it seemed unbelievable that a man could stalk the wrong person for a week, let alone years. Something was definitely rancid about the guy, and it went way beyond his stench.

Link picked at his breakfast.

Jacqueline's appetite seemed to have failed her, as well.

When Capolucho stuffed the last slice of muffin-cake into his mouth, Link made his decision. "If you'd like to get your gear while we strike camp, you're welcome to join us. The more company, the merrier." And the easier it would be to keep on eye on him.

Capolucho nodded eagerly, got to his feet and purposefully hiked upstream. When he was out of earshot, Jacqueline turned to Link. "Never in my life have I met someone that had so much go wrong."

"Sure took the edge off my appetite."

"His story has so many similarities to— "

"I don't buy his story," Link said.

"It does seem unbelievable, but the way Envirohab bur— "

"If he torched it, he cou— "

"You think he killed Adam?"

"What do you think?" Link demanded.

"He seemed so sincere."

"The best con men do."

"Why would he lie? He's discovered I'm not who he thought. What's his motive?"

"I'm not a mind reader." Link glared at the receding figure and shook his head. "His story just doesn't add up."

She frowned at Capolucho's receding, stooped form. "Link, do you believe me about how Adam died?" He nodded. "The situations are similar."

"Maybe a little too similar ... Do you think that

could be because he based his story on the lab?" White dominated her eyes. Link cleared his throat. "My mother always told me that 'people figure they'll find the devil lying in the sewer with the other drunks. Not so. His work is done there. You'll find him sitting in the front row of church, where he has lots of misinformation to spread and doubt to cast'."

"What does that have to do with this problem?"

"Distraction is a good way to calm a person."

She gently touched his hand. "Thank you."

"For what?"

"Helping me. I don't think I'd have managed to get through that meeting if it hadn't been for you...When I saw his hands." She crossed her arms over her stomach and shook her head. "It was terrible, I wanted to throw up. Then it was like you knew exactly what I was going through and you helped me get past it."

To his surprise, she leaned forward and kissed the corner of his mouth. Pleasure, hot and strong, surged through Link's veins. He wanted to take her into his arms and give her a real kiss. But now was neither the right time nor place. Fearing he might give into his body's demands, Link got to his feet. Reaching down, he lightly patted her hair. "Anytime. Right now, we need to start packing."

She nodded. "I'll do the tent. You do the food. OK?"

"Sure." Whenever she suggested chores, she switched them every other day. It made him feel like they were equal partners. Link liked that.

Jacqueline cast another look upstream as Capolucho disappeared behind an accumulation of boulders and driftwood.

"I wonder why he hasn't bathed," Link said.

"I've been wondering how long it's been. If it's just

been recent, I figure that maybe he hates icy water, or he didn't pack soap. Not everyone has the nerve to wash with glacier melt." Jacqueline turned to Link. "What do you think?"

Link rubbed his chin. "I hope it's lack of soap and if I offer to share mine, he'll take me up on it."

"We should have offered before breakfast." Jacqueline shivered. "I can still smell him. I wonder if he's got lice or anything else nasty buried in all that hair."

"I don't think we want to know."

Jacqueline's mouth flattened. "Every time he moved, a shower of crud flew out of his hair and went into my food. Who'd have thought dirt had such good aim?" She grimaced. "Between trying to eat around that and the smell..." She crossed her eyes. "It was the best breakfast you've made, but it was a wonder I managed to swallow anything."

"Poor baby." Link hugged her. Once she was in his arms, it felt right. Too right. "The muffin-cake was especially good. And the second pot of coffee tasted first-rate. I can't thank you enough for tipping the first one." His arms tightened for a moment.

She caressed his spine. "We'd better get things organized before he gets back."

Link didn't want to let go, but knew he had to. As he packed the food chest for transport, he wondered what the rest of the day would bring. He'd just finished loading the canoe when Calpolucho's kayak drifted into sight.

"Ready?" Link asked.

Jacqueline climbed into the bow. "Whenever you are." She gripped her paddle as if preparing to bludgeon someone with it. Perhaps she distrusted Capolucho's story, too.

23

As the campsite receded, Jacqueline wondered if the shaky sensation in her stomach was anxiety or relief. She'd felt an odd kinship to Capolucho when he was sitting there, looking so pathetic, but then Link had voiced his doubts about how the man's story was just a little to close to her own for comfort.

Worse, she hadn't been able to get past the worry that he could be correct.

Worse, the more she thought about it, the more holes she noticed. Link was right, there were just too many parallels.

Capolucho could have burned his hands while murdering Adam. But why would he have done that? What sort of a relationship had he had with her husband?

What if the messages had originally been for Adam and not for her?

"Jacqueline," Link murmured. She turned. He placed his paddle across his lap. "I know you like the guy, but I don't trust him." He glanced back at the kayak, which was still out of hearing distance. "Have you noticed the way he avoids answering questions?"

Jacqueline nodded. "Like that restraining order. He brought it up twice, but never explained it. I think that's very fishy."

"What about his claim of two Jacquelines? Cardew

isn't that common of a name. Now that you've seen him, do you recognize him?"

"I'm having a hard time looking at him." Jacqueline admitted as she rubbed warmth into her arms. "I thought that once I met my stalker, everything would fall into place and I'd understand why he's been pestering me. Now, I'm wondering what gave me that stupid idea." She jerked her hands away from her upper arms and gripped her paddle tight, wishing she could dig into the water or do anything which required physical movements so she could shake off the eerie sensations hovering over her.

"None of this is logical."

She nodded in agreement. "I can't figure out how he could have known another person well enough to live with her for two years, then not recognize the difference right off."

Link's reaction indicated that he'd noticed that, too.

"But the thing that really worries me is what man in his right mind would make up such a story."

"It is improbable."

She placed her paddle across her lap, then pressed her aching temples. "On one hand, it's so off the wall that I figure it has to be true; but on the other, it sounds like the worst fiction I've ever heard." She rubbed her temples. "I've never been to Hawaii, not that I wouldn't like to go, but there's never been time." Or money.

"Same here," Link said. "Do you know anyone who lived the high life or vacationed there?"

"Hawaii? No. High life? Yes," Jacqueline said. "My freshman roommate, Nora, lives for laughs and fun. After she dropped out, she started living a jet set life in Europe. And no, I don't think it could be her. Wrong ocean for one thing, plus she never stays anywhere for two months, let alone two years. She sends me occasional postcards."

"From Hawaii?"

She shook her head. "A state would be too passé for her. She lives in exotic places like Turkey, Paris and Greece. The last postcard was from Nicosia, Cypress. Her husband owns some sort of shipping line and they travel a lot, but it's almost always around the Mediterranean and I don't recall her ever mentioning Hawaii."

Link looked like he was going to ask something, but wind gusted from upstream and ruffled his hair. His nose quivered. A moment later the stench reached her. Link turned and studied the approaching vessel. "Capolucho, you lead the way." Capolucho gave a short nod and the kayak skimmed past.

Jacqueline didn't know she'd been holding her breath until she exhaled.

"Ever wish you could trade lives with her?"

"Who? Nora?"

He nodded.

"Not since I realized how empty and superficial her life seemed. But when I got her first letter from Morocco, where she'd found some great copper pots in the Market, and I was still stuck in college, studying for finals, yeah, back then I would have traded."

Link smiled and her heart did a flip.

Eventually, she'd find an isolated cottage and settle into a nice comfortable existence. She'd make it a cozy home with good security and wouldn't worry about finding strange notes. Alaska would be a nice. Hawaii would be, too. Anywhere there was water. Until this trip, she hadn't realized how much she missed the simple joy of canoeing and listening to the soothing murmur of a stream.

This would have been a wonderful vacation, if it hadn't been for her stalker and Tempest. She studied Capolucho's back. It felt good to have him where she could keep an eye on him. But before she could plan her future, she needed to figure out why he'd picked her. She rubbed her temples. Had he followed her thousands of miles, and then made up the ridiculous story to cover up the fact that he'd murdered Adam and was still after her because he thought she had whatever he'd wanted or could his story possibly be true?

Before he paddled out of sight, Jacqueline dipped her paddle in the water and helped Link align their canoe in the current far enough behind so they'd have breathable air. Her initial impression of Capolucho had been of a man who acted like a rabbit ready to flee from a fox. She'd tried to give him the impression she believed him so he'd quit treating her like she was a predator. In all her fantasy outcomes, she'd never visualized confronting a cowardly man. Could his fear be an act to make them feel secure? But what would he gain? A canoe, tent and food chest? Those seemed like small recompense for such an elaborate hoax. Of course, a lunatic would probably think his plan was intelligent, while it looked absurd to everyone else.

Jacqueline scrutinized grimy plaid flannel covering her stalker's back. Unreasonable as it seemed, his story could be true. He might be just as cowardly as he appeared. A timid person could conceivably have chosen odd poetry and silly origami creatures as a means to contact her – or Adam. Her fingers tightened around her paddle.

What if he was insane and had concocted the outrageously false scenario as part of some mind game he was playing?

Regardless of the reasons for his story, the man probably needed psychiatric counseling. Jacqueline grimaced. If she kept thinking in circles, she'd need a session or two herself.

In mid-afternoon, Link maneuvered their canoe so close to the kayak that Jacqueline nearly gagged. Gesturing with his paddle, Link indicated a rocky beach. "That looks like a good spot to camp."

Capolucho eagerly nodded.

Jacqueline would have preferred postponing the inevitable, since being near the man's disgusting odor during breakfast and lunch had been bad enough. She couldn't imagine spending an entire evening with the stink. Jacqueline glanced back at Link, whose expression radiated geniality. She tried to match his demeanor and fervently hoped her nose didn't permanently wrinkle. "I need time to scrounge for fruits and veggies before we start dinner," she said.

"And I need to catch something."

As they tied the vessels to a rock, Capolucho asked, "How come you always camp on sandbars? Aren't you worried there'll be a flood?"

"This is the dry time of year," Link said. "Next spring, during breakup, the floods will wash away any sign that we were here."

"That way we don't leave anything behind," Jacqueline said.

"Sure we do," Link teased. "Footprints and bits of charcoal from the fire, but those are natural and won't have an environmental impact."

"I suppose you're right." Jacqueline grabbed the tent. "It's my turn to set up." She left them as quickly as she could, knowing that if she'd stayed one more minute she would shove Capolucho into the water and dump detergent on him.

Link strolled up to her and deposited their duffel bags. "I'm going to catch dinner." He gave her an intense look, then raised his voice adding, "After I clean the fish, I'll wash up."

Silently, he pointed to his shirt and made a scrubbing motion. She frowned, as she tried to grasp his meaning. "You want me to wash your clothes?"

Link grinned. "Well, yeah, if you want. I'd appreciate it." He gave her a conspiratorial wink, then turned to call over his shoulder, "How about you, Capolucho? It's Jacqueline's turn to do laundry. Want her to wash your things?" Her hands closed into fists. Since when did she wash Link's clothes? She pulled her elbow back and aimed a punch at his stomach. Then it dawned on her. This was Link's solution to the stench problem. Her hand opened and she patted Link's bicep in appreciation.

When she looked at Capolucho, he refused to meet her eyes. She thought she detected a faint flush beneath his hairy facade, but she couldn't be certain. "I don't mind," she said. "I have to do both of ours. One more person's stuff won't make a difference." It seemed to take forever for him to respond. She bit her lip and hoped God would forgive her for her impatience.

"I better not. I ran out of repellent." Capolucho's expression seemed sheepish.

"We have plenty of bug repellent," Link assured him.

"I meant bear repellent."

"Bear repellent?" Jacqueline asked, in confusion. "What's that?"

"The pilot that flew me up here sold it to me. Said that since I was a pacifist and wouldn't carry a gun, I'd need something to fend off the bears. I almost think it'd have been better to get eaten or carry a gun."

Link had a sudden fit of coughing.

Jacqueline blinked rapidly. Could a pilot's prank account for the stench? Knowing bears' fondness for dumps, she suspected they would view the smell as ambrosia or an invitation to dine, instead of something disgusting. Surely a bush pilot couldn't have been that deceitful! She cast a quick glance at Link, who was coughing so hard that his eyes were tearing and she suddenly realized that he was trying to cover up a fit of laughter. How could he think someone putting another person's life in danger was amusing? She resisted the impulse to kick him. "Don't worry about that," Jacqueline told Capolucho. "Link and I are armed." A look of relief spread beneath the ragged beard. "Do you know how to make a fire pit?" Capolucho nodded. "If you could do that, after you set up your stuff, we could get hot water quicker. Trust me, bathing in glacier melt isn't something you want to do."

He studied her silently for such a long time that she began to worry she'd gone too far. Finally, his mustache quivered. "You're much nicer than my Jackie."

"Thank you, I think."

His beard trembled, and she had the impression he'd smiled. Capolucho turned and began putting stones in a ring near the water, just as they'd done every day.

Jacqueline blinked in surprise. How many times had he watched them set up camp and why hadn't they spotted him? Jacqueline picked up Link's fishing gear and shoved it at him. "Hurry up with the fish. I'll finish the tent, then find whatever food is nearby." Lowering her voice to a hiss only Link could hear, she added. "If I come down with some dread disease and die washing his stuff,

I'm going to come back and haunt you."

Shoulders still shaking in silent laughter, Link nodded.

By the time Jacqueline was satisfied with their tent, Capolucho had a placed small stack of dry driftwood beside to the rock. Next, he gathered dry grass. "Do you need anything else to start this?" he asked.

Her back stiffened. "You can light it."

He vigorously shook his head. "I haven't lit one in years. It was all I could do to unbury the embers this morning."

Remembering his hands, she didn't need to ask why. For the first time, she felt true empathy for him. They shared an unseen bond; both were haunted by fire. "What exactly caused your burns?"

For the longest time, he crouched next to the wood and rocks gazing at his scarred hands. Slowly, he lifted his head. "My Jackie said I set it on purpose. But I don't remember doing that." He shrugged. "Maybe I did." He heaved a sigh. "We'd been out celebrating, and I was drunk. So drunk that I can't remember much of what happened." His mustache drooped down. "Don't even remember drinking more than one glass of champagne, but it had to have been a lot more because I had one hell of a hangover."

He fell silent.

Jacqueline looked over Capolucho's bowed head toward Link, who appeared to be concentrating on fishing, but she thought he was close enough to overhear their conversation. That fact gave her courage. "What were you celebrating?"

"A gallery wanted to give me a one man show." He hung his head and shrugged.

Why this humility for such a monumental event?

Did his modesty hide a lie? "If someone thought I was good enough to give me my own show, I'd print it on a T-shirt for the world to read."

Capolucho gave her a sad look. "It was a long time ago."

"Didn't it turn out well?" A look of pain flashed deep in his eyes. "Forget I asked. Link or anyone else that knows me will tell you one of my worst faults is sticking my nose in other people's business."

"It never happened. My paintings burned along with the shack. There wasn't time to create more, so I tried to get the others back." Capolucho raised his deformed hands and moved them before her eyes. "I can write, but I don't have enough feeling in my hands to paint like I want to paint." Everything about Capolucho's tone and body language proclaimed that he was telling the truth.

"I'm sorry," Jacqueline said. While his situation might not be as fatal as Adam's, in his own way, he had lost his life to fire, too. He certainly smelled dead.

"It was a long time ago," Capolucho said.

She bit her lip. "So you haven't painted since?" He shook his head; small dark particles showered the ground. She tried not to inhale too deeply. "I'm no artist, but it seems to me that if you were good enough for a showing before the accident, you still have the talent. You'll just need to develop a style to suit your current abilities."

"Maybe someday." His tone and body language were evasive.

Sensing she had pushed enough, at least for the moment, she changed the subject, "If you give me your clothes, I'll start the laundry." He stared at her. "Do you have any other things that need to be done?" He slowly shook his head, through the beard, red splotches deepened. "Do you have a towel, soap, shampoo?" Again, he shook his head. No wonder he smelled so bad. "In that case, I'll loan you mine." She made a face. "That is if you don't mind smelling like lemons."

"It would be an awful nice change." His understatement sent such a flood of relief rolling through Jacqueline that she felt suddenly lighter. She got the items and handed them to him. A few moments later, he gave her his clothing, then, wrapped in her soft pink towel, he headed for the river. "I don't care if it's ice water, I'm going to wash." She stared after him in astonishment as he walked straight into the water until it came up to his knees, then he began to soap the washcloth.

Poor man had lived with the stench longer than they had and obviously wasn't as desensitized to it as she had expected.

Pensively, she looked down at the tinder he'd collected. If he could wash in ice water and save her nose, the least she could do was light a fire. Her stomach contracted. A small fire. Surely, she could manage that. It took her five tries, but she finally stilled her hands enough to strike the match. The euphoria felt incredibly liberating. If she could light a match and hold it to dry moss, she could do anything - even wash reeking clothing.

When she picked them up with the tips of her fingers, a small bundle dropped to the ground. She peered at the zip lock bag. It contained his wallet. Jacqueline bit her lip, then glanced toward the boulder, behind which Capolucho had disappeared. Quickly she stooped down, unzipped the bag, flipped open the wallet and extracted a New Mexico driver's license. Though Ray's photo was of a clean-shaven man with one eyebrow, he'd given them his real name. Or at least the one that matched this piece of identification. When she tried to shove the license back into place, she noticed a photo. She took a peak. A couple stood against a backdrop of palms, sand and clear blue sky. Hawaii? She squinted at the tiny faces. The man, tall and well built, was dressed in a wild tropical print shirt, sandals, sunglasses and a straw hat, which hid his face in shadows. Wild orphan Annie curls concealed most of the petite redhead's face. Between the flowing muumuu and the way she was glued to the man, it was impossible to determine her body shape.

Still, there was something vaguely familiar about the couple. Had she known them in the past? Jacqueline didn't think so, but she couldn't be sure. The backdrop looked familiar, yet she'd never been anywhere that had dark sand.

Her temples began throbbing, so she tucked the picture away, rezipped the bag, then tossed the wallet inside his tent.

Scrubbing the fetid clothing gave her ample time to think about the photo. With every dunking she gave the fabric, she became more certain she'd seen that photo before.

But where?
When?

24

Link caught two dolly varden. Neither were prizewinners, but they were still nice fish. Normally, he felt content after fishing, but today the closer he got to their camp, the more something felt wrong. Yet everything appeared normal: damp clothes were draped over a clump of knee-high shrubs near on the edge of the bank, and best of all Jacqueline was mixing something in a bowl, which undoubtedly would be heaven on the tongue. Judging by his slicked flat hair, and the fact that he had Jacqueline's pink towel wrapped around his waist, as he huddled close to the fire, Capolucho had bathed.

Without the seedy clothing, the man looked muscular and fit.

Link frowned. What was wrong with this picture?

Striding even closer, he saw that the disfigurement of Capolucho's hands and forearms was only a fraction of the trauma he'd suffered. It was a wonder he'd survived burns over that much of his body. As Link advanced toward the fire, Capolucho said something to Jacqueline. She glanced up and smiled at him. An unfamiliar emotion formed in the pit of Link's stomach. The scene seemed too peaceful. Too domestic. Link felt like an intruder in his own camp. He looked at the fire. Soon the embers would be ready to cook dinner. The wildflowers were another homey touch. Had Capolucho picked them for Jacqueline?

Link's jaw clenched.

"Those are beautiful fish," Jacqueline said. "Is that big one trophy size?"

Link shook his head. "It isn't even eight pounds."

"What a shame." Jacqueline sounded genuinely sorry. She turned to Capolucho. "Link is one of the best fishermen I've ever known."

"Never been fishing," Capolucho said.

"You should try it sometime," Jacqueline said. "It's wonderfully relaxing, at least it is for me, but I'm not sure it is for Link. He's always trying to catch the big one and that seems stressful." While Link honed his filleting knife, Jacqueline's casual but accurate comment replayed like a broken record.

Had fishing ever been relaxing?

Not since he was a kid and forced to eat macaroni and cheese twice a day because it was all they could afford. The first time he'd brought home a string of bass, his mother had called him her little breadwinner. There had been pride mixed with relief in her voice. Two decades later, Link fingered the blade of his knife and considered the day when fishing had ceased being fun: the day he'd begun fishing for survival. Compulsive fishing had made sense when his father was ill, but why was he still doing it? It had been years since anyone in his family relied on his catch to eat.

He'd stopped fishing when he went to college, then he and Stone formed Linkstone and as their success grew, so did the compulsion to catch a trophy. Link frowned, as he filleted the Dolly Vardens, and wondered why it had taken so many years to realize he didn't enjoy his obsession.

Jacqueline finished blending the batter in the bowl. Mixed emotions fought for dominance, as he contemplated how Jacqueline had noticed what he couldn't see for himself. He had the feeling that in many ways she saw him more clearly than he saw himself. He also sensed that she liked him for who he was.

He liked her, too.

Unwilling to ponder the ramifications of that thought, Link finished filleting the fish. He put the pan on some embers to heat, then realized that he hadn't lit the fire. He frowned. Capolucho could barely hold a fork. Matches should be too small for him to deal with. That meant there was a good chance Jacqueline had ignited it. Had she faced her fear and conquered it?

Link flipped the fish. Hot grease popped and sizzled. He felt more compatible with Jacqueline than with anyone he'd ever known, but he also wanted her more than he'd thought it was possible to want anything and he was getting damned tired playing the roll of protective friend.

Still, pissing off Mavis would be a really dumb move.

Link sprinkled seasoning on the fish.

Jacqueline, who was checking their laundry, looked at him and smiled.

Link grinned back.

Her beam widened.

His heart warmed. In fact, his entire body warmed. Definitely lust. Link dropped his gaze back to the fire. While he prodded the fish, he wondered why Jacqueline seemed so special. To avoid pondering that question, he made a mental list: on his next birthday, he'd be thirty; he was financially stable, not a millionaire, but comfortable. Even if something happened to him, his share of the profits from Linkstone could support a family. He wouldn't have to worry about that.

What was he thinking?

Jacqueline used a stick as she retrieved the aluminum wrapped biscuits from the embers. As she opened the foil, their aroma blended with the scent of cooked fish. Next, she reclaimed the Dutch oven, which was filled with roasted carrots and potatoes, seasoned with onion. It was beginning to look like a feast.

So was she.

Capolucho leaned forward and sniffed. "Heads up." Jacqueline tossed Capolucho a steaming biscuit. He caught it, tossed it back and forth between his hands for a moment, then wolfed it down, like he was a starving dog.

She handed Capolucho a plate. He piled on the food until it threatened to fall off, and then dug in as if he hadn't eaten in weeks. Link scratched the back of his ear and wondered if Capolucho always ate like that.

Jacqueline placed her hand on his forearm. Her skin felt good against his. "Ray is an artist," she said. "A good one." She nibbled a sliver of fish.

"Not that good," Capolucho protested, his mouth full of food.

"They were going to give him a one man show," she added, "but his paintings burned before they could be exhibited." Did she have to sing the man's praises while he ate? Link bit into a biscuit.

Capolucho shifted uncomfortably. "It most likely would have been a flop."

"You're too modest," Jacqueline said.

Link swallowed. He coughed. Jacqueline patted his back. Eyes tearing, he wondered if fate was teaching him a lesson. When he recovered, he took Jacqueline's hand in his, then asked Capolucho, "What style do you paint?"

"Surrealistic."

"Ariel paints impressionism."

"Did she paint the callas?" Jacqueline asked.

Link nodded. "The caribou, too."

"Oh, she's really good. Ray, you should talk to her."

"Who is she?"

"My partner's wife."

Jacqueline grinned. "Maybe she could inspire you to get back into painting."

"Not likely." He held up his disfigured hands. "I can't hold a brush. Can't do much of anything that I used to."

"Then change your style," Jacqueline said. "Surreal stuff doesn't have to be detailed. I should think that if you can write notes, you can do something. If you were good enough for your own show, the talent is still there. From what I understand of art, which admittedly isn't all that much, it's more a matter of line, balance and color than detail."

Capolucho silently studied her for several minutes. "It's been a long time."

"I bet painting is the same as riding a bike." Jacqueline made a funny face. "Besides, what have you got to lose? You might find out you like your new style even more."

Capolucho smoothed his misshapen hand over his scraggly beard. It reminded Link of the way Stone petted his dogs, while he was trying to figure out how to discipline Tempest.

Slowly, the eyes under the shaggy brow began to brighten. "Maybe."

"No maybes about it," Jacqueline said.

"When I get back, maybe I'll give it a shot."

Link cleared his throat. "When we get back, I'll introduce you to Ariel."

"Are you sure she won't mind?"

"I don't think so."

Capolucho continued stroking his beard. "I suppose it doesn't make sense to keep this any more. I'm never going to find my Jackie, not after this long."

Jacqueline blinked in confusion. "I don't follow."

"When I was in the burn unit, my Jackie came in and cried over the way my hair had been singed off. Said she always loved it long and she told me she'd always wished I'd grow a beard."

He stared into the distance, remembering another time and place. "I have some scars on my face from the sparks." His beard quivered. He took a deep breath and his hand clutched his whiskers "It's time to cut it."

Link nodded. Capolucho wasn't just talking about his hair; he was telling them that it was time to let go of the woman who had preoccupied his thoughts. He hoped the man hadn't switched his fixation to Jacqueline.

"I brought along a small pair of scissors," Jacqueline said. "If you'd like, I can trim your hair." She grimaced. "I've never tried to do a beard, but I'm game if you are."

"Get them," Capolucho said. "It can't look worse than it does now." Jacqueline eagerly hurried to their tent.

Link raised an eyebrow. "Just like that? I'd have asked for references."

"If I had a decent haircut, like you, I'd worry. If she butchers my hair, could you give me the name of your barber?"

He nodded. "Provided she doesn't scalp you." Capolucho's eyes widened. "It was a joke. I don't even think an enterprising Indian could scalp anyone with her scrawny scissors." Link began cleaning up the pan and plates.

Jacqueline returned and without preamble, began combing Capolucho's tangled hair. Whenever the teeth stuck, she studiously snipped away with her cuticle scissors until the comb was free. Soon, a mound of whiskers and hair big as a beaver carcass surrounded Capolucho's seat. Jacqueline stepped back to survey her efforts. The remaining hair lay in rough-edged layers. She returned to her project and began by running her fingers through his hair.

Link's jaw tensed until his molars hurt. Why was he resentful? He'd never experienced this particular emotion, but he had the uneasy suspicion he was feeling jealousy. What had Jacqueline done to him?

Nothing.

She treated everyone with decency, kindness and respect. That was the crux of it. He didn't want to be treated like everyone else. He wanted to be special. Link knew that what he was feeling came from deep within him. The problem was, he wasn't sure how to deal with it.

He stretched the kinks out of his spine. Getting to know Jacqueline felt like being whirled inside an emotional tornado.

Jacqueline's brow furrowed in concentration, as she began shaping the remaining hair. He wondered if she had special feelings for him. He'd thought so until he saw how good she was to Capolucho. Link surged to his feet. "I'm going to clean up and wash my hair."

Capolucho grunted, but Jacqueline ignored him. Link stomped away. Dunking his head in the icy river took his breath away. There was no reason for Jacqueline to give him special attention. Still, he despised not being first. Loathed that he didn't know how she felt. Detested that he couldn't understand his own mind or actions when it came to her. Link worked the shampoo into his hair, rinsed it and took a sponge bath. His teeth chattered so hard that he was afraid he would crack the enamel. Then he slipped on a clean pair of sweats.

Walking back to the campsite, he reflected that loving someone was never easy.

25

As the sun touched the western horizon, a mystical shimmering light spread out over the land. Jacqueline sat on a blanket watching the display, her heart expanding with pleasure as radiant salmon-colored rays uncurled over the frozen tundra like a benediction. When the bottom of the sun slipped below the tree line, Link strolled toward her; the departing light formed a halo around him, making him look like an enchanted being.

She sighed. It wasn't fair; when she wore a sweat suit, she looked shapeless, but when Link wore one, it accentuated each muscle of his magnificent body. Quickly, she shoved the thought aside and looked away.

Link stopped a foot away from her. His bare feet remained motionless on the permanently frosty ground. She looked up. There was a strange gleam in his eyes, which seemed to kindled by an inner blaze as strong and hot as the departed sun. His gaze centered on her face, caught her attention and held it.

Heat poured through her from head to toe.

No one had ever looked at her with such intensity. Her skin tingled. Her heartbeat accelerated, then began to beat a wild cadence as Link knelt in front of her and lowered his head, and the heat intensified so much that a kernel of apprehension sprouted. She tore her gaze from his when she realized she couldn't think straight.

His palm gently caught her chin and brought her

close, then Link's lips met hers in a gentle possessive kiss. Feelings, hot and primitive, ignited inside her. Jacqueline wrapped her arms around Link's neck.

Link groaned softly as he shifted closer to her.

Jacqueline's body turned into a shimmering torrent as he deepened the kiss. Nothing had ever felt so good, so right. In fact, she'd never felt such intense, all-consuming emotions. Her hands caressed his strong back. Link mirrored her movements.

Link groaned as he tightened his hold. Abruptly, he stiffened, then released her and moved away.

Resentment boiled within her. Link was no different from Adam. The moment she responded, and her body began to cry with need, it was over. Poof. One minute hot need, the next frustrated emptiness.

"I'm sorry," said a voice behind her. Jacqueline stiffened with embarrassment when she realized they had an audience. "I was just getting a drink of water." Capolucho's face appeared crimson in the fading light. He shifted uncomfortably, and reminded her of a little boy, who had been caught playing a prank that he expected to be punished for.

"It's all right." Every nerve in her body disagreed, but intellectually, she knew his presence had saved her from making a terrible mistake.

Link settled on the blanket next to her, and wrapped his right arm possessively around her waist.

"I shouldn't have joined up with you." Capolucho scuffed his feet. "You wanted to be alone. That's why everyone else left."

"No," said Link. "They left because we wanted to contact you, and figure out what your messages meant, but we didn't know what to expect."

The massive eyebrow contracted. "You serious?"

"Yes," Jacqueline assured him. Her fingers stroked Link's hand. "I'd had enough of the one-sided exchange."

"It was the only thing left," Capolucho muttered. "If I'd known there was two Jackie Cardews, I'd have made sure you were the right one." He shifted his weight back and forth, faster and faster, giving Jacqueline the odd impression that his movements were a clumsy dance.

"Are you referring to the restraining order?" Jacqueline asked. He hung his head. Clipped, washed and clean, he bore little resemblance to the man who had pursued her, yet he was still reticent.

Jacqueline hoped Capolucho was telling them the truth and that there really had been a terrible mix up, but she still didn't understand how it could have occurred.

"Sit down." Link pointed to an unoccupied spot on the blanket. "Tell us about it."

For a moment, she thought he wouldn't do it, but slowly, Capolucho sat on the farthest possible corner of their blanket. "I told you about the fire," he said softly. She nodded. "I was in the hospital for months."

"Burns can take a long time to heal," Jacqueline agreed.

"My Jackie came to see me once."

"Only one time?" Link sounded surprised.

He nodded.

"Was she hurt in the fire, too?" Jacqueline asked.

Capolucho shook his head.

"Why only once?" Link asked.

"She had a job offer in the states and needed to leave."

Capolucho's eyes glistened. Jacqueline didn't know if it meant tears were beginning to well, or if the final quivering rays of sunlight were merely reflected in his eyes. "I thought we'd always be together. That's why I gave her the infernos. We'd talked of marriage, but she wanted to wait."

"You gave her the infernos?" Jacqueline repeated, feeling as if she were tantalizingly close to finally understanding what this entire fiasco was about.

"How long had she been looking for a different job?" Link asked.

Capolucho shrugged then shook his head. "I didn't even know she wanted one, or wasn't happy living in my shack."

"You lived in a shack, and had lots of infernos," Jacqueline said.

"It was more like an airy studio with areas for cooking and sleeping." He shrugged. "I loved the view, the lifestyle." He cleared his throat. "Then, I wake up in the hospital and my Jackie tells me she's had enough of slumming with a wannabe-Picasso and living in a hovel." He studied the rocky ground like a crystal ball would pop up and give him the answers to life's mysteries.

Link raised a brow. "She waited until you were flat on your back to hit you with something like that?" Capolucho's head moved in assent. "What a monster," Link muttered.

Capolucho's head jerked up. "No. The timing was wrong. That's all."

"So, what about the infernos?" Jacqueline tightened her fingers on Link's shin, warning him to back off. "And how is the restraining order you keep talking about come part of this?" she asked.

"I got out of the hospital a couple months later, and managed to convince the cops that I hadn't set the fire. They dropped the charges against me." He grimaced. "I don't think they really cared, since the only stuff that got destroyed was mine. By the time I got out, she was gone.

I managed to track her to L. A." The muscles in his face moved, but no words emerged.

"And?" Link demanded.

"I found her. She still had the infernos and boy was she furious that I'd found her. Said that she didn't want any part of me, that I'd tried to kill her in the fire." His eyes bored into Jacqueline's. "I didn't. I swore that to her and the cops."

"I believe you. Now, about the infe— "

"She said my scars turned her off." Jacqueline willed herself not to nod in agreement. She felt Link's muscles contract. "But I loved her, I couldn't let go. My skin was— " He gestured silently with his grisly hands. "I might look different on the outside, but I'm the same on the inside."

"She sounds shallow." Jacqueline didn't add malicious or insensitive.

"I suppose she was, a little," Capolucho agreed.

"She sounds cruel," Link said flatly.

Capolucho's strange, glittering eyes studied him, and then he slowly nodded. "Maybe, but she didn't start out that way. When we first met, she was different. I don't know when she changed."

Sympathy welled within Jacqueline. "Your scars aren't that bad, but some women can't stand any blemish."

Capolucho shook his head. "She loved horror movies, the grislier, the better. Whenever we watched one, they turned her on. I figured she wouldn't mind my scars."

A memory that Jacqueline couldn't quite grasp nagged at the back of her mind.

"She told me it was over," Capolucho said. "That I was part of her past. It upset me, and I tried to argue with her, to make her see how much I cared."

"Like writing love letters?" Jacqueline said.

The muscles in his face worked. "She called the cops. Told them I tried to kill her before and had threatened to kill her again. They arrested me."

"Like I said, Satan incarnate." Jacqueline swatted Link's arm for being so rude, but privately thought he was right.

"I spent the night in jail, and at the hearing the next morning, the judge told me that my Jackie feared for her life and had filed a restraining order against me." A tear trickled down his cheek, but it was quickly lost in his short beard.

"Of all the nerve," Jacqueline said.

"I tried to phone her, but she kept hanging up on me." He swallowed. "That's when I wrote the first poem." The original messages had been filled with pain and yearning. "Two days later, she moved to Arizona," Capolucho concluded.

The hair on the back of her neck quivered. "Did you immediately follow her to Arizona?"

"Yep. That was just under three years ago."

"But I'd been there almost a year before I got the first note." Heat crept up her neck. "I thought my husband had sent the tulip to me." She quoted the first note, "Burning desire, heat of the night, passion's fire, give them back." She gestured in frustration. "Coincidently the note arrived the morning after my husband and I had our first fight. I forgave Adam, and thanked him for the cute note, but he denied writing the 'foolish drivel'. I didn't know what to think. The only explanation I could think of was that Adam had written it, then been ashamed of showing a soft side."

"No, I wrote that."

She glared at Capolucho. "You should have signed it."

Capolucho rubbed his temple with his fist. "So, I got mixed up when she moved." He stood up and began his odd shuffling dance.

"How?"

He came to stop in front of her. "I don't know."

"I started my job in June, right after graduation."

"Damn," Capolucho muttered. "I'm sorry for the mix up."

Jacqueline was too. The tenderness of the earliest notes and the sweetly scented flowers had given her hope that Adam deeply loved her, but couldn't show it. Now that she knew who'd written the note, she realized her suspicion that Adam had only wanted a good research assistant with benefits was more likely.

Capolucho cleared his throat. "Do you happen to have a sister-in-law or cousin or anyone with your same name?"

She shook her head. "Adam wanted to keep our marriage a secret, so I kept my maiden name." She couldn't keep all the bitterness out of her tone. "I wish you'd talked to me instead of leaving the notes, we could have had this straightened out years ago."

"My Jackie had threatened to kill me if I did. It wasn't the way she told the judge, though. She always told them I made the threats."

"Three years is a long time to devote," Link said.

Capolucho nodded. "I couldn't find work close by, so I was only able to drive down about once a month."

It had seemed more frequent than that. "Where did you go?"

"Santa Fe. I went to live with my parents until I got back on my feet." Capolucho scuffed the dirt. "My mother doesn't mind the scars; in fact, she tries to smother me."

"Mothers can be that way," Link agreed. "Ask my father."

Capolucho's eyebrow arched into a J.

"So, now that you know I'm not the right Jacqueline, what are you going to do?"

"I'll go back to Santa Fe and keep working with my Dad." He paused. "Try to rebuild my life." Capolucho shifted his feet. "Forget about ever getting Scorching Strand, the Inferno Series or the rest back. Maybe I'll try to paint again." He grimaced. "Just to see if I can, but I've got to accept that my Jackie hasn't been part of my life for years and won't be."

"The infernos you talk about are paintings?" Jacqueline asked.

He nodded. "I gave them and some others to my Jackie, but figured that if she'd just lend them back to me, I could get my career back on its feet."

"They weren't in the house when it burned?"

"She'd taken them to a framer."

"What's your dad do?" Link asked.

"He builds rammed earth houses. It's hard work, but it hasn't been that bad. He hated it when I went into art." He looked at the ground. "Thought it was sissy to want to paint. But I've been experimenting with the pours, and he likes the results." Ray stopped his restless movement. "I just realized that I never stopped being an artist."

"How so?" Link asked.

"For the past couple years, I've mixed the earth we pour. I've been adding colors." His grin was sheepish. "Natural ones from the earth. They form patterns, creating abstract designs in the walls." His scarred hands moved, delineating peaks and waves.

Jacqueline silently studied Ray and hoped he'd get back to the reference he'd made to scorched strands and infernos, since they'd been the focus of most of his notes.

"I don't need to paint on canvas," Ray enthused. "Not when I can build the color into the walls. I've got to think this through." He turned on his heel and walked down to the shore.

As Jacqueline watched him go, she was tempted to run after him and demand answers to her questions. When Capolucho was out of earshot, she leaned toward Link. "He's the strangest person I've ever met. I like him, though. Do you think all artists are like him?"

"Ariel isn't, but then art is more of a hobby with her." Link's left hand moved to trace her arm from shoulder to fingertip. "Want to resume where we got interrupted?"

Did she? Her heart told her that Link appreciated her while Adam had never really cared for anything except his work. Logic told her that all men were essentially created the same and that whatever deficiencies existed were her fault.

Link's right hand moved up to caress her side. The sensation traveled all the way to her toes. A second kiss would be far too dangerous. In fact, she didn't know how she'd get any sleep, after the first one. Jacqueline wet her lips. "Link, I won't lie and say I'm not tempted, but the truth is if we did, I'm not certain I could control things and it's just not right." He raised her hand to his lips and placed a gentle kiss on it. Jacqueline felt the tender touch all the way to the soles of her feet.

26

The harsh caw of an arctic raven woke Link from a fitful sleep. As he stretched, he felt Jacqueline's warmth. A vivid memory of the previous night's kiss flashed across his memory. He forgot to breathe as he watched the gently undulating nylon ceiling, which reminded him of how Jacqueline felt in his arms. As if reading his mind, she sighed. Her hot, damp breath caressed his shoulder, and then grazed his ear. Chilblains broke out over his body. His lungs burned for air. Link took a deep, shuddering breath. He had to get out of this tent before he did something he'd never forgive himself for.

He turned onto his side and reached for the sleeping bag's zipper. As Link sat up, he noticed that her hair was in a wild tangle, which made her appear erotic. He stopped in mid motion. Couldn't he think of anything besides sex? Why was this his basic response to her? Though everything about Jacqueline seemed seductive, she had a great mind and intellect too. Why couldn't he focus on that instead of her perfect skin?

Perfect, except for the dark smudges under her eyes. Bruises? Link leaned closer to make sure the dim light hadn't distorted his observation. It hadn't. He moved closer, until his finger hovered over the telltale discoloration. The signs of exhaustion were as distressing as black eyes would have been.

She sighed in her sleep. It was the sound of weariness. If she hadn't gotten any sleep, it was his fault for thrashing all night. He should never have kissed her.

In the past, on the occasions when women had infatuated him, the lustful fantasies had quickly dissolved during the resulting affairs. It was as if having sex revealed how little he had in common with the woman.

Link laid back down, turned his back to Jacqueline, and stared at the tent's wall. He could still feel heat radiating from her peaceful form, hear her soft sensual breathing, smell her lemony musk aroma. He felt feverish. Not giving in to temptation had had the reverse effect, this time. Link pressed his fingers to his forehead, but it was cool.

Thank God he wouldn't have to share a tent with her much longer.

Jacqueline rolled over, wrapped her arm around his waist and snuggled close. The heat against his back pounded desire into every cell. He defined torture as lying in a tent with the woman he loved and resolving to stay celibate.

The spot between his shoulder blades became hot and damp. He told himself it was sweat from the sleeping bag. He knew he was lying, that all he had to do was roll over and start caressing her. Feel her soft, hot skin beneath his probing fingers.

Link stifled a groan and clenched his hands so tight that his nails dug into his palms.

She murmured in her sleep.

Agony.

He defined misery as thinking about how Jacqueline tasted and vowing never to kiss her again.

Again, she murmured in her sleep. This time, she followed the sensual sound by nuzzling his nape.

Perspiration broke out on his forehead.

Torment.

There was no way he was going to get any more sleep, and he refused to interrupt hers. Link carefully positioned his pillow under her arm, and then he escaped temptation. The cool dry morning air quickly evaporated his perspiration, and left him chilled, but it was a welcome relief after the overheated condition he'd been in.

Link stoked the fire then scraped embers into a cooking ring and filled the coffeepot. As he waited for it to perk, he sat down and leaned back against a boulder. Dawn's peaceful serenity seeped into him. Gradually, the residual sexual tension drained away, and he slept.

Capolucho woke him when he poured himself a mug of coffee. He stretched. Muscles moaned; joints complained, and his entire body tingled. Link suspected that his backside had frozen solid. Yet, as the circulation returned, he decided he felt much better than the first time he'd awakened that day.

"Mmm. This is great." Capolucho smacked his lips. He blew into his mug, then took another sip of coffee and savored it before he swallowed

Link poured himself a mug of the thick, brew that resembled molasses. He gulped without thinking. The sour substance landed in his stomach like an acid bomb. Capolucho took another swallow, his expression rapturous as he relished the sludge.

Link put his mug aside. "I'm glad you like the coffee." He could taste the bitter brew with every syllable and prayed he wouldn't disgrace himself.

Capolucho fondled his enameled metal mug. "Reminds me of my Jackie."

If she made coffee like this, why hadn't he celebrated her departure? Link tossed a scrap of wood onto the embers. "Tell me about her."

Capolucho slurped his coffee. "She was beautiful. Exciting. Sexy."

And brewed acid strong enough to ulcerate the nose with one whiff. "Too bad she left."

Capolucho's nod was jerky. "I guess I always knew it was temporary." He grimaced and shook his head. "She was high class. A real jet setter. Born to money and all that. I still don't know why she was willing to live with me. I lived on hot dogs and beans." He sighed. "Mostly beans. She was used to caviar."

Link tossed another chunk of wood into the fire. It barely missed the coffeepot, again. "So, your Jacqueline was rich."

"We never talked much about money. Every few months, I'd sell a painting and we'd stock up on the basics, then party 'til we were broke again. She loved to party."

"When you first met her, you said you thought she was contemplating suicide. What made you think that?"

"She looked like she didn't have anything to live for. Then there was the way she was looking at the lava; like she was possessed by it or maybe in love with it. I can't really explain it, but she felt something." Capolucho swallowed a large gulp of coffee and stared silently off into the distance.

Link suspected that he'd learned all he was going to about the other Jacqueline.

"My Jackie reminded me of Princess Di. Spirit wise, not looks. She had this refinement to her. I knew she was more than I deserved, but I loved her. At least I thought I did. The last couple days, I've wondered if she was only a fancy face. You ever felt that way?"

"In high school." And a couple times since.

Capolucho stared at him for a long moment, then looked at the ground and nodded. "There was a dark side to my Jackie, but I ignored it."

"Depression?" If the woman was mentally ill, there were lots of opportunities for help. The man slowly shook his head. Then again, the woman had apparently loved lava or the fire goddess or whatever she'd seen in the volcano. Link arched a brow. Possession? For that Capolucho could have sought the aid of a priest.

"She hated dogs." The short whiskers on Capolucho's chin undulated as if he was gnawing his words. Perhaps he was just chewing the coffee. "Was always throwing things at them. Even wanted to buy a pistol to shoot them, but I refused." He lowered his gaze, then peeked back up. "I like dogs."

"So do I," Link said.

"I like myself better without her."

Big surprise. "When did you figure that out?"

"Watching you and your Jacqueline," Capolucho said. "You complete each other. You accept each other for who you are. Work together. You're a team. My Jackie and me was never like that. My Jackie always stage-managed me .... made up stories or just plain refused to tell me where she'd been and what she'd been doing. Or else she was trying to change me. And she never lifted a finger to do much of anything, neither. Sat around all day reading about soap operas and other rich people. Or she'd do her nails. It seemed like she always had wet polish on them." He shrugged. "I had to do all the shopping, cooking and cleaning."

"Sounds like a real piece of work."

Capolucho shook his head. "She was high class, and worth every bit of effort."

Link had an image of a high-class whore or at least

a woman who was only good in bed. Lest he articulate the thought, he took a gulp of coffee. He gagged and spit it out. "Sorry," Link said. "It went down the wrong way."

Jacqueline emerged from their tent and stretched.

"Want some coffee?" Capolucho asked, as he reached for the pot to pour himself a second cup.

Her nose twitched and her eyebrows rose. "Smells wonderful, but I'm in the mood for tea."

Why hadn't he thought of that excuse? "That does sound good." Link threw out the coffee. "I'll put on some water." Rising, he gave her a quick hug and pecked her cheek. She glanced at Capolucho and blushed.

Every fiber in Link's body urged him to give her a real kiss, but he knew better than to follow through on that temptation. Link found that he was suddenly anxious to get home, where he could lock the door and have time to figure out if this was love or lust or whatever the feeling was without distractions.

What if this was real love, and she shared his feelings? What did he want to do about it?

What if she did not share his feelings?

There were too many unanswered questions.

Five hours later, Link spotted the distant bridge and knew they'd almost completed the final leg of their journey. He glanced at his watch. "If Stone is on time, he'll meet us in four hours."

"We couldn't have timed it better," Jacqueline said.

Suddenly, Link remembered that going home meant demands on his time from Carmen, Stone, Ariel and Tempest. He grunted at the thought of Tempest. His job would intervene, too. He groaned louder.

Jacqueline looked over her shoulder. "Still suffering from Capolucho's coffee?"

"I brewed that pot," he confessed. "Unfortunately, I

fell asleep." He glanced at their companion. "Fortunately Capolucho thought it was ambrosia." As she began to turn forward, he asked. "How would you like to drop Capolucho off with Stone and spend another week or so on the river?"

She swiveled back. "Why?"

"So we can have time together."

Jacqueline wet her lips with the tip of her tongue and Link inhaled. "It's probably better if I go back to Grandma's."

"Why?"

She took a deep breath. "I need time and space."

"What do you mean?"

"For months," her gaze darted to the kayak, "actually, years, I've thought of my stalker as some sort of villain." Her upward-turned palms signaled her discontent. "Now I finally meet him and I realize Capolucho is more of a victim than I've ever been."

"So this is about Capolucho?"

"Sorta."

"I'd like to explore— " Link paused, wondering how to phrase his thoughts and feelings without offending her.

"I thought I loved Adam, but since he died, I can't even remember what he looked like."

"What's that got to do with spending another week on the river?"

"Everything," she said quietly. "When you kissed me—" She bit her lip. "Last night's kiss was the most wonderful thing I've felt in my entire life." She blushed scarlet.

"That's why I think we need more time. Time to figure out what—"

"Link, please, I said no." She ended the thought with a helpless gesture.

"I thought you were attracted to me."

"That's the problem." Her tone was so soft he could barely hear her over the water lapping the sides of their canoe.

"Why?"

"Link, I think I lo— " Her blush deepened as her voice got softer. She cleared her throat. "I should never have kissed you." As she raised her voice, her chin went up.

"Are you sure?" Hadn't she felt it, too?

She chewed her lower lip. "Right now, my life is in chaos. I don't even have a place to live."

"Live with Mavis." Better yet, live with me. For a second, he thought he'd said it out loud and she might throw her paddle at him or at least douse him with river water.

"I need to feel as if I'm contributing something." Jacqueline paused. "The earth is being destroyed by overpopulation, misuse of resources, greed, misinformation and pollution. I want to make things better for future generations. That's my calling. And if I don't do my part, there might not be a future for any living thing." She wrinkled her nose. "Except maybe cockroaches."

Why was she avoiding discussing any feelings she might have for him? What if she didn't like him and was simply too polite to say so? 'I should never have kissed you.' Link tried to swallow past the lump of fear in his throat. "You're right, you should pursue your calling."

"Right now, too many things have turned topsy-turvy."

He nodded. Unspoken emotion formed a choking lump. "Jacqueline, I don't want to lose you."

"Link, I don't know what I think or feel about anything."

"Are you still in love with Adam?" Her eyes widened. She quickly looked at the frigid water, then slowly returned her gaze to his.

"I don't know if I ever was in love with him." Her regretful tone confused him.

"But you married him."

Jacqueline nodded. "In retrospect, I think I was in love with his dedication to saving nature."

His gaze locked with hers. "So that's it? One kiss and good bye?"

"If that's my only option, I guess it has to be." She looked ready to cry. "Link, I know I gave you the wrong impression with the way I kissed you, but I'm not—" She looked away and bit her lip.

Link hadn't cried since he'd watched the bittersweet ending of Schindler's List. He vowed that he wouldn't cry now. He cleared his throat. "Does this mean we won't see each other again?"

"After spending so much time with you over the last few days, I can't imagine being completely cut off from you." Jacqueline blinked rapidly and he saw tears in her eyes. "You still owe me a flight to Valdez, unless you have other obligations." She swallowed. "Perhaps, if I can find a job in Valdez, we'll see each other once in a while."

"Count on it. And while you're at it, you might want to look for work in Fairbanks, too."

Jacqueline gave Link a lopsided smile before she turned her attention back to the river.

Beads of perspiration broke out on his forehead. The tension was broken, but he might have lost her in the process. Link couldn't imagine his life without her and he felt as if he'd lived his entire life waiting for her. What if she didn't share his feelings? What if she didn't share her grandmother's moral convictions and was the type to go from one affair to the next?

He gazed at Jacqueline's straight spine and wondered if she wanted babies. He never had before, but it would be nice to have a miniature Jacqueline to cradle in his arms. How had he gone from wondering what he was feeling to babies?

Link felt like dunking his head in the river's glacial melt.

27

As Stone landed the Cessna on the desolate road, mixed feelings assailed Jacqueline. Part of her wanted to spend another week on the river, alone with Link and without the stress Capolucho had provided.

Spending a few days with him while Capolucho had followed them had been tempting enough. But the lure had quadrupled since he kissed her. Jacqueline shaded her eyes and watched Linkstone's Cessna taxi closer. Had the news that she and Link were alone in the wilderness gotten to her grandmother? Probably. But at least she wasn't sitting next to Stone with a shotgun in her lap.

Did that mean she was pleased, angry or indifferent? Opinionated as her grandmother was, the latter seemed unlikely. Still, her grandmother adored Link and she couldn't get past the suspicion that she'd been forced into this trip just so she'd fall for him.

Jacqueline glanced at the hard planes of Link's face and focused on the tension in his jaw. She knew she'd hurt Link's feelings. Jacqueline sighed and remembered the time she had whacked her brother with a baseball bat. Her grandmother had lit into her with a fury. Never mind that Rory was bigger and had swiped her sled.

She looked at the river. She still felt like she was

ten years old. She cared deeply for Link, but couldn't tell him because her future was so uncertain. Even when she'd tried to hint at her feelings, he hadn't grasped what she meant and she didn't know how to make him understand how terrified she was of romance and ending up committed to another loveless relationship.

If only she could put her vague sense of insecurity into words and explain that it wasn't him; it was her and her disillusionment with marriage. But to do so would force her to admit her failure as a wife.

Jacqueline glanced at Link. The melancholy in his beautiful brown eyes tore at her heart. Better to break a possible relationship off before anything happened than to be stuck in another lifetime commitment and make Link miserable.

If Capolucho had been the malevolent man she'd believed, she might not be so confused about Link. How could she trust her character assessment of men when the mysterious one she'd feared actually turned out to be sweet, meek man while the person she'd admired enough to commit her life to ended up being an emotionless workaholic? When she'd thought her stalker was threatening her life with fire, Capolucho had only been asking for his paintings to be returned.

Whatever passion she'd felt for Adam hadn't been enduring. What if she discovered the same truth about her feelings for Link?

If breaking contact with Link was the right choice, why did she feel like crying?

The Cessna's propellers slowed, then stopped. Jacqueline stayed back while Link introduced Capolucho to Stone and told him about their week. Capolucho looked like a different man than the one who had pursued her. Part of it was due to the removal of the stench and excess hair, but his attitude change and the resulting way he held himself made the real difference.

After all their gear was loaded, Stone motioned for her to climb aboard. Moments after she buckled her seat belt, Stone increased the rpms. The plane launched down the road, then leaped into the air.

Jacqueline pressed her forehead against the window and watched the silvery ribbon of the Yukon River recede behind them. The emotions that had been humming inside her took on a dreamlike quality. Once they were above the cloud cover, Jacqueline sat back in her seat and closed her eyes. The next second, Link was shaking her arm. "Wake up." She opened her eyes and saw him smiling at her.

Warmth flooded through her. When he leaned a fraction closer, her heart pounded with anticipation until she trembled all the way to her toes. It was easy to remember how his lips could make her feel so alive.

"Shake a leg, Link," Stone hollered.

Link leaned away and stroked her jaw line with the callused pad of his thumb. "Morning, sleepyhead," he said softly. Then he raised his voice. "You know, you've given Stone a swelled head. No one has ever managed to sleep through one of his crashes, er, landings before."

"I heard that," said Stone.

Link gave her a conspiratorial wink. "Do you know that once he even blew out all the tires when he smashed onto the runway just so he could wake Tempest?"

"Really?" Jacqueline asked. "No wonder I passed out. It must have been from acute fear."

Link laughed.

Stone's face appeared over Link's shoulder. His left eyebrow arched so high that it merged with the dark waves over his forehead. "Are you trying to tell me that you didn't like the curly cues and rolls?"

For a moment Jacqueline wondered what Stone was referring to, then she realized he was teasing. She pretended to shiver. "I didn't think planes were supposed to fly upside down."

Stone's dimples deepened. "Taught you, then, didn't I?" He ducked back out of the plane, but she could plainly hear his parting statement. "Never met anyone who snored when they passed out."

Jacqueline lunged after him, but was held in place by her seat belt.

Link laughed. "Relax, you don't snore."

"Guess he won that round, huh?"

Link nodded.

Jacqueline unclasped her restraints as Link ducked out the Cessna's door.

When Link parked in his driveway, Tempest rushed out to greet them. Tempest threw her thin arms around Link as soon as he stepped out of the cab.

"Uncle Link, I missed you so much," she squealed.

"I missed you, too." Link ruffled Tempest's hair. Tempest's face assumed a look of abject disappointment. It must be frustrating to love a person and not have them love you in the same way.

The next moment, Tempest's eyes widened and a new, raw emotion filled her expression. Jacqueline looked over her shoulder and saw Capolucho. "Are you the kayak guy? The one that sent her," Tempest's thumb jabbed Jacqueline's stomach, "those weird notes?"

Ray's face flushed. "I got mixed up."

"You sure are a weird poet."

"Tempest," Ariel warned.

"Well, he is. His poems were weird. That's why Jacqueline wanted to meet him. Guess she likes lousy poetry."

"The notes were actually lists," Jacqueline said.

"Apologize this minute," Ariel said.

Tempest stared at Ariel, then looked down at the dirt and traced a line with the toe of her sneaker. "Sorry. It's just that I don't like poems of any sort."

Stone placed his hand on Tempest's narrow shoulder. His grip tightened as he looked at Capolucho. "Sorry for her behavior. We should have given her a rabies shot."

"It's okay." Capolucho's florid face belied his soft words.

"Ray Capolucho may not be a poet, but he's a good artist." Jacqueline patted his arm. "Before he hurt his hands, a gallery offered him a one man show."

"That's wonderful!" Ariel said. "What are you? A sculptor? Painter?"

Capolucho straightened his spine and squared his shoulders. "Oils."

"They're my favorite, too, except for the drying time."

Stone smiled. "Come inside." He let go of Tempest and steered Capolucho toward his townhouse. "I'll show you some caribou she painted for me. They look so alive, I keep expecting them to jump into the room."

"Yes, do." Ariel hooked her arm in Capolucho's empty one. "Come inside, I'd like to show you my work. Normally I do impressions, but I knew Stone would like realism, better. Of course, I just paint for a hobby, so I'm nowhere in your league. Except for the florals I did a few years ago, I try to paint souls in motion. What do— " The door closed behind the trio and ended the chatter.

Tempest looked ready to detonate.

Link shook his head. "Trust Stone to find a way to

avoid hauling this junk inside."

Free from Stone's grip, Tempest squeezed herself between Link and Jacqueline, then demanded, "How soon do you go back to your grandma?"

"Tomorrow."

Link gave her a sharp look. "I'll be flying to Valdez on Friday. Stay until then."

Tempest's face took on a fierce look as she whirled to Link. "If she wants to go tomorrow, let her."

"I don't think she does," Link said as his gaze locked with Jacqueline's and he gave her a penetrating look. "Do you?"

Jacqueline's stomach made a tiny bounce. Part of her wanted to get far enough away from Link so she could think rationally, and didn't feel tendrils of desire growing. The other part never wanted to leave.

Tempest looked ready to kick her. "She wants to leave? Let her."

"I think tomorrow will be best." Jacqueline picked up her duffel bag and headed toward the O'Banyon's townhouse. Link grabbed her arm and stopped her. "Stay," he said. "We need to figure things out."

Tempest fled into her home and slammed the door.

"Link -"

"She'll be fine," he cut in. "Right now, she's mixed up." Tempest wasn't the only confused one. "Say you'll stay."

"I can't."

"Tempest thinks she loves me." He sighed and kneaded the muscles at the back of his neck with his free hand. "She probably does. Eventually, she'll figure out that there are many types of love, and what she feels for me isn't the 'until death do us part kind'." He gave her an intense look.

Jacqueline wondered if he was trying to tell her he felt confused, too.

Link dropped his arm, and then after a moment of indecision ran his palms up and down her arms. Delightful currents of energy coursed through her. How could she think when he was so close?

Phillip came out of Link's back door. "Welcome back." Phillip waved. "How'd things turn out?"

Jacqueline said. "Just a case of mistaken identity."

"That makes sense." Phillip grabbed her duffel bag and headed toward Link's door. "Desert's a long way from 'Frisco."

She frowned, wondering what the odd remark meant, but before she could question the comment, Link asked, "How's Carmen?"

"Fine." Phillip didn't pause as he walked toward Link's townhouse. "I've had a fascinating time on your computer. By the way, I hope you don't mind that I added RAM and updated your programs." Link shook his head, the gesture half acceptance, half perplexity. "I came up with some really interesting stuff." Phillip stopped in front of the door. "But telling can wait. I'll get back to work." He rubbed his hands together. "I'm close to getting an identity on the stalker."

"Don't bother," Link said. "He's next door talking art with Ariel. Goes by the name of Ray Capolucho." Judging by his tone, Link didn't give much credence Capolucho's story.

"What did you mean when you said a case of mistaken identity made sense, then mentioned the desert and Frisco?" Jacqueline asked.

"Simple. There are two of you." Phillip scratched his head. "The only thing I don't understand is how he managed to get on your trail instead of the other one's.

It's not like you lived next door." Phillip shook his head. "It was really strange, until I figured out there were two."

A tremor that had nothing to do with Link's proximity ran up and down Jacqueline's spine. "Capolucho told the truth."

Link grunted.

Phillip frowned. "It could have been caused by a major bureaucratic snafu. Frankly, I've never seen anything like it."

"What do you mean?" Link asked.

"Same birthdate, same name, different addresses."

"You're joking." An ominous feeling began to expand in Jacqueline's core.

Phillip shrugged. "Your counterpart lives in Frisco – San Fran, that is. She's been there for the last couple years, but seems to have moved around a lot prior to that."

"I have a double."

Phillip nodded. "At first I thought the computer had a glitch. It took me a couple hours to figure it out."

"Unbelievable," Link said.

"It's the truth."

"I believe you."

"I don't understand why the government didn't catch it when they issued the social security number." Phillip shrugged.

"But what can you do?" Link said, "Bureaucracies mess up details all the time."

Jacqueline gasped. "Did you just say that she uses my social security number?" Phillip nodded. "I've been battling with the IRS for over two years about a refund. Do you think— "

"I'd bet money on it," Link said before her question was fully formed.

"You really should straighten out the mess," Phillip told her.

Jacqueline blinked as she tried to assimilate the notion that somewhere in San Francisco there was another Jacqueline Cardew. Should they tell Capolucho they'd found his Jackie? Heartless as the woman had sounded, it probably wouldn't be in his best interests.

But someone needed to deal with her. The confusion caused by having the same name gave her the second viable reason to confront the woman. She didn't have the problem of an emotional involvement and a shared past or the problem of a restraining order. And it certainly would be nice to get that $1,674.27 that the IRS owed her.

While it was tempting to simply alert the IRS that they'd made a mistake, getting a look at her double was even more enticing. Jacqueline closed her eyes and imagined the encounter. She wouldn't introduce herself, but pretend to bump into the woman. They'd chat a moment, as was so common in casual encounters, then, at some point, she'd introduced herself and watch the woman's reaction. What would it be? Shock? Laughter, as if it was a joke? Amazement?

How many other women had doubles that they didn't know about? Same birth date, same name, different addresses. According to the photo in Capolucho's wallet, the other Jacqueline was short, too. Jacqueline shook her head at the similarities.

28

Phillip said, "Cardew is not a common name. What are the odds of there being two Jacqueline Cardews? Two Jacqueline Cardews with the same birthdays and social security number?" As Link listened to Phillip, he became convinced that someone had orchestrated events.

"But someone should have figured it out." Jacqueline hunched in the easy chair and stared past Phillip to the picture window.

"Less than if your name was John Smith," Phillip said.

"I wonder how many John Smiths have the same birthday and social security number," Jacqueline muttered.

"The government is big," Phillip said. "Some lazy bureaucrat could have mistakenly given the same social security number to two people if they had the same name and birthday."

"Not likely," Link said. The more he thought about it, the less probable it seemed, and the more suspicious he became of a diabolical plot.

"There's something really fishy about this." Phillip adjusted his spectacles, then gestured to four untidy piles of printouts on the coffee table. "What confounds me is how Capolucho came to follow the wrong one."

Link sat up straight, impressed that Phillip had

noticed the disturbing coincidences, also.

Phillip plucked a printout from the jumble on the coffee table and flipped through it. "I can't stop wondering how two people with the same name could live so close to each other at some periods of their lives and never meet." Phillip shifted irritably as he impatiently looked for something in the text. "You don't have a cousin with the same name, do you?"

Jacqueline shook her head, her expression worried and confused. "What do you mean about us being in the same place?"

"I'd like to read those," Link said, leaning forward, but unwilling to pick up anything for fear there was some sort of unidentifiable organization to the mess.

"Me, too," Jacqueline said.

"There are plenty more upstairs." Phillip tossed the printout at the coffee table and got up. Link followed Phillip up the stairs and into his normally immaculate office. It looked like a bomb had exploded and spewed paper everywhere. Link looked from the mess to the needlepoint his mother had given him as a housewarming gift. *'Have a place for everything and keep everything in its place'*. Obviously Phillip's mother had never given him such valuable advice.

Link picked up the papers, which were scattered on the floor and began collating them. Having a cyber-geek for a husband wouldn't be Carmen's only problem. That was assuming she would agree to marry someone who seemed to view chaos as comfortable.

Phillip dodged a foot-high stack of newspapers, which were piled in the center of the room, and swept a jumbled heap of printouts off the seat of the desk's chair. Turning back to them, Phillip's elbow caught the pencil holder. It tipped, and then slowly rolled off the corner of his desk. Pencils and pens scattered in every direction, but Phillip ignored them.

It took all Link's willpower not to say anything about the disaster Phillip had made in such a short time.

Phillip triumphantly held up a fistful of papers and waved them like a victory flag. "Here they are. Fascinating stuff."

Jacqueline held out her hands and Phillip proudly handed them to her. Link managed to ignore the mess by reading over her shoulder.

At first glance, the information in the two columns seemed muddled, but as he continued reading, he realized the right side was a timeline of employment and movement for his Jacqueline and the left side chronicled the same activity for Capolucho's girl. "I don't get it. How come it lists your employment as being both at Envirohab and that nursing home, then later, this hospital?"

She shrugged.

"That's what I wondered," Phillip said. "When I started this timeline, I thought you were the hardest working woman I'd ever known. But that was before I figured out that there were two of you. Arizona and California share a border, so initially I figured you had a job on each side of the state line."

"Envirohab was miles from the border. Hours from San Francisco," Jacqueline said.

Phillip waved his hand. "I figured that out when I found out where the lab was and thought about it geographically. Southern Arizona and Frisco are too far apart to commute."

"This is wild," Jacqueline said. "I wonder if my namesake knows about me."

"I'd bet money on it," Link said.

Phillip looked startled. "You gamble?"

"It was an expression of certainty."

"Maybe I should write to her and see if she'll help me get the IRS straightened out." Jacqueline shuffled through several more sheets. With each one, her frown deepened. "This stuff goes back for years."

"I don't think contacting her would be a good idea," Link said.

"Aren't computers wonderful?" Phillip asked. "With the right programming, you can find out almost anything you want to know without leaving home."

"This seems too orchestrated," Link said. "I think she knows about you, perhaps even stole your identity. It's the only scenario that makes sense for the way Capolucho got on your trail."

"That's a scary thought," Jacqueline said.

Link pointed to several entries. "You and your duplicate were practically neighbors here. Then you moved. A few months later, she filed the restraining order against Capolucho and told him she was moving; despite the fact that you'd been gone for months, he ended up following you. Doesn't that seem suspicious?" She bit her lip and shrugged. Link jabbed the printout with his index finger. "Regardless of what she told Capolucho, this timeline of Phillip's indicates that she stayed in the L.A. area for at least a year." Either Capolucho was lying or his Jacqueline deliberately orchestrated the switch. Either way, he didn't like this.

Phillip pushed his glasses to the top of his head and stared at Link. "Is that when the mix up occurred?"

"Only if you believe Capolucho," Link said.

"I believe him," Jacqueline said softly. "But it doesn't resolve how Capolucho got mixed up in the first place." She sighed. "His sheer persistence and honoring of that restraining order— along with my belief that Adam was the writer— explain why things never got resolved before now."

"Assuming that she knows about you, she might have gotten the restraining order so he couldn't get close enough for a good look at you," Link said. "What if she purposefully left hints and clues to get rid of him?"

"You think she didn't have the nerve to confront the man and tell him to go his own way?" Phillip asked.

Or she'd tried to kill him once and didn't dare a second attempt. As if reading his thoughts, gooseflesh erupted on Jacqueline's arms. Link stroked warmth back into her clammy flesh.

Phillip grabbed the printout from her trembling hands. Link wrapped his arms around her, willing heat back into her body. "There were other crosses." Phillip ruffled through the pages. His finger jabbed another paper. "Here, a few years earlier, she got an Associates in nursing. Two years later, you earned a Bachelors of Science. Same college. Probably same class. It's a wonder that UCLA didn't boggle your records, like the IRS did."

Jacqueline shivered. "Both degrees were mine." Phillip gaped at her. She nodded. "It's true. I earned that Associates in Nursing, but I've never used it." Link stared at her until she explained. "During my sophomore year, I decided I didn't want to become a LPN, which is what I started out to do, but since I only had a couple of months to go, I completed the degree anyway. Most of the credits went toward Animal psychology, plus I figured I'd have nursing to fall back on if worst came to worst." She massaged her temple.

Link rubbed the knotted muscles in the back of her neck. "I don't like this."

She pursed her lips. "We've got her address and

know where she works. Do you think we should let Ray know?"

"That's not a good idea," Link said.

"I didn't really think it was, either." Jacqueline sighed. "Over the past couple days, he's gotten used to the idea that he's lost her. I'll let it be; it's better for him."

Link wrapped his arms around Jacqueline and hugged her close. After this long Ray's girlfriend might not hesitate over a second murder attempt. That assumed he was correct about the fire at his beach hut being arson. In light of the new information, he suspected the one at Envirohab was arson and murder. But what would her double have gained by setting the fire? "The woman doesn't want Ray," Link said, as he tried to think through the situation. "She made that perfectly clear when she had him arrested. She emphasized it when she filed a restraining order against him."

Phillip perked up, fished a small notebook and stubby pencil out of his pocket and wrote something down.

"Ok, you've made your point," Jacqueline said. "I won't breath a word about what Phillip found."

"Good," Link said. "Ray will make it without her and the paintings. I think he's probably a whole lot better off without reminders of what might have been."

Jacqueline tilted her head to study the printout. "I still don't like this." Her forefinger tapped the paper. "I don't know what bothers me, and I can't put this elusive feeling into words, but something doesn't feel right."

Link knew exactly what she meant. In black and white, things looked mundane, but in real life, the situation didn't feel ordinary; it felt bizarre, immoral and deviant. Coincidence could only go so far. Link tried to remember what Capolucho had said about his girlfriend's character and couldn't understand why the man had put up with the suicidal demon for so long, much less remained devoted for years. The more Link thought about it, the less he liked it, and the more the apparently meaningless pattern began to look like a contrived plan.

Jacqueline looked up from shuffling the papers. "I can't believe all these parallels. I'm trying to find earlier entries to see if my namesake worked as a white water guide in the summers." Phillip stared at her as if she'd sprouted a second head. "It was a great way to earn tuition. Fun, too," she added as an afterthought.

No wonder it had felt so right to have her on their trip. No wonder she seemed so perfect in a camp. "If I'm right," Link said, "you won't find any work record for her prior to the year you earned your Associates Degree, because I'm betting that's when she assumed your identity."

Phillip relocated his glasses to the top of his head and stared at Link. "How'd you put that together?" He grabbed the papers out of Jacqueline's hands, flipped through three, then jabbed his index finger at the timeline, where items started appearing in both columns. "That's exactly when it all started." He thrust the papers back into her hands, and spoke to Link as if Jacqueline wasn't in the room, much less between them. "The other one has only worked sporadically for the past five years. Short term jobs all over the place. That's why I initially figured Jacqueline was earning extra cash on the side." He switched his attention to Jacqueline, "But if some woman took on your name, faked an ID..." Phillip's voice trailed off, then he snapped his fingers. "It makes sense."

"You couldn't have enrolled in the same college without the registrar's office flagging the files," Link said, as he held her close, giving her support. "The obvious explanation is that you didn't."

"And I should think I would have met her, if she was in the same program." Her spine straightened.

"Someone is using your name and degree."

"Basically this other person stole my identity." She quivered, with pent up anger.

Link said, "That's it in a nut shell." Jacqueline whirled out of his grasp, and began pacing. She shook the papers. "Why me?" she fumed. "If this person wanted a new identity, why be satisfied with a two year degree? Why not go for something better?"

"Perhaps because you got the degree but never went into nursing," Link said.

Jacqueline stopped, her expression showing surprise at the thought. "Which would mean that she'd heard about my course change, like she worked in the office or something."

"There's always a need for nurses, and there are so many that there's little likelihood of discovery," Phillip said. Link nodded. "Plus, I think she adopted your identity as soon as you earned that degree."

"Like you said, it had to be someone who knew about you or maybe even knew you personally," Link said. "Maybe someone who couldn't hack school, but wanted to be a nurse. Know anyone that dropped out of your class, but knew you didn't plan to use your degree?"

"No."

"Maybe she just liked the name," Phillip said.

"Oh, please! Do you have any idea how much teasing I got over Card Ew, Car Dew and at least ten other variations when I was a kid?"

"Maybe she figured she could pull off nursing," Link said.

"She obviously adopted my social security number,

but I've only been having problems with the IRS the past couple years. Jacqueline frowned. "I wonder what she originally went after - the degree or my identity."

"What confounds me is how she found out what your social was." Phillip pushed his hair out of his eyes and knocked his glasses off the back of his head. Using a gesture that looked well rehearsed, Phillip caught them before they hit the floor.

"You must have given your number to someone," Link said. Jacqueline shook her head. "Sure you did. People in the registrar's office had it. When tax forms get mailed, it can be on them. Anyone who had access to your mail or college files could have gotten it."

"I bet it was someone with access to the college archive," Phillip said. "After all, that seems to be where this began."

Jacqueline closed her eyes and concentrated. "Correct me if I'm wrong, but didn't Ray say that he'd met his Jacqueline about five years ago? That would have been about the same time I got my first degree."

"I thought it was three years," Link said.

"No. He's been following me for three. He said they lived together for two. That makes five."

"You're right." Link caressed her shoulders. "One heck of a coincidence, wouldn't you say?"

She nodded.

"That substantiates my theory that someone working at the college adopted your identity," Phillip said. "Then later took the degree. Perhaps as a continuation of their cover, perhaps for some other reason."

Jacqueline rubbed her arms as if she was chilled. Link moved behind her and covered her icy hands with his own, willing his warmth back into her. Gradually, her flesh responded and he was forced to still his hands so his mind could concentrate on the problem.

Suddenly, she jerked her hands free and began pacing, again. "But why did this person need a new name?" Jacqueline shook her fist at the papers. "That's still the question." Those papers didn't explain how the other one managed to keep her job. "Nursing isn't as simple as slapping a Band-Aid on a cut. It's not something you can decide would be fun, then apply for a job and get it. Nursing takes knowledge. You do the wrong thing and whammo, at the very least you're fired. This person has worked several places and moved around a lot. I don't like the implications at all. What if she's taken my good name and..." Jacqueline couldn't go on.

Again, Link wrapped his arms around her and settled her against him. Despite the fact that he understood how she felt, he suspected that she could not say, '*What if the woman who took my name has killed someone with the wrong medicine?*' Her body quivered against him. Link vowed that his Jacqueline would never be held accountable for the other's actions. He even felt a chill at the possibility that the authorities might charge her with a crime some imposter had done in her name.

Worse, Link feared Jacqueline would decide to follow the pattern, which had worked with Capolucho: confront the situation and get it straightened out. But the woman had probably tried murder at least once, that they knew of, she might be willing to try a second time. A cold knot formed in his stomach and he cuddled her closer. "We'll give this data to Windy and have her contact the correct authorities."

"But— "

"This isn't something you can work out," Link said. She glared at him. "Think about it, why was she in

Hawaii? Why couldn't Capolucho learn anything about her past, even after two years of living with her? Don't you think this situation of yours seems contrived?"

"I don't like what I'm thinking." Phillip sounded as worried as he looked. "What if this other woman was a nurse and had her degree, but something happened and she couldn't get a job under her own name. Somehow she assumed your identity." Phillip frowned.

"But according to Ray, she didn't work as a nurse while she lived with him, so I really don't think she took my name to be a healer, at least not at first." Jacqueline chewed her lower lip.

Phillip nodded. "And it still doesn't explain why she chose you or how she managed to get the information she needed."

Again, Jacqueline pushed Link's arms away and began to pace. "If she was standing in front of me this minute, I'd make her eat that darned diploma." Link fought the urge to chuckle. Jacqueline plopped down on the desk chair, which was the only uncluttered thing in the entire room. "Go ahead and laugh," she said. "I know it sounds like a stupid solution." Jacqueline exhaled. "I still want to do it, though. I can even picture rolling that tasteless piece of parchment into a tight little tube, smothering it in gravy, and ramming it down her throat until she choked on it."

Link took a steadying breath. "Why gravy?"

"Gravy, grease, slug-slime - whatever'd make sheepskin go down easier." Jacqueline swiveled the chair toward the computer and took several deep breaths, before calmly asking, "Phillip, is my entire life stored in computer files?"

"Just about."

"And you learned all this from the few things I told

you." Jacqueline glared at the blank monitor.

Phillip's nod was reflected on the dark screen. "It was child's play. Once someone gives you his or her social security number, you can find out just about anything."

"I don't like this at all." Jacqueline massaged her temple. "My privacy has been violated."

"You gave me the— "

"Not you," Jacqueline interrupted, "her."

"It's worse than a privacy violation," Link said. "Someone took your life, your name, your past."

"Exactly." Jacqueline nodded.

Link watched her mentally wrestle with the facts and his apprehension grew. Gut instinct told him that whomever had taken Jacqueline's identity would want to hang onto it at any price. It was time to ask for help. "We need to phone Windy and tell her what we've found."

"Stone's sister? The FBI agent?" Phillip asked.

Link nodded. "Identity theft isn't her department, but she'll know who we need to contact."

"No." Jacqueline shook her head.

"What do you mean, no?" Link demanded.

Jacqueline shook the sheaf of papers at him. "Some woman stole my life. My life. She's been me for at least five years. We don't have to deal with this today, or even tomorrow. I imagine that by now, she's feeling pretty confident." Jacqueline paused to catch her breath, and Link saw fury in her expression. "Ray's Jackie may be comfortable with my name, but I need time – time to think and decide exactly how I want to handle this. When I decide how I want to proceed, I'll do it and I won't go running to Stone's sister."

"Please," Link said, "don't even think of personally confronting the woman." She glared at him. Acid seeped into his stomach and he felt his core begin to writhe in misery. Instinct told him that if Jacqueline decided on a personal confrontation, things wouldn't turn out well.

His apprehension went past his desire to keep Jacqueline with him. Yes, he wanted her to spend the rest her life with him, but he was afraid to hold too tight, and simultaneously not to hold tight enough.

The intensity of his thoughts brought him up short. Link had never felt that way about anyone before. Not even Stone. While he couldn't imagine not having Stone as a best friend or business partner, it had been a relief when he'd married Ariel and moved next door. He knew he'd never feel that way about Jacqueline. He didn't know why he was so certain about that, he simply was.

He was certain of two other things: one, he knew Jacqueline would want to confront her imposter, as she had Capolucho. Two, if she followed her inclinations, it could turn out badly. The thought of losing Jacqueline terrified him. Somehow, he had to convince Jacqueline to let the authorities deal with her imposter. The question was how to do it without locking her in a closet or handcuffing her to the bed. He blinked at that tantalizing solution, then shook his head.

Perhaps Mavis would help him talk sense to her. He'd phone her right after he laid this entire mess out for Windy to analyze.

29

Her parents had espoused education above all else by continually telling her that higher grades equaled a better job, more money, a lovely home … success … things they wanted for her, but she had never been sure she wanted for herself. Jacqueline's teeth ground together as she thought of how often she'd forsaken fun with her friends in order to study for tests or rewrite her notes. Her father praised every big fat A she brought home; her mother equated whatever she did to either Aesop's grasshopper or his ant.

Ants got privileges.

Grasshoppers didn't.

Straight A's were given money.

Every B meant fifteen extra minutes rewriting homework for a week. She had never dared to discover how a C or worse might affect her privileges.

Until today, she'd been proud to be the industrious ant. Now, the more she thought about it, the more indignant Jacqueline became. How dare some stranger, possibly a grasshopper, steal the degree she'd worked so hard for! It didn't matter that she'd given up the career-goal of nursing. She, Jacqueline Cardew, the *real* Jacqueline Cardew, was the one who'd made the Dean's list every semester and been offered the coveted job at Envirohab.

What had her counterpart done with her life?

Was Phillip right about the imposter administering the wrong medication? Had the phony Jacqueline Cardew killed a patient and lost her job? What other reason could there be to steal someone else's good name? The more Jacqueline thought about it, the more plausible it sounded, and the more she wanted to punch the phantom imposter square in the nose. Punch her again and again – at least once for every blasted note Capolucho had written and every fear she'd felt because of his miserable attempt at righting the wrongs done to him.

The idea of an incompetent woman ruining her own reputation, then appropriating another name, was infuriating. The only thought that upset her more was the fear that the woman had made mortal mistakes as Jacqueline Cardew and she, the real Jacqueline Cardew, could be accused of the imposter's crimes.

How could she go to the authorities and prove she was the real Jacqueline Cardew? Would her driver's license and birth certificate be adequate to prove her identity? Since her counterpart had purloined her birthday and social security number, she was certain it would be extremely difficult to prove her identity. If the woman had stolen her diploma, she probably had access to her bachelor's degree, too. Would the situation come down to depositions from family to verify her claim?

If she needed to prove who she was, this was the worst possible time for her parents to have disappeared on their sailboat. Jacqueline wanted to hit something. Someone. A specific lying, cheating someone who lived in San Francisco.

She glared at the blank computer-screen, willing it to give her a solution instead of the reams of disturbing facts compiled on the lists Phillip had strewn around the room. But, she wasn't some sort of computer wizard, like Phillip, and all she knew how to use computers for was write papers and check her e-mail.

'I need to know why she chose me, and if she's done harm using my name.' She closed her eyes, and attempted to control the rage curling within her. Abruptly, she remembered the photo in Capolucho's wallet. There had been a coed with curly red hair in her freshman chemistry lab. Jacqueline frowned. Though she couldn't recall the girl's name, she had always seemed overly friendly. That oozing, syrupy sweet friendliness had repelled her. Was it possible that she was the woman who'd stolen her identity? Access codes for the computers had been social security numbers. If the redhead had wanted to, she could have looked over her shoulder when she was entering it.

Could it have been that simple to steal her life?

Jacqueline seethed with self-recrimination, as she recalled how little value she'd placed on security when she was a co-ed.

Link moved behind her chair and began to massage the tense muscles at the back of her neck. It felt wonderful. "What are you thinking about?" Link asked softly.

Jacqueline gestured toward the offending pile of papers. "Her. I'm praying she hasn't murdered anyone while she was pretending to be me."

His hands paused for a moment, and then resumed their tender kneading. "I tried calling Windy, but her service said she'd be away from the phone for at least four more hours. So, after dinner I'll try, again."

"What good will that do? How could I even prove that I'm not some nut? Or that I'm the real Jacqueline?"

"Windy will believe you, especially when she hears Mavis was the one who introduced you."

Grandma! Why hadn't she thought of her or Rory? Relief, warm and sweet, flooded through Jacqueline. Reaching up, she touched Link's hand. "Thanks."

"For what?"

"For helping me look at the whole picture. With my parents sailing wherever the wind takes them, I was wondering how to prove to the authorities that I'm who I say I am." His fingers twined with hers. She swiveled the chair and tilted up her head until she was looking at him. "Can you imagine how debilitating it is to wonder if you can prove your own identity? To wonder if the imposter is so good that if you take her to court, she'll somehow be able to turn the situation back on you and convince the judge that you're the imposter?"

He grimaced and shook his head. Jacqueline placed her palm over his hand and squeezed.

Phillip cleared his throat. "I hate to interrupt, but could I have that chair? There are a few other leads I want to follow up on before we leave on Sunday."

Jacqueline sprang out of the chair. "It's all yours. I want every scrap of information you can find."

"Figured you might." Phillip settled into the seat and touched the mouse. As the dark screen cleared, Phillip deftly opened the Internet connection and began pointing and clicking. Though he had seemed awkward and somewhat incompetent while camping and canoeing, he suddenly had an air of confidence. It was a side of him she would never have suspected.

The man probably even knew how to put spangles on e-mails.

Link tugged on her hand. "Come on. Let's let him concentrate." The expression on his face stopped her from protesting. As the door closed behind them and they stood in the small hallway, Jacqueline could almost sense Link's relief. Dropping his voice, he whispered, "I couldn't stand that mess any longer."

"I take it that your office is generally tidier?" He nodded. "How on earth does he ever find anything?"

"Some people find order in chaos." Link looked to the ceiling.

"Since you don't, it's good we left."

He gave her a lopsided grin. "In a couple more minutes, I'd have started cleaning."

"Well then, it's good that we closed the door so you can't see the chaos."

"You don't need to confront that other woman, either." Who was he to tell her what to do? "That is what you were thinking of, isn't it?"

She shook her head, but now that he'd mentioned it... "You were right, the law needs to do its part." She simply intended to get a look at the woman *then* let the law have her.

He smiled and hugged her. Jacqueline clung to him, amazed at how quickly she had learned to depend on his presence. He hugged her closer. "I want you to stay here. With me."

Jacqueline swallowed hard. Within the past two weeks, Link had become such a large part of her life that she couldn't imagine him not being part of her future. "I don't— "

"Marry me."

Surprise, terror, joy, and panic burst through her like fireworks. She opened her mouth to speak, but didn't know what to say. Part of her wanted to say yes, but feared what she was feeling was chemical attraction. A bigger part remembered Adam. Granted, what she felt for

Link was different from anything she'd ever experienced with her husband.

His smile faltered. "Well, will you? Marry me?"

"I-I need to think about that."

"Why? Do you need time to think up an easy way to let me down? Look, I know that was probably the worst proposal in history, but-"

She put her fingers over his lips. "We've known each other for two weeks. Granted, I got to know you better than I've ever gotten to know anyone in that amount of time, but-" At a loss for words, she stopped. How had Link gotten so firmly entrenched in her life so quickly?

He nodded. "It took me by surprise, too. Take all the time you want."

Jacqueline studied Link. Was he an emotional crutch, only necessary for the troubled times just passed?

Or did she want him with her at all times?

What if their relationship had already exceeded its limits? If so, she needed to get out and put the canoe trip in the past, as quickly as possible.

But, what if Link was the right one? If so, she should say yes.

30

Link silently stared at the repaired crack in the massive chainplate.

"Something wrong, boss?" Trevor asked.

Link jerked. "No. Thinking about something else."

"That's good." Trevor gave the inspection checklist in Link's hands a significant glance. "Thought I did something wrong."

Link shook his head. "Everything here is fine." He quickly finished checking off the items, then signed the form. Trevor's smile widened with relief. He wished adding his signature to something could relieve his own mounting anxiety. But nothing could block the building feeling that something was wrong, so by the time he drove home, his dread had escalated until it felt like someone was pounding his temples with an annoying little hammer. After he parked his truck and turned off the engine, his relief at surviving the trip home was so overwhelming that he closed his eyes and laid his head on the cool steering wheel.

Someone knocked at the passenger window. "Uncle Link, are you okay?" Tempest's face pressed against the glass, her nose flattened until it looked ridiculous.

Now that his muscles were more relaxed, the hammering in his temples had eased. He smiled. "Hop in." She landed on the passenger seat with a bounce, then slammed the door shut. "What's up?" Link asked.

Tempest ran her teeth over her lower lip. "Is it true that Jacqueline is going back to Valdez tomorrow?" Anticipation brought a flush to her cheeks.

"Where'd you hear that?"

"She was talking to Stone. Is she going to stay there?" Tempest's eyes gleamed. "Or only going for a visit?" The corners of her mouth turned down. "I hope she never comes back here."

He felt like a cad, but Jacqueline had taught him that living with fiction was not good. "Tempest, you're my family and I love you." Her smile turned radiant. A faint, but annoying drumming began in his temples. "I love Jacqueline, too, but how I feel about her – it's different."

"Don't say that."

"Don't you want the truth?" She shook her head. "Then I doubt if I can explain it." Link got out of the truck. Tempest exited even faster. He peered across the Dodge's hood at her pouting face. Tempest turned her back to him and sniffed. "There are many faces of love and it's hard to figure out which one we feel. I love you as a niece. I care for Jacqueline in a different way."

Her shoulders shook.

Link closed his eyes and pinched the bridge of his nose. "One of these days you'll meet the right man and know what I mean. Until I met Jacqueline, I didn't understand the concept, either."

Tempest stared down at the sparse grass surrounding her feet. "Sometimes I hate her."

"Only sometimes?" he teased.

She nodded and turned back to face him. Though she was no longer crying, her cheeks were still damp. "When I forget about being jealous, I find myself really liking her. Then I hate her twice as much, because she's nice enough to like."

Link went around the truck and gave Tempest a hug. "Believe me, you'll find yourself liking her more and more. Eventually, you'll forget you were jealous. But it might be a while. Don't force it."

"I'll try," she said with a trembling voice. Breaking out of his arms, she fled to her townhouse.

Link sighed. Had their talk done any good? The only thing he was sure of was that it had taken his mind off his fear of losing Jacqueline. Link entered the kitchen door, and sniffed appreciatively. Chocolate and lemon combined in a mouthwatering scent. A Devils food cake sat next to a lemon pie on the counter. Carmen didn't bake. Jacqueline swore she could only cook on embers, but the fallacy of that statement sat right in front of him. Link felt warmth deep in his soul, as he envisioned Jacqueline making herself at home in his kitchen. She must feel comfortable here to do so. And if things worked out the way he hoped, they would be sharing this kitchen for the next fifty years or so.

Optimistically, he went in search for her. She wasn't downstairs. As he went upstairs, he heard Jacqueline's muffled voice. "I know that, Grandma." After a pause, she added, "Of course, I do." Link stopped outside the closed door of his office. "This is the right thing to do." Phrase by phrase the tension in her voice increased. Link frowned. "Grandma, I have to do this."

What were they disagreeing about? He hoped Mavis wasn't against their relationship, because he'd rather climb Mt. McKinley buck naked in the middle of December than go nose to nose against Mavis.

"Grandma, I know you're always right."

Link gulped and wondered how he could win

Mavis' favor and get her to support him instead of advise Jacqueline to leave him. Unable to listen to more, Link slipped back down the stairs.

After popping seven salmon steaks in cold water to thaw, he began making a salad. Moments later, Jacqueline appeared. "I didn't hear you come in. Have you been back long?" He stiffly gestured to the vegetables. "Long enough to get this done. How was your day?"

She gave him a searching look. "Apparently, a lot better than yours."

Link shrugged and focused on slicing a tomato.

"Phillip and Carmen went to see the murals downtown and said afterward they were going shopping." Jacqueline's perky tone sounded phony. "I used your computer to type a resume and cover letter."

"You heard about a job?"

"Sort of. Grandma told me about an opening with Wildlife Management. She overheard one of their people talking about retiring. It might not be anything." Her voice trailed off. For a moment, the only sound was the rhythmic thunk of the knife hitting the cutting board. "Did your project get finished?"

"Right down to the final inspection." He stopped cutting and looked up at her.

"Tempest told me you plan to go to Valdez tomorrow." Jacqueline blinked in surprise. "She hoped she'd be rid of your competition – her concept, not mine - permanently. For what it's worth, I talked sense to her."

Jacqueline shifted uncomfortably. He tensed and waited for the rejection he knew Mavis had ordered her to give him. "Being a teenager is emotionally hard," she said.

Being an adult was no picnic, either. "So I've

noticed." On the river, silence had seemed peaceful; this silence felt oppressive. "I assured her that you were only going for a visit."

"Why'd you tell her that?"

"Because I want it to be true. I want this to be your home. Permanently."

"Oh, Link." His heart constricted at her somber tone. "This thing with us." Jacqueline made a helpless gesture. "I can't think straight with you around. I need time and space."

"Jacqueline— "

"Don't disagree with me. This is how I feel. Can you understand that?"

Link gave a choppy nod. He theoretically understood; he just didn't like it. If Mavis was against their relationship, and Jacqueline went back to stay with her, it would not be good. Mavis would have twenty-four hours a day to convince Jacqueline she should find someone else. No matter what Jacqueline had said about Mavis liking him, Link knew that all he was to Mavis was the person who signed her paycheck.

He was also the person that occasionally irritated her to the point of threatening to quit or do bodily harm. Try as he might, Link couldn't envision Mavis as his ally. He focused on his hands. They looked empty. He picked up a tomato. "How much time do you think you'll need?"

"Maybe an hour; maybe a year." She smiled up at him, but something deep and unidentifiable in her eyes disturbed him.

The hour he could live with, but being separated from her for a year? No way. Tomato juice dripped from his clenched fist. He opened his hand. The tomato had become unrecognizable pulp; the image of how he felt. "What can I do to make you see things my way?"

"Quit pushing me. Let me have space." Jacqueline rubbed her temples. "When I'm with you, I see everything your way. You're so dominant that I don't know what I think or feel when you're around. Your emotions are so all-consuming that you somehow transmit them to me. I feel what you feel."

"And you don't like that," he said flatly.

"At times, it's not bad. But right now, when I'm feeling such intense frustration radiating from you, I don't. Is that honest enough for you? Can you understand?"

Link nodded. Desolation grew in the pit of his stomach. He was going to lose her. And all because he loved her too much. "So," he said tightly, "after you get back to Mavis, you don't want any contact with me." He hoped he'd misunderstood, and she would protest his stark statement.

"At least for a week or two."

That sounded like eternity, but at least it was better than a year. He held onto that thought. If she could go from a year to a week in the space a few minutes, hopefully, she would go from a week to a day. An idea came to him and burst like warm sunshine in his soul. Maybe if he could show her he was willing to give her the time here, she wouldn't leave.

Something his mother had often said came to mind. *'If you hold the ones you love tight, they'll never be able to spread their wings and soar. Hold the ones you love in an open hand.'* Her advice had originally been given in relation to raising baby ducks, but had been repeated on so many other occasions that Link suspected loving with an open hand was essential for all types of love. Was it possible Jacqueline felt smothered by him? Held captive by his tightfisted hold on her? Link hated to let go long enough to find out. Yet to keep her, he had to give Jacqueline her freedom. He carefully placed the knife on the cutting board. "I'll give you all the time you need. But I'll miss you."

A soft, radiant smile slowly spread across her face. It should have convinced him that everything would turn out right.

It didn't.

Something deep within her eyes told him that he'd lost her. As she went back upstairs, he felt worse.

Link washed the tomato pulp from his hands and hoped she'd return. She didn't. His heart felt as if all the despair in the world lodged there. Strange. He hadn't realized that he lacked something before he met her, and now … He didn't want this to be the conclusion of their relationship.

This might be his last day with her. Forever. A tremor of fear radiated through his stomach.

The following morning, voices outside the window woke him. Looking out, he saw Stone toss Jacqueline's duffel bag into the back of truck. A moment later, Ray loaded his gear. Just what he needed; Capolucho in Valdez with Jacqueline, while he kept his distance and gave her time. Link punched his pillow, then leaped out of bed and dressed. He slammed the kitchen door as he exited.

Stone glanced up. "About time you got up." Link glared at Stone, then gave Capolucho's gear a pointed look. "I told Capolucho he could live on the boat as long as he wanted."

Link arched a brow.

"I plan to head home by Sunday morning, at the latest." Capolucho gave him a lopsided smile. "As long as I'm here, I want to check out the local architecture."

"Great," Link muttered.

Later, as Stone piloted the plane to Fairbanks, Capolucho and Jacqueline sat cozily in the back talking softly. Link kept his gaze focused on the horizon and silently prayed that she wouldn't stay away very long. He pleaded that he'd done the right thing by letting her make the decision and that she would choose him.

The decisive factor would be Mavis. He had to figure out how to get Mavis to accept the idea of him as a grandson-in-law. Or at least be fond of him; something he hadn't been able to do since he met her, no matter what Jacqueline said. The sheer hopelessness of his situation felt monumental.

31

Link sat behind his desk and stared out the window at Valdez's afternoon traffic until his dry eyes ached. Only then did he turn back to the requisition order in front of him. Though he tried to concentrate, his acidic stomach felt as if it was riddled with ulcers and tied in knots, which made focusing impossible.

Across the room, Stone absentmindedly twirling his pencil while he read a contract. Periodically, he shifted his weight causing the leather to squeak as he stretched his legs. A readjustment of his reading glasses and a sigh always followed the chair's plaintive squeal. Papers crackled and snapped as Stone crisply added the contract to his finished pile. Link ground his teeth. "Can't you keep the noise down?"

Stone looked across their shared office. "What bit you?"

"Nothing." Stone's brows arched over his blue eyes and receded under his thick black hair. Link's jaw tightened. "Forget I said anything."

"Nope. You don't get off that easy." Stone's attention centered on him. "Talk. Tell me what's been gnawing at you since you got back. Was it Tempest?"

"There's nothing to talk about."

"She did get to you. Look, if I'd known the kid had a crush, I wouldn't have suggested you take her."

"This has nothing to do with Tempest, I just have a headache and an upset stomach." Christ, he sounded like a wimp.

"I'd tell you to take a couple aspirins." Stone winked. "If I knew you were talking about the head between your shoulders." Link grabbed the requisition order and swiveled his chair in the other direction, but not before he saw Stone's grin widened. "Aspirin won't work on what ails you, but talking might." Link hand clenched on the paper so hard it crackled. "Thought so."

Link glared at Stone, then laid the document on his desk and gestured toward the open door between their office and Mavis' domain. The last thing he needed was Mavis overhearing something and misinterpreting it. An all-knowing expression suffused Stone's face and his wolfish smile grew.

Link pushed back his chair. "Aspirins sound perfect." He went into the small bathroom, slugged down half a bottle of Mylanta, then swallowed two Tylenol and a glass of water. His goal was to win Mavis' seal of approval, not get on her bad side. Link stayed in the claustrophobic room and counted. When he got to one hundred, he figured Stone had refocused his attention on paperwork.

But when Link opened the door, Stone had his glasses off, feet on the desk and was leaning back in his chair, obviously waiting for him. Worse, the door between their office and Mavis' domain was shut. Stone put his feet on the floor and leaned forward. "What do you think of Capolucho?"

"Jacqueline anticipated a villain. He's too pathetic to be one. Ariel hit it off with him," Link added.

"I noticed." Stone got up and began to pace; two strides east, pivot, two strides west. "For a while, I thought they were going to start a mutual admiration society." Stone snorted. "Capolucho liked her work." His tone was angry. "I'm not sure if that's good or bad. He wants to contact a gallery owner he knows."

"You don't approve." Link settled into his chair, smoothed the wrinkles out of the requisition order then picked it up.

"Sure I do." Stone's sarcastic tone had a hard edge. "I just don't want her hurt." The last admission was barely above a whisper.

"How so?"

"Dashed dreams." Stone shrugged. He leaned against his desk and folded his arms across his chest. "Why's Jacqueline going back?"

Why didn't Stone sit down and get back to the darn papers? Link gave a negligent shrug. "She came here to visit Mavis, not us."

"I meant back to the Lower 48," Stone clarified.

Link's stomach knotted. "What gave you that idea?"

Stone's eyes narrowed as he studied him. "Maybe I misunderstood."

He went around his desk and sat down. "What are you talking about? Is Tempest still having a fit about Jacqueline?"

"Drop it, okay? We've got a mountain of paperwork to do." Stone put on his reading glasses.

Link fisted his hands so he wouldn't rip the papers to shreds. "Spit it out."

"It's nothing." Stone picked up a contract and pretended to read it. The sham didn't last long. He sighed and put aside the document. "I overheard something. Perhaps I misunderstood."

"Yeah, right," Link snapped. Stone looked pointedly

at Mavis' door. Link lowered his voice, "Who did you overhear?"

Stone peaked around the papers. "Capolucho and Jacqueline."

"And?"

"They were talking about him driving back. She asked if he had space for a passenger. Look, Tempest gave me the impression that you had the hots for her and I was wondering how a looser like him could get two women interested in him so quick. But I probably missed something. Drop it."

"No," Mavis said, as the door swung inward. "Don't. The discussion was just getting interesting." Mavis' pale, piercing, blue eyes focused on Link. Link glared at Stone. Stone carefully took off his reading glasses and massaged the bridge of his nose with his thumb and forefinger. Mavis calmly walked across the room until she was in front of his desk, leaned forward and turned off the intercom. "What did you do to my granddaughter?" Mavis placed her hands on her hips and glared at Link.

He felt the hair on his nape quiver. At least she didn't have her letter opener. "Nothing. What did she say I did?"

Mavis straightened her already military posture. "Very little. It's what she didn't say that concerns me. Why is she leaving with that artist? Furthermore, why did she insist that I pretend she was staying with me incommunicado?"

Link shook his head, partly to deny the implication behind her words, partly to clear his head. The facts as he knew them rearranged themselves and his stomach tightened into a hot, heavy ball of despair. "I don't know what you mean." But he did know.

Jacqueline had said she needed time and space.

Now she was leaving with Capolucho and drafting her grandmother as an accomplice to cover her, so she had weeks to disappear in. Jacqueline had never told him she loved him because she didn't love him.

Still, it didn't make sense for Mavis to confront him as if Jacqueline's leaving was his fault. The hot acid ball sent jabbing spears into his gut. He wanted to curl up in pain.

Mavis's hands came away from her body, revealing the miniature Celtic sword actually was in her throwing hand. She shook it at him. "I think you do know." Link clamped his jaws together and shook his head. She switched her attention to Stone. "Why else would she act like Link was the only other person on earth?"

"Beg pardon?" Stone said.

"Yesterday, Jacqueline phoned me and told me she planned to hitch a ride with some artist. She made me promise not to breathe a word of it to your partner." She turned and glared at him. Link shook his head and shrugged. Mavis' attention returned to Stone, her posture stiff with fury. "Perhaps you can shed some light on this."

"What do you want to know?"

Mavis cleared her throat. "Could you tell me why Jacqueline feels there's a reason for her to get a good look at this imposter of hers without your partner knowing about it?"

"Is that what she's planning?" Stone's surprise was evident.

"Yes." She straightened. "We had a lengthy phone conversation on the subject." Mavis' shoulders squared, as if she was trying not to look back at Link. "During the course of it, she mentioned something about a certain individual being overly protective and not allowing her to face her problems on her own. Could you elaborate on that?"

Stone's eyes darted to him. Link held up his hands and shrugged. Stone looked like he'd rather be wrestling a grizzly. "You talked to her. Why ask me?"

"Because she made me swear not to speak to a certain individual."

Link looked at the ceiling and silently beseeched God to help him figure out the Cardew women. A sudden thought nearly took his breath away, Mavis was concerned about Jacqueline, too, and doing the best she could to understand the problem, while keeping her word. Link sat forward.

Stone cleared his throat. "I may be out of line, but it seems to me that some people act protective when they care about someone."

"I hoped you'd say something like that." There was warmth in her tone. Link wanted to join the conversation; instead, he clamped his teeth against the flood of words. Mavis settled into the visitor's chair in front of Stone's desk, placed the letter opener on his desk, acting as if they were the only two within miles. "My granddaughter has always thought of herself as being invincible. In some ways, that's a good thing, in others." She shook her head. "What disturbs me is her single-minded resolve to track down an old college acquaintance of hers. I tried to tell her that time cures everything, and though she agreed in theory, she still seems determined to deal with this person."

"From what I've heard," Stone's blue gaze briefly connected with his. "Jacqueline isn't the sort that runs from problems and someone knows that, but due to past problems, this other person has been trying to contact my sister." He frowned. Link nodded. "I think she's on an assignment, though."

"Precisely my point," Mavis said. "Which makes me wonder why she would ask – no -" She frowned. "*Insist* that I cover for her." She leaned toward Stone. "Only to a certain person, while she pursues this old acquaintance, mind you."

Link was fed up with the game. "Mavis, spit it out."

She turned to face him. "Oh. You're back. I thought you'd left." She gave him a glacial look. "I was having a private conversation with Stone."

"You've made your point; I didn't hear anything from you. Now tell me exactly what I didn't hear. Start with the phone conversation you had yesterday. What was she referring to as the right thing to do?" Mavis got up and took a step toward her office.

He'd pushed it too hard.

She turned back, grabbed the letter opener and twirled it between her fingers. "Do you always eavesdrop on our private conversations?"

"No. Yesterday, when I got home, Jacqueline was upstairs talking to you. I didn't think anything of it, then. Now, I'm wondering if she called you from my place so she'd have privacy or in the hope I'd overhear and stop her."

The letter opener stilled. "So you heard what she was telling me."

"I overheard half a conversation." Mavis raised a brow. "I'd like you to clarify the subject," Link said. The letter opener began to oscillate. "You seem to be into games today. Maybe you'd like me to WAG it and tell me if I'm warm."

"Wag?" Mavis asked.

"Close to a SWAG," Stone said. "A SWAG is a scientific wild assed guess."

Mavis caressed the letter opener. "What's your

wag?" Was that amusement mixed with irritation in her expression?

"Jacqueline felt that she had to do something, personally, while I suggested that she let the proper authorities handle it. And since she didn't want to argue, she is using deception."

"My, but its warm in here." Mavis fanned her face. This had to be the most frustrating conversation he'd ever had.

How much had Jacqueline told Mavis? Did she know someone was impersonating her? That the person may have torched both Capolucho's home and Envirohab? Mavis stared at him, as if willing him to speak. Mavis had always been a woman of her word. Since she'd brought up the subject, she must be more concerned about Jacqueline than keeping her promise. His frustration dissipated.

Stone cleared his throat. "Theoretically speaking, I think it's safe to say that we're all on the same side."

"Which is?" Mavis asked without turning. "Theoretically speaking, of course."

Stone stared at him.

Link cleared his throat. "You love your granddaughter." Mavis inclined her regal head. Link took a deep breath. Link squared his shoulders and prepared for possible repercussions. "So do I." While he expected Mavis to have a strong reaction, he hadn't anticipated gloating.

"I knew you two would hit it off."

"You did?" Stone asked.

She had?

"Of course," Mavis said to Stone. "Why else did you think I asked your partner to take her along?"

Link didn't think matchmaking had been Mavis'

sole motivation, but before he could figure out why he felt that way, she turned toward him.

Mavis smiled. His blood chilled. "I told you that you wouldn't regret taking her."

"I think I might be," Link muttered.

Her pale, blue gaze pierced him. "You don't mean that."

"Mavis, I said that I loved her." Link swallowed. "I never said she returned the affection."

She frowned. "Jacqueline has never trifled with people's feelings."

"Do her actions sound like something a person in love would do?" Link took a deep breath. "Think about it. When you were dating your husband and he told you that he loved you, wasn't your response, 'I love you, too?'" Mavis' shoulders slumped. She frowned, then nodded and sat down. Link had never seen her so subdued. "And if you'd had a personal problem, wouldn't you have shared it with him?" The deep burgundy leather chair across from his desk seemed to swallow Mavis. The tip of her tongue moistened her lips, but no sound came out. She nodded. "Even if you thought he was domineering?"

Her smile was mellow. "When Rhys and I were courting, he overwhelmed me with emotions. It was difficult to tell how I felt. Maybe Jacqueline feels something similar." Mavis cleared her throat. "I'm sure she shares your sentiments."

For the first time since meeting her, he thought Mavis was wrong about something. "Obviously, you eventually sorted out your feelings," Link said.

Mavis nodded.

A squeak announced that Stone had taken off his glasses, put his feet on his desk, then leaned back to enjoy the entertainment.

"Let's assume there is a hypothetical situation wherein someone is trying to decide how they feel about another person," Link said. "In that situation, would it be logical for one of them to completely abandon the other person? To try to make them think they were one place, doing one thing, when in fact they were somewhere else?"

As Mavis' shifted backward into the leather chair, her frown deepened. "I knew I wouldn't like this conversation."

"That's your answer?"

"If I were the individual in question, I would stay until I knew how I felt." She gave a decisive nod.

"Exactly." Link pantomimed firing a gun and clicked his tongue.

"However," Mavis continued, "in this speculative situation, let us assume there are other outside factors. Let's say that the person somehow believes they've lost something very personal."

Stone asked, "A husband?"

Mavis glared at him. "If it's been your life's work, an institution or governmental agency can be motivating."

"The IRS," Link said.

"That is also a possibility. Perhaps the person didn't want to bog down a new relationship with governmental red tape. Perhaps someone thought she should deal with the personal problems before they soured a future relationship."

Link was relieved to realize Jacqueline had told her grandmother about the imposter, but stung to discover that she'd been unwilling to tell him her true plans. He leaned toward her. "In which case, once the governmental mess is untangled, the person would return and feel free to explore potential new relationships?"

Mavis leaned forward. "That would be my hope."

"So, what should I do? Let her deal with the IRS and her imposter her own way, and hope she comes back to me? Or follow her and give her support?"

"This doesn't sound speculative any longer," she said.

"Forget the game," Link said.

"Have you been sleeping with her?" Mavis asked.

"No, but if I can convince her to marry me, I hope to for the next fifty years or so."

"Good," Mavis said.

"Not good," Stone said.

"Why not?" They both demanded.

Stone blinked. "I wasn't referring to the relationship. I'm all for that. I was referring to Jacqueline's decision to confront this other woman."

Link's stomach felt like a bomb had gone off in it.

"What are you talking about?" Mavis demanded.

As if stalling for time, Stone picked up his pencil and began to twirl it. "It's something Capolucho said last night at dinner." He shrugged. "I'm sure it's nothing." Mavis tightened her grip on the miniature sword and took a step in Stone's direction. He scrambled to his feet, his chair shooting backward to collide with the wall and dropping his pencil in his haste.

"Out with it." Link stood shoulder to shoulder with Mavis as he planted his hands flat on Stone's desktop.

Mavis shook her lethally sharp letter opener, Perspiration popped out on Stone's forehead. "Last night," Stone began, "I asked Capolucho if he planned to try to find his Jacqueline. He said no. Then he said that since he'd actually met the real Jacqueline and gotten a new direction for his life, he'd gotten over his obsession enough to be objective and see that his Jacqueline was nothing but a vicious, vindictive, opportunistic, selfish woman." Mavis stared at Stone. He held up his hands. "Those were his words, not mine."

"Why did he use the terms vicious and vindictive?" Mavis demanded.

"I don't know." Stone inched backward. "At the time, I didn't question it. But now, I wonder if it's a good idea for her to be alone with the woman." Link's sense of doom escalated. Stone rubbed and old wound just above his heart where a bullet meant to kill Ariel had struck him. A quarter inch lower and he would have died instantly. Link wondered if the old wound was bothering Stone, or if he, too, sensed danger. "Capolucho told us about his shack burning down. He confided in Ariel that he believed his Jackie had drugged him and set the fire." Stone cleared his throat. "Ariel's theory was that once Jacqueline, er, his Jackie found out his paintings were valuable, she tried to kill him for them."

"Ariel has always been paranoid," Link said, despite the fact that he'd come to the same suspicion.

"True," Stone said. "But how often is she right?"

"Too often," Link admitted.

"Yeah, well, I had the feeling Capolucho would have dumped the broad once he healed from the burns, except some pal of his told him about an exhibit he'd seen in L. A. where the artist's style mimicked his. Then the guy told Capolucho the paintings were of some volcano." Mavis sat down, and serenely folded her hands over the miniature weapon in her lap, but her hawk-like gaze never left Stone's face. Stone kept talking, "Rayboy decided he wasn't going to let his Jackie get away with everything, so he followed her to California. I guess when he found her, things got nasty. She managed to get a restraining order against him. He still tried to get his work back, but adhere to the letter of the law."

"And that's when he somehow ended up following the real Jacqueline." Link sat on the edge of Stone's desk. "We couldn't get him to talk that freely. How'd you get all that?"

"Bits and pieces. Interpolating. He mainly opened up to Tempest and Ariel."

"Trust those two to make a guy talk," Link said.

"Link, if this imposter is as vindictive as that poor man said," Mavis' tone was tight and controlled, "it's possible that the woman who stole her identity may have set more than one fire."

"And succeeded in killing Jacqueline's husband?" Link voiced the theory he had spent days speculating about.

Stone leaned forward. "What if she killed Adam, but was actually trying to murder Jacqueline?"

"She was the one who normally checked the lab at night," Link said, "but she'd gotten hurt." Had that twisted ankle saved her life?

"To think it was probably Adam's bad luck to die because he decided to be a gentleman just once in his life. How ironic." Link's attention swiveled to her. Mavis grimaced. "I've never known such an egotistical ass. Jacqueline is great at tech writing, I think he only married her so she'd make a name for him." The knuckles of the hand holding the letter opener turned white. "He would never let her take his name, never acknowledged her as his wife and he was the worst user I've ever met."

Link frowned. "What do you mean?"

"Adam treated Jacqueline like an exasperating employee. Or maybe a slave. Sometimes I didn't think he even realized he had a wife. At least I didn't think he knew what a wife was really for."

"Jacqueline blames herself for Adam's death," Link said. "She thinks he'd still be alive if she'd checked the lab. She said the accident happened because he smoked and it wouldn't have happened if she'd done her job because she doesn't smoke."

Stone scowled in confusion.

"She had a schedule and always stayed with it," Mavis said.

"Like her grandmother." Stone eased back into his chair, but stayed alert.

Mavis gave a regal nod. "Every evening, she'd check the lab before turning in. That day, she sprained her ankle and for the first time in his miserable life, Adam decided to be gallant."

"She told me the fire marshal said there must have been a gas leak and his cigarette ignited it," Link elaborated. "Jacqueline feels it was her fault because she doesn't smoke and if she'd checked the building, she'd have found the leak and everyone would have been safe."

"The official report stated arson/suicide."

Stone's scowl deepened. "But it might have been a set up by someone else. Someone who knew her schedule. She might have been the intended victim. And it might not have had a thing to do with cigarettes."

Mavis nodded.

Link forced himself not to panic. "We need Phillip's printouts to find out where this other woman is."

"I'll call Ariel and have her go next door to get them," Stone said, as he punched the quick-code into his phone.

Mavis shook her head. "Jacqueline didn't want you to follow. She took them with her."

Link and Stone looked at each other. Stone found

his voice first, "What do you mean 'took them with her'? Isn't she at your house?" Mavis bit her lower lip and shook her head. "And Capolucho isn't at my boat?" Tears shimmered in Mavis' eyes, as she shook her head.

"Both that artist and Adam were supposed to have died in fire." Link's throat constricted.

Stone grabbed the phone. "I'll try to catch Windy – claim it's a family emergency."

32

Jacqueline stood in front of Valdez's airport and waved a final farewell as Ray's battered blue truck merged with traffic. A passenger hurrying into the small terminal jostled her. With a sigh, she shouldered her duffel bag and turned toward the entrance.

Inside the building, a baby's wails echoed over several conversations. Most people were queued in an impatient line for the next flight to Anchorage; emotions ranging from anticipation to dread marked posture and expressions. A white-haired woman bustled away from the counter, a ticket clasped in her veined hand. In one corner of the lobby, a few people huddled in a small group, which looked like a family being torn apart by the impending flight; in another corner, two others were quietly reading. She hadn't realized Valdez's airport would be so busy. Jacqueline scanned the departure lists, found a flight to San Francisco, and joined the line.

"But I don't wanna go," a child's high-pitched voice stated the sentiment of her heart as something hit her thighs. Jacqueline glanced down. A little redheaded boy raised a belligerent fist at the person behind her. She took a quick look back as a balding man grasped the child's hand and urged the kid's pointy elbow away from her legs. "I won't go." The high-pitched tone made her ears cringe.

"Quiet," the man said.

"I'm not going."

"Yes, you are. And you will behave."

The battle between boy and man raged. Jacqueline stood on tiptoe and tried to see if San Francisco was listed anywhere else. It wasn't.

"You can't make me."

"Perhaps not, but you must visit your mother and this is the only way possible."

The queue seemed to move slower than the process of evolution. Finally, it was her turn. "Round trip to San Francisco." She shoved her Visa card to the service rep. The child let out a screech. "And a pair of earplugs, please." The woman laughed.

Despite the child's continued complaints, she dozed on the flight. Later, in her hotel room, she sank into a deep, restoring sleep. By the time Jacqueline awoke, it was two o'clock the following afternoon.

After a shower and snack, she took a taxi to her namesake's street, then walked down the twisting lane – twice – before she accepted the fact that the house number didn't exist. Hoping on a cable car, she headed to St. Francis Memorial Hospital. She'd expected a simple building, not something over ten stories high, or with all sorts of specialized clinics. Where might her namesake work? The Melanoma Center? HIV Care? Perhaps the Burn Center or the Alzheimer's and Dementia Clinic. She, personally, would have chosen to work in the Clinical Research Center.

Standing on the sidewalk, she gazed up at the high tan walls and the regimented windows. What had possessed her, to want a glimpse of the woman so badly that she'd come all this way without a plan? Until now, she'd been under the illusion that it would be an easy matter to somehow deliver a box and covertly watch as her imposter picked up the gift.

Dumb, dumb, dumb.

Jacqueline stared at the hospital, which seemed to grow larger by the moment. Could she walk into something that huge and ask the information desk for Jacqueline Cardew?

No.

Go to their personnel department? It was doubtful that anyone would tell her anything about an employee. Worse, whomever she spoke to could turn hostile and accuse her of being the pretender. Jacqueline wiped her clammy hands on her denim-clad thighs. She needed a plan that wouldn't spook the imposter until the authorities could deal with her, but she wanted a strategy that would explain why she'd been chosen. Deep in thought, Jacqueline began to pace the sidewalk.

People carrying flowers, balloons and bags jostled past her, as they hustled into the building. Others departed, most now empty-handed. Nurses occasionally came out to sneak a cigarette, or simply stretch their backs and look at the sky. A child started crying, then buried its face in an older woman's paisley skirt. A baby, in a passing stroller, wailed at the top of its lungs.

Jacqueline wished she could scream in frustration, too.

"Jacqueline? Is that you? Eek! It is you." She knew that voice from somewhere, but where? "What a surprise. This is wonderful." She focused on the face barely visible behind a large pot of yellow chrysanthemums in a gaudy red paper-covered pot. The blossoms clashed with her florescent pink T-shirt.

She'd know that bouncing enthusiasm anywhere. "Nora? What are you doing here?"

"Oh, Jacqueline. It is you!" Nora's screech of

delight made Jacqueline's eardrums cringe. Nora jumped up and down, her white-blond curls bouncing wildly. The chrysanthemums began losing petals. Nora juggled the pot. "Are you here to visit Clarissa, too?"

Jacqueline knew that if it hadn't been for the plant, Nora would have bowled her over and hugged her senseless in the name of reunion. As it was, Jacqueline was astonished that Nora hadn't dropped the pot and grabbed her anyway.

"Who?" Jacqueline stared at Nora.

"Clarissa Wells. She used to be our dorm supervisor."

"Petite, red hair, green eyes?"

"She's Clarissa Boulet, now. Silly me, I still think of her as Wells."

"I didn't know you kept up with her."

"My Sugarbunny and I got a place here in Frisco last year. Clarissa works here, except she's just had surgery, but then, of course, you know that."

"Actually, I was here for something else."

"You aren't sick, are you?"

"No."

"I can't believe it's you. I haven't seen you in years. What a great tan. The desert looks like it agrees with you."

People were staring at them. "It did for a long time," Jacqueline said.

Nora stopped bouncing, shifted the pot and grabbed Jacqueline's wrist with her free hand. "Let's go somewhere and talk. Or are you waiting for someone?" She looked suddenly somber.

"Just thinking."

Nora glanced around. "This is a strange place to think. But I guess that must'a been what caught my attention. Everyone else was going somewhere. You were pacing. I just can't believe this. Finding you here. You gotta visit Clarissa while you're here. She'll love seeing you."

Nora had always been annoying, yet enviable, with her sexy voice and bottled energy. "Don't let me keep you. Tell her I'll look in, if I get the time."

"Nonsense." Nora tugged her toward the street. "I can see her any time. How long are you here for? Is the person you're visiting really sick? Dying? Is that why you looked so sad and upset?"

"They work here," Jacqueline said.

"And you're waiting for them to get off." Nora changed the grip on Jacqueline's arm to a comforting pat. The pot slipped and Nora grabbed it.

Jacqueline took a step away and tried to smile politely. "Actually, she doesn't know I'm in town. I planned to surprise her."

"Great," Nora enthused as she made a little jump of delight and clicked her heels. A flower head splatted onto the sidewalk; Nora stepped on it, slipped and grabbed Jacqueline's arm, almost wrenching it from her shoulder.

"Don't let me keep you."

"Can't we at least have a cup of coffee or something? I've really, really missed you. I should have kept in touch better. But I never knew where I'd be, or how long. Postcards were the best I could do." Nora giggled.

Jacqueline's nerves cringed. The chrysanthemum lost more petals and a leaf. Jacqueline wished she could throw down petals of protest, too. She felt guilty for not being able to share Nora's excitement, but she and Nora had been opposites in college, and probably still were.

Initially, Nora had fascinated her, because she was so different, but by the middle of their freshman year, Jacqueline couldn't wait to get away from Nora's chaos, veneer of vitality and frivolous core.

As if sensing Jacqueline's lack of enthusiasm, Nora giggled and pressed her fingernails deep into flesh. Jacqueline ground her teeth.

Nora wrestled with the chrysanthemum; another yellow flower head broke and fell to the sidewalk. "It's so wonderful to see you. Do you have time for an early lunch?"

Jacqueline decided chatting over a cup of coffee would satisfy her social obligations for the next few years, plus give her time to formulate a plan. "I have time for coffee." Jacqueline turned toward the hospital.

"Where are you going?" Nora asked.

"Hospitals have cafeterias."

Nora wrinkled her nose. "Yuck. They brew toxic sludge. And anyway, who wants to catch up on years' worth of gossip in a cafeteria stinking of antiseptic? Even if they used Colombian, you'd still have to smell that..." she grimaced, "that smell. You know what I mean, that disinfectant, sick person, medicated smell, while you drank. Eek. My apartment isn't far from here. We can go there and have some privacy."

Reluctantly, Jacqueline allowed herself to be towed away. The farther they got from the hospital, the more Nora bubbled and danced. By the time they arrived at the front steps of an apartment building that seemed to cling tenuously to the side of a hill, Jacqueline thought she would stuff a pillow in Nora's mouth if she heard the phrase, 'E*ek! I can't believe you're here*' one more time. Glancing at the yellow chrysanthemum, Jacqueline decided the poor plant was worse off than she was; en route, it had lost at least half of its blossoms.

Nora fumbled with the pot as she keyed her access code into the pad. Two more flowers dropped as she opened the door. Nora danced with excitement as she climbed the steep stairs. "I'm on the second floor. This place isn't in the best neighborhood, but it has a great view, I can even see part of the bay."

And how many rooftops?

The flowerpot lurched as Nora shoved her key into a doorknob. When it wouldn't easily turn, she jiggled it. A yellow petal dropped, then another and another, until a crescent of petals lay on the gray carpet. Finally, the door groaned open. Nora stepped back and swished the pot. Two leaves dropped. "Go on in. It isn't much, but it is my pied a terre in 'Frisco."

Jacqueline edged inside before dirt started spilling out of the pot. The power of a huge painting on the opposite wall captured her attention.

"Sit down. Make yourself comfortable. I'll go make that coffee." Nora thumped the chrysanthemum onto the island-counter, which separated the galley-kitchen from the living room end of the elongated room. The two remaining blooms nodded wildly. Jacqueline looked away from the pitiful plant and surveyed the area. The ultra modern colorful upholstery looked like Nora and gave the area the feeling of being an artist's studio more than an apartment. If someone had homes and apartments on practically every continent, as Nora had often bragged of, something like this could be fun.

Candles seemed to be everywhere and a heavy vanilla aroma permeated the room. She settled on the edge of a vibrant red overstuffed chair, which had a lush zebra fur draped over the arm. She looked around the colorful room. Across from her, an acid green sofa was festooned with purple pillows. In between, an arrangement of thick candles along with piles of newspapers and magazines topped a large piece of circular glass, which was held up by a huge white Doric column, which looked more like sculpture than furniture.

"Nice apartment," Jacqueline said.

"Thanks."

"I thought you lived either on a sailboat in the Mediterranean or in one of your European homes."

"We do, sort of. After a couple years smelling salt got old. Henri wanted to stop partying and I wanted to start a family. Plus, his dad was pushing him to take a bigger interest in the family business. So when Henri agreed to run things from this post, we sold the boat and bought this."

Nora, a mother? "I can't imagine such a dramatic change."

"Caf or decaf?" Nora called.

"Whatever is convenient." Jacqueline shifted on the too-squishy seat and studied the column's detail. A giant turquoise-colored floor pillow was plopped against it. Jacqueline leaned forward and touched it. The silky texture felt cool and soft. A vivid purple pillow lay next to the turquoise, plus two emerald ones were piled next to her chair. Somehow, the gem-tones and the shaggy white carpet all worked perfectly together.

She looked around the rest of the room; the wall-to-wall, floor-to-ceiling windows on the far end of the room caught her attention. She got up and went to them. True to Nora's claim, a sliver of the Bay could be seen in the distance. Though the view was superb, the huge abstract painting, which had initially caught her attention, diminished its impact.

Jacqueline moved away from the panorama of the

city and stood in front of the six-foot by six-foot abstract drama primarily painted with black and flaming orange-red. The canvas seemed to radiate heat and power, especially when contrasted with the cityscape out the window.

"Like it?" Nora handed her a funky lemon-shaped china mug, which emitted the rich aroma of coffee.

"It's certainly primordial."

"It's my favorite." Nora settled into the sofa's arm and sipped her coffee. Her face took on a look of rapture. "Mmmmm. This is a treat. I rarely allow myself to dip into this special blend." Nora took another sip and Jacqueline dutifully lifted her mug and pretended to sample the hot liquid. "Tell me everything," Nora commanded. "Eek, it's so wonderful to see you."

"There's not much to tell." Jacqueline perched on the wide arm of the red chair.

"Do you live here in 'Frisco?" Nora's feet tapped the thick white carpet with barely suppressed excitement. "Or are you still living in the desert?"

"Right now I don't live anywhere. Envirohab, the organization I was working for, folded, after my husband died in a fire." She shrugged. "I've been visiting my grandmother."

Nora wrinkled her nose. "Bummer. No one wants to be stuck with the blue hairs."

"I like Alaska. I'm seriously thinking about moving there."

"How soon do you go back?" Nora leaned farther forward with interest.

"As soon as possible." Jacqueline took a tiny taste of the bitter coffee and immediately wished she could spit it out. "How long have you lived here?"

"A couple years."

Funny, hadn't she said they'd moved last year? Jacqueline smiled. "I'm having a hard time with the concept of you settling anywhere and starting a family."

"Why?" Nora struck a long fireplace match and lit a fat ivory candle. As the tiny flame licked upward, Jacqueline hoped her distaste didn't show.

Jacqueline shrugged. "I guess I remember how things were in college. You were always so beautiful and full of energy that guys flocked around you." She gestured with the mug. "When I think about you, I think of a free spirit."

Nora nodded as she lit a second candle. This one was tall and thin. "Actually, I've been married twice. The first didn't last a month. Eek. I still can't believe I was dumb enough to marry Antonio." Nora lit three more tapers, then, as the flames licked her fingertips, she blew out the match and her feet ceased their tapping. It was almost as if Nora had extinguished some of her own animation.

The scent of vanilla became overpowering and Jacqueline's head began to ache.

"The party-a-day life gets old after a while," Nora said. "Maybe Henri is right. Maybe we should— " She shook her head. "Nah. Don't listen to me. I must be feeling nostalgic because you're here."

"What do you do, now?"

Nora gestured toward the canvas, which had captivated Jacqueline. "Some painting." A manicured nail pointed to the bedraggled chrysanthemum on the thin island separating the long narrow kitchen from the main room. "Florist, sometimes. Actually, I kind of like not being tied down to any one thing, then I can travel with Henri."

"It sounds like a wonderful life. It suits you," Jacqueline said. She sighed, grateful that the conversation seemed less stilted. All this time, she'd thought Nora was living the jet set life. To think that she'd been married twice, and then actually grown up and finally settled down. "I've enjoyed your postcards."

Nora's face dimpled with pleasure. "You got them. I was never sure." The tapping of her feet resumed.

Jacqueline nodded. "That's one reason I was so surprised to see you here. I thought you were in Europe or some other exotic place."

"I almost didn't stop and speak to you. I told myself that really couldn't be you."

"Well, it was." Jacqueline pretended to sip her coffee. The silence between them grew. Nora's foot tapped faster and faster. "Whatever happened to that guy you went to the island with?"

"Travis?" Nora laughed. "I lived with him almost half a year. Then I met someone I liked better." Nora drank a loud slurp of coffee. "Eventually, I was stupid enough to marry Freddy." Jacqueline blinked and looked down, lest Nora see her confusion over the way names and tine-lines didn't match. Nora continued. "He turned out to be a worthless drunk, and abusive, too. Jerk was bad as my father. Fortunately, Freddy only lasted six months. Men like him and my dad just aren't worth spit."

Jacqueline waited for her to go on; when she didn't, Jacqueline gestured toward the window. "Your view is beautiful."

Nora's face took on an odd pinched expression and her tone lowered. "Everyone in that crowd lived life on the edge." Nora's darting gaze momentarily focused on the cluttered coffee table, then it dropped to the floor. "I got into drugs and booze."

"I'm sorry," Jacqueline said.

"Don't be. Another guy sobered me up."

Nora seemed so high strung that Jacqueline wondered if she was still on drugs. "Henri?"

Nora snorted. "No. Raysy. I thought he had promise, but he never amounted to anything, so I left."

A cold shaft of dread speared Jacqueline's heart. Was it simply a coincidence that she'd met Nora in front of St. Francis or that the man that had rescued her had been named Ray C.?

Suddenly it was difficult to breathe.

Could Nora be her imposter? No. There was no reason for Nora to want to become her. Nora had everything including rich parents and a fascinating life, then a jet set husband and even more money. Yet the location of their coincidental meeting couldn't be ignored.

Jacqueline cleared her throat. "How are your parents?"

"Dead."

"I'm sorry."

"I'm not. After I flunked out of college, they cut me off. As far as I'm concerned, they got exactly what they deserved."

Jacqueline blinked at the pure venom in Nora's voice and her inner chill grew. "What happened to them?"

"They burned to a crisp." Nora grinned.

It was all Jacqueline could do not to keep a calm tone. "When?"

Nora made a terminating motion with her hand. "Years ago." Her voice hardened. "Would you believe that they'd been living it up on my money?"

"I beg your pardon?"

"You remember how they were always living it up? Taking cruises? How my mother always wore designer clothes?"

Jacqueline didn't, but she nodded anyway.

"When they died, they left me with a mountain of unpaid bills." Nora took a gulp of coffee and the rhythm of her dancing feet picked up.

Assuming Nora was the imposter, had she just been told the reason Nora had adopted her identity? Jacqueline had to get out of the stifling apartment and find time to think this mess through.

"How would you like it if your folks did that to you?" Nora demanded.

"I wouldn't." Could Nora have begun impersonating her and using her nursing degree to pay off the debt or had the debt motivated her to walk away from her own identity?

Nora lunged to her feet and began pacing in a gait reminiscent of a caged tiger. "God, I hated them. I almost wish they were still alive so I could have the satisfaction of killing them myself."

"Surely you don't mean that."

"Bet me! They taught me, though. Oh, yes, they taught me. I've never let anyone ruin my life since."

Jacqueline placed her mug on the cluttered coffee table. As she did, she read the address label on The Artist's Magazine. The subscription was to Jackie Cardew. Her worst suspicions were confirmed. Feeling shaken, she straightened. "Nora, it's been good to see you again, but I really have to run. The guy I'm supposed to meet should be off work soon. I'm sure you understand."

"Oh, you bet I do." Nora's voice took on a hard edge. "You said you were meeting a girl, not a guy. You've finally figured it out. Haven't you?"

It was difficult to get enough air into her lungs. "Figured what out?"

Nora gestured to the coffee table. "It took you long

enough." Nora's cornflower blue eyes made contact with Jacqueline. The insanity and hatred in their depths terrified her. "You always were so naive and stupid. But you've served your purpose." Nora gave a high-pitched demented laugh. "Oh, yes, you've served your purpose."

Jacqueline tried to stand, but Nora leaped at her and roughly pushed her into the red chair. "Sit down, dammit. I need to figure out what to do with you."

Jacqueline took a deep breath to settle her stomach. "Nora, we can work this out."

"You don't get it, do you?"

"Get what?"

"That there can't be two of us. One of us has to die. And it isn't going to be me."

Fear transformed into controlled fury. Jacqueline sat very still and watched Nora resume pacing. *Dear God, what am I supposed to do?* "Nora, if you want to pretend to be me to keep your parent's creditors off your back, fine. I don't care. I'd just like some help with the IRS."

"You never were any good at lying. You still aren't. There's no IRS problem. How'd you really find out?"

"Actually I've had problems with the IRS for the past two years, plus I met Capolucho."

"That loser." Nora snorted. "He really put one over on me. Eek. Do you know that at one time I actually thought he'd be somebody?" Her fists clenched and unclenched at her sides. "He turned into a big nothing."

"Maybe if he'd gotten his one man show," Jacqueline ventured.

"Forget it. His work wasn't worth spit. I should know."

"No one will ever know. Everything he did burned in that fire."

"Nothing of value burnt." Nora's glittering eyes studied her. "You really don't get any of it, do you?" Jacqueline shook her head. "I set that fire. His work was ugly. Nothing but big ugly splotches of color. Anyone could do it." Nora gestured toward the immense canvas, which had captured Jacqueline's imagination. "See what I mean? Passion's Fire, my ass. Worthless piece of crap is more like it. And you know what? That asshole gallery owner told Ray he was going to be famous. Wealthy. Eek. For that shit. Can you believe it? I asked myself why it should be Raysy and not me. Now do you get it?"

"What happened?"

"Nothing. I couldn't take the stuff to the same gallery after the jerk didn't die in the fire. No one else on the island wanted it."

"You intended to kill Capolucho?"

"Of course I did, you stupid fool. It would have worked, too. I made sure of that." Jacqueline started to stand. Nora grabbed a fat candle and flailed hot wax at her. "Sit." She sat.

Jacqueline forced her voice to remain calm. "It seems like none of your fires ever accomplished the goal you wanted."

Nora's eyes gleamed with a maniacal light. "Maybe you aren't so stupid after all." She leaped across the space separating them and grabbed Jacqueline's wrist, pinning her to the chair with a surprisingly strong grip.

"Who'd you tell where to find me? Raysy?"

"No. No one."

Her laugh was tinged with hysteria. "God, I was wrong. You're still as stupid as I remember."

In light of the circumstances, Jacqueline was inclined to agree with her. "Nora, we can work this out."

Hysterical laughter was Nora's response. With

horror, Jacqueline realized Nora was insane; probably criminally insane. A small part of Jacqueline wanted to help her. The larger part wanted to pull free from the bruising grip and flee. "Nora, you're welcome to use the nursing degree and my name. I never really wanted to be a nurse, but you were always perfect for it."

"You really believe that, don't you? Eek. Don't you know why I wanted to be a nurse?" The pressure of the fingernails increased on her biceps.

Jacqueline blinked as she chose her words. "To help people?"

Again, Nora's insane laugh rippled and echoed through the living room and seemed to surround Jacqueline with coils of doom. "Help people? Only for my own good. I wanted to meet a wealthy doctor." Nora made a wild gesture with both hands, which served to simultaneously free Jacqueline and throw her toward the sofa.

"Why a doctor?"

"God, what a stupid fool you are. To marry him, of course. Plus doctors have great access to drugs."

"So drugs aren't something new."

"I've been using since junior high. Oh, eek, does that shock you, Miss Goodie Two Shoes?"

Now that she thought back on Nora's behavior, it didn't. Jacqueline shook her head, then tried to steer the conversation in a direction that would calm Nora. "Have you met any nice doctors?"

"Why in hell would I want nice? Nice is for sissies. Nice can't get it up. But you probably wouldn't know about that, would you. Prissy as your man was, I'll bet you're still a frigging virgin."

Jacqueline's teeth ground together. She should have listened to Link and stayed in Alaska.

Though she kept her attention on Nora, she glanced around the room, assessing it for possible dangers and useful weapons, the powerful colors in Passion's Fire held her attention for a moment. "Tell me about that painting. What's it supposed to be?"

"Don't you know anything? It's lava. The asshole was painting it when we met."

"Oh." Jacqueline felt woozy from breathing the sweet, heavy scent, the flickering light, and the sheer stress of the situation. She'd never buy vanilla, again.

"I was swamped with bankruptcy, courtesy of my parents, and good old Freddy had gotten royally smashed the night before and beat the shit out'ta me. All I wanted to do was kill myself once and for all and have it done with."

"I'm so sorry."

Nora's shiny eyes focused on Jacqueline. The sheer insanity in their depths made her skin crawl. "You should be sorry Raysy saved me from that beautiful, hot, cozy lava." Nora laughed. "Freddy sure was. You should see how he looked when the flames started licking his body. Particularly some parts, know what I mean? A little oil in just the right places does wonders!" She looked like she was talking about one of the high points of her life. "I loved watching that wimp die." Nora licked her lips and snatched a candle. "Now I can watch you die."

"You aren't a killer." She hoped it was true.

"Bet me."

"Capolucho is still alive," Jacqueline said softly.

Nora snorted as she brandished the candle. "So what? Your worthless husband isn't. And Raysy taught me to use a stronger drug."

The bitter taste! What had been in the tiny sip of coffee? Poison? A sleeping potion? "Nora, please sit down. Watching you pace makes me dizzy."

"It won't hurt once you're dead."

"You aren't going to kill me here."

"How would you know?"

"In your own living room? I don't think so. Right now you're upset, but we can work this out."

"Stupid. Stupid. Stupid. Eek, I can't believe how stupid you are. The only way is for you to die."

"Then why haven't you killed me already?"

To her horror, Nora reached behind her back with her free hand and pulled out a butcher knife. "You want it here and now? Fine!" She moved both hands back and forth. Candlelight glinted off the knife's shiny surface.

Though I walk through the valley of the shadow of death, I will fear no evil for thou art with me. You are with me, aren't you?

Suddenly, Nora thrust her arm high and stepped back, finally freeing her arm.

Jacqueline edged away, childhood memories echoed in her mind, *'Whenever you're facing an opponent, keep your attention on their eyes. You'll know what they're going to do.'* It worked with animals. She hoped that it worked with maniacal people. Nora looked like a rattler ready to strike.

Jacqueline steadied her nerves and tried to appear calm, even though she was prepared to tip the chair over, if that's what it took to get away. "This is nice furniture. It would be a pity to stain it with blood."

Confusion flitted through Nora's eyes.

"Killing me in your own apartment is a really bad idea."

"You're giving me advice on how best to kill you? Unbelievable. Eek, what a stupid, stupid, stupid fool. I suppose you're going to tell me the best way to do it."

"Only if you'd like to listen." Jacqueline hoped her tone sounded unruffled and rational.

"I'm listening," Nora hissed.

"If you kill me here, you'll leave traces. Think about all the technology the homicide department has. Even if you think it looks clean, they'll be able to find traces of blood, maybe other things, too."

"Like what?"

"Hair. Clothing fibers."

"Why would they look here?"

"I'm not the only one who knows about you. Besides, you can't leave my body here. That would create quite a stink in a day or so. How would you explain it to Henri?"

The knife wavered as Nora laughed. "Henri! Henri was a freaking mutt."

"Aside from the smell, you'd have the problem of moving me. Alive, I can walk. Dead, you'll need to drag or carry me to get me out of here."

"I could hack you up and cart you off piece by piece." Nora licked her lips.

"Of course you could. But that would leave blood. Really, it's not a good idea. And it would be a shame to ruin your carpet."

"Fine! I'll burn you." Nora grabbed the burning taper in her free hand and thrust the candle at her.

Jacqueline held her ground. The taper stopped a fraction of an inch from her stomach. She could feel a pinpoint of scorching heat grow, but didn't dare glance down to make certain her shirt hadn't ignited. "That is an alternative." Amazing how calm she sounded. "However, if I burn, so does your own home and furniture."

"So what?"

"This is a great apartment."

"Bullshit! It's a dump."

Jacqueline ignored the comment. "When my body is found, they'll eventually identify me as Jacqueline Cardew. How will that help you? If I'm dead you'll have lost the use of my name. Alive, you can keep it."

"You're lying."

"Am I? Envirohab was a government project. My DNA, dental records and fingerprints are on file." At least she hoped they were.

"That's a lie. Your stupid project wasn't that important."

"Maybe not, but the government loves paperwork, and they made us take all sorts of tests." The knife lowered, but remained clutched in Nora's white knuckled hand, while the candle was gripped in the other and still held too close for comfort. She tried not to visualize blisters bursting on her skin. "Once my body is identified," Jacqueline continued, "your life as Jacqueline Cardew ends."

"Then no one is going to find you." Nora took a step backward. "Go." Jacqueline didn't like the idea of turning her back on Nora, but rose and casually did just that as she put the chair between them and took a step toward the door. "Don't even think of trying to get away." The hissed words sent a shiver down her spine.

With a wild yip, Nora leaped over the chair.

Jacqueline jumped, but Nora grabbed her. She felt heat at her back. "Where are we going?" The stench of scorched hair burned her nostrils.

"Wouldn't you like to know!" Nora made a slashing motion with the knife. The tip of the blade missed Jacqueline's wrist by a hair. "Walk to the door, but not too fast. I don't believe your fucking meek act, but since you seem to like the idea of dying, I'd just as soon not have a mess here."

This was the best opportunity she was likely to get and it was imperative that Nora drop her vigilance. Trying to appear indifferent, Jacqueline shrugged and took a step toward freedom. Before her second step, her ponytail was yanked and the blade swished through the air. As she tried to catch her balance, locks of hair fell around her feet and short tresses flew everywhere.

"Why'd yo— "

Nora laughed. "The door." The tip of the blade bit into her lower back and she cringed as Nora's maniacal cackle shrilled. "This is fun. Better than fire. I can watch you die piece by piece and still burn you."

"You like fires, don't you?" Jacqueline said.

"Love them." Nora chortled. "Except they don't always work right. First Raysy gets out alive, then that jerk, Adam, dies instead of you. At least I got it right with the rest. Good ole Freddy'll never beat me again."

She really had set Envirohab's fire. This couldn't be real. "You were trying to kill me even back then? Why?"

"You're so smart, figure it out yourself."

"Because of taking my name?" Jacqueline asked as her fingers circled the doorknob.

"That was part of it. Mainly I needed to get rid of Raysy once and for all. That jerk really messed things up for me in LA."

"How?"

"I had a surgeon interested in me, and was even making some money on those lousy paintings, until Raysy showed up."

"I'm surprised you didn't simply murder him."

"That would have been more fun, but I didn't have a chance, because the fucking quack made me use legal means. Then the jerk doctor dumped me anyway. He got his reward, though."

"How?"

The knife tip dug in and Jacqueline took a step forward.

"Ives was a plastic surgeon. I got my boobs from him and gave him the best ass he'd ever had, but then he found out about Raysy." The knife hit a nerve and Jacqueline flinched. "He dumped me and took up with a two-bit piece of fluff." Nora's laugh made Jacqueline cringe. "I toasted them both in bed. It was beautiful. The fire got so hot that the flames were lavender."

Jacqueline tasted bile. "How many people have you burnt?"

"Everyone but you and Raysy, but don't worry, I plan to make it a clean sweep." The knife tip bit deeper into Jacqueline's vertebra. "Open the door. Slowly."

Pretending to comply, Jacqueline held the door with her foot and rattled the knob. "It's stuck."

"It can't be."

Jacqueline rattled it again.

Nora shoved her aside.

Jacqueline stumbled, but quickly regained her footing and grabbed the chrysanthemum's pot. She swiveled and smashed it against Nora's knife hand.

Nora shrieked with pain and fury.

The knife dropped to the floor.

The pot burst and a shower of petals, leaves and dirt covered the knife.

Nora screamed and hurled the candle at her.

Jacqueline ducked, but hot wax sprayed over her hair and back, several drops singing her cheek.

Nora lunged at her.

Jacqueline jumped sideways. Her left foot slipped on a floor cushion and she fell backward, toward the coffee table. She twisted and managed not to hit her head.

Nora jumped her from behind, one hand yanking her hair, the other clawing her nose.

Jacqueline rolled under the table. The thick glass edge hit Nora's temple, but Nora continued coming at her with slashing crimson fingernails.

Jacqueline tried to roll out of the way, but collided with the column. She kicked Nora's hands away, then rolled out from under the table.

Nora jumped on her stomach and wrapped her hands around Jacqueline's neck. She fought the pressure, but it increased. It felt like her entire head was being torn from her body.

Jacqueline used her legs and flipped Nora off.

Nora landed with a thud.

Jacqueline scrambled out of reach.

Circling away from Nora, Jacqueline was grateful for all the wrestling matches she'd lost to Rory. He'd been a much larger, heavier and stronger opponent, so she'd had to learn ways to compensate. But she'd never learned to fight dirty enough to deal with this situation.

"What, no more advice on how to kill you? Eek, I can't believe how stupid you are."

Nora grabbed the coffee mug and hurled it toward her face.

Jacqueline ducked.

Nora seethed with rage.

Coffee spattered the room, then the cup smashed against the wall.

Nora threw a magazine. Jacqueline deflected it with her forearm. It ricocheted and hit a candle. Hot wax and flame spewed across the white shag carpet.

"Stupid. Stupid. Stupid. Eek, I can't believe how

stupid you are."

Flames licking her ankles, Jacqueline scrambled behind the red chair. She glanced down and stomped on the fire, but it suddenly seemed to be everywhere.

Abruptly, the knife ripped into her right hand. Jacqueline grabbed the fur blanket and tried to throw it over Nora.

Nora laughed as she cut it to ribbons.

The room looked like it was rippling. She tried to wipe the tears and smoke from her eyes. A large teal pillow smacked her head. Jacqueline hit it away.

Nora turned her back and grabbed the fat ivory candle. She aimed at her face. Jacqueline ducked, but couldn't miss all the hot wax.

Nora's fury filled the room with curses. She snatched a purple throw pillow from the sofa. Jacqueline leaped over the chair and ripped it from her grasp. "Stop this. We have to put the fire out."

"I hate you. Hate you. Eek. Hate you." Nora lunged for her neck.

Jacqueline jumped out of her way. Her uninjured hand connected with the remaining mug. Grasping it, she threw it. It sailed past Nora's face and crashed through the window.

Nora laughed.

Flames shot up from the magazines.

Jacqueline rolled to her right and scrambled to her feet. The knife was back in Nora's hand. Jacqueline centered her attention on the insane blue eyes.

"What's the matter, stupid? Don't you wanna give me more advice? Huh? Come on, tell me the best way to kill you."

Was that a siren she heard in the distance? Jacqueline prayed it was.

"You aren't going to hack me up." She forced her dry mouth to form words. "This isn't the way you should do things." Demented laughter accompanied her opponent's lunging form. Jacqueline leaped to safety and landed close to the door. "Fire is the way you do things."

The wild look in Nora's eyes intensified as her blue gaze went to the wave of flames spreading across the carpet. The blaze surged up the arm of the sofa. Six-foot-high-flames exploded from the tattered fake fur throw.

Jacqueline leaped backward, her spine slamming hard against Ray's painting.

Nora began to sway and croon. "Fire. I love fire. So pure. So beautiful. Flames burn away filth and leave nice clean ashes." Nora held her hand toward the licking flames, as a lover to her beau.

More lines of flame erupted between her and escape. They seemed to be living things as they leapt from place to place. Immobile with horror, Jacqueline stayed splayed against wall and stared in frozen horror.

Nora turned from the blaze; madness filled her expression. When the knife slashed toward her throat, Jacqueline fell to her left.

A shriek of fury erupted from Nora.

Jacqueline jumped behind the island counter. Nora slashed over the counter, and her high pitched, drawn out wail of defeat mirroring the approaching siren.

Jacqueline grabbed the blender and threw it. The base connected with Nora's shoulder with a sickening sound. She fell. Jacqueline dashed past Nora, heading for the door.

Nora grabbed her ankle.

Jacqueline fell, kicking.

Nora let go.

She scrambled to her feet and lunged the rest of

the way. The doorknob scorched her fingers. Not again! She gritted her teeth and yanked at it, again. The unmistakable stench of burning flesh made her gag. She twisted harder. Nora laughed with delight.

Jacqueline looked back. Nora stood up, spread her arms wide, and stepped into the flames. She twisted toward the door, but a jet of flames shot up the doorframe. She leaped backward. Flames were everywhere. Her lungs felt like they were on fire. Her eyes stung.

Nora laughed as the blaze danced over her clothing and leapt into her hair.

It was Jacqueline's worst nightmare come to life, but Nora acted like she was enjoying it.

With superhuman strength, Nora picked up the armchair and threw it. Jacqueline jumped out of the way, but it hit her leg and she fell behind the counter.

The chair landed on her ankle, pinning it. A burning sensation ran up her leg. Nora's laugh sounded like the hounds of hell baying.

Jacqueline twisted and yanked her foot free.

"Stupid. Stupid. Stupid. You can't get away." Nora's clothing and hair were engulfed in flames. She looked like a nightmare come to life.

"You're on fire," Jacqueline croaked.

Nora laughed and spun around in a dance step. "Fire. I'm on fire." She twirled and fanned the flames. "I love, love, love fire." Nora crowed with delight.

Jacqueline sucked in a lungful of poisonous black smoke. Frantically, she tried to crawl to where she thought the door was. Something thudded behind her. Nora's demented laugh echoed. *Dear God, please don't make my last vision of this life this glimpse of hell."*

33

The day Jacqueline vanished, Link flew back to Fairbanks, and discovered she'd not only taken all the printouts, she'd wiped out all of Phillip's history files by reformatting his computer.

Phillip started with reprogramming, then tried to rebuild the data file, but it seemed impossible without her social security number.

Link phoned Mavis, but she scolded him about being overprotective and refused to help. Next, he phoned UCLA and got put on hold for half an hour. Finally, he presented his case to a syrupy-voiced woman. She hung up on him.

The third day, Link stood in his home-office's doorway and watched Phillip, the only one who seemed able to do anything about the problem. It felt like his entire world had turned upside down. As St. Francis Memorial Hospital's website materialized on the CRT, Link inched closer. Soon, he was reading over Phillip's shoulder. Though the information about the facility was innocuous, a sense of impending doom chilled his soul.

Phillip swiveled around, his expression annoyed. "Do you mind not breathing down my neck?"

"Sorry." Link started to tidy up his office. Phillip kept glancing back at him, malevolence in his glare. Link turned his back and kept clearing the clutter.

"Look, I know you're worried," Phillip said. "We all

are, but I need to concentrate."

Link went downstairs, sat on the sofa and stared at the blank television screen. Perhaps he should have gone with everyone else to see the pottery exhibit.

His sensation of approaching doom increased.

He turned on the television and tried to accept the fact that he'd driven Jacqueline away. Though their lives had only crossed for two weeks, he'd believed that destiny had brought them together for a permanent purpose.

As if to emphasize his guilt, the images on the screen turned to a laughing couple, holding hands as they walked along the beach, waves lapping at their bare toes while the announcer advertised perfect sex if he'd just chew their brand of gum. He changed the channel several times, and then tossed the remote onto the coffee table.

If he hadn't forbidden Jacqueline to go confront her imposter, maybe she have stayed with him.

Allowed him to help her, at least?

Told him where she was going? She would probably have told him something, at least, if he hadn't tried to dominate her.

How could he have been so foolish and overbearing?

An annoying signal brought his attention back to the television. A Special Bulletin announcement trailed across the screen. Then the car chase changed to a somber woman standing, microphone at the ready, on a desolate city street. In an effort to think of something else, Link tried to identify the city, but he didn't recognize it. In the background, flames in front of the sunset made it look like the sun had set fire to the entire area. He squinted to read the ticker tape. It was a transmission from the lower forty-eight.

"Are we on? Good evening. A fire, which started earlier today in an apartment building on Randor Street, has now burned down an entire block of San Francisco. Due to winds, firefighters were only able to contain it within the last hour."

A story like this would have terrified Jacqueline. Link grabbed the remote, intending to change channels, but inadvertently increased the volume. The newscaster gestured to someone off screen. "Jason Roberts, who lives on Randor Street, initially called 911."

"Randor Street sounds familiar," Phillip said. Link looked over his shoulder. Phillip was in the doorway, balancing a club sandwich on top of a sweaty glass.

"Why?" Link said.

"Something about the imposter. Seems like a credit card listed that street or something similar."

Cold sweat bathed Link's body and he suddenly knew Jacqueline had been in the building. He didn't know how he knew. He just did. *'Please God, let that address just be an awful coincidence.'* But it felt like he was being given a message.

"Course, I could be wrong. It could have been Pandor or Tandor or— "

"But it was probably Randor."

"Could be lots of variations of Randor, lots of different streets. Things like that mess up fire departments, ambulances, all sorts of stuff."

Phillip shrugged, then took a big bite of his sandwich as he watched the television, for a moment. "Well, I won't figure it out staring at the boob tube." Still chewing, he sauntered toward the stairs.

A shy looking man clutching a large white Persian cat joined the newscaster. "Mr. Roberts, can you tell our audience what alerted you to the crisis?" She tilted the microphone toward him.

Link leaned toward the screen.

"The woman upstairs from me come home in the middle of the day. She had someone with her. I only heard her talking. She was real mad. Made a big commotion with lots'a threats bout about killing and such. I called the police because I figured someone was trying to do her harm, but then I saw the smoke, so I grabbed Goddess and ran." He hugged his cat tighter.

"Thank you, Mr. Roberts."

"And thank you, Sarah." Another reporter joined her. This one had taken the time to comb his hair. "As you can see," he gestured to the scene behind him, "fire broke out in a second floor apartment earlier today. Thus far we have confirmation that four people have died and many others were injured. Unconfirmed sources say that the fire hydrants in this once picturesque area had been sabotaged and arson is suspected." The reporter paused for a beat to look at his notes, then added, "Here with me is Carla Hastings, who lived across the street."

A rotund woman wearing gym clothes and a trench coat stepped next to the reporter. "Ms. Hastings," the reporter said, "you phoned the fire department."

The woman bobbed her head like a dashboard Madonna. "To begin with, I was gonna call the police, 'cause of all the caterwauling and such, then I smelled smoke an' looked outside. When I saw flames up there, I phoned the fire department instead."

Link stared at the screen. The lump in his chest expanded until it was suffocating.

"While I was talking to the dispatcher," the woman continued, pleased to be the center of attention, "I heard someone laugh. Crazy-like, not ha-ha. Then I heard breaking glass and shards started pelting the street. I looked up and it looked like flames were beating the glass. It was hard to tell 'cause black smoke was everywhere. Then the whole windowpane sorta exploded out. For a minute it looked like the room was solid black and she was flame. I guess that's because her clothes were on fire. She was screaming, but not like she was scared. More like a high-pitched laugh. She kinda did some dance steps and shouted, 'I'm the fire goddess.' And then she jumped out the window," Hastings stared at the camera.

"You saw a woman jump?" the reporter said.

"Sure did. She sure was somethin'. Black smoke was billowing out the window; it was somethin' to see." Hastings pointed to a distant spot behind the thick yellow barrier tape.

"Landed right there."

"Thank you, Ms. Hastings." The reporter tried to take the microphone back, but the woman grabbed his hand.

"The fall didn't kill her. Just knocked the wind outta her. After a minute of lying there, burning, she got up and started dancing around and singing about being a fire goddess. It was an amazin' sight. Just as the fire truck arrived, part of the roof caved in. It was like forth of July."

"Thank you for your vivid account, Ms. Hastings." The scene switched by to the news desk. Link snapped the television off and slammed the remote onto the coffee table.

He knew there was no rational reason to believe the disaster had anything to do with Jacqueline. But Link knew she'd been there. He grabbed the phone to call Windy. Just as his hand touched the receiver, the phone rang. Link flinched.

The phone rang two more times. He took a deep breath, then picked it up. "Hello?"

"Link." Mavis' voice sounded tormented.

"Mavis?"

"Oh, Link, I got— I got a, a, a f-f-f-f-phone call. I hate phones," she wailed.

"It was about Jacqueline, wasn't it?"

"How did you know?"

"I just do."

"Oh, Link, she's dead."

Tears burned his eyes. "She burned, didn't she?"

"Did they call you, too?" Mavis sobbed. "Oh, what am I going to do? I need to go and claim her body after they're done with the autopsy, but I can't leave Valdez."

"I'll come with you."

"They said it'd be a few days. This is all my fault. My pride brought my beautiful girl to this."

"Don't blame yourself. It's my fault because I ordered her not to confront the woman."

"It was my fault," Mavis insisted. Heartrending sobs echoed over the phone line. Link had never imagined his militaristic little office manager held such deep emotions. "I told him where you were going. Don't you see? It's my fault."

"Take a deep breath and explain."

After several moments of sniffling and a hearty blow of the nose, Mavis sounded calmer. "That man, Capolucho, came to my house the morning after you and Jacqueline left. He explained that he loved Jacqueline, but that they'd been fighting and he needed to put matters right." Mavis sniffed. "He was scruffy, but seemed decent and I had to go, so I told him you'd gone to Fairbanks and would be continuing north that same morning."

"You gave him the time of day?"

Mavis sobbed harder. "I haven't dared take my hearing aid off."

Link rubbed his temple and wished he understood.

"Oh, Link, my pride killed my dear baby."

"Mavis— "

"It did. If I'd been wearing my hearing aid, I wouldn't have had that accident and if I hadn't had that accident, I wouldn't be spending my weekends doing community service and if I hadn't wanted to hide my conviction, I wouldn't have insisted that Jacqueline go with you and— " Sobs stopped the flow of words.

"Mavis, it was destiny."

"I told him where to find Jacqueline and let her leave with him. Twice. He killed her, Link. I just know he did. I saw his hands— they'd been burned. What if that happened when he the lab burned? What if he killed Adam so he could have— " She couldn't finish the thought.

"Mavis, Capolucho was a victim. I'm ninety percent certain the same person that tried to kill him, killed Adam, and now her. If anyone is to blame, it's me. I should have been with her, helped her. Instead, even though I had no right, I ordered her."

He swallowed. "And now..." Tears flowed in scalding trails down his cheeks.

34

The following day, Stone punched Link in the shoulder and told him to get his act together. When that didn't produce a response, Carmen tried to smother him with sisterly concern and Ariel plied him with a casserole. After three days of noodle-laced sympathy, he was ready to spend eternity alone.

After a week, Tempest was the only one brave enough to deliver a casserole. When she slammed it onto the counter, Link turned from the open refrigerator. She put her hands on her slim hips, jutted out her chin and took a deep breath. "You're better off without the witch." It was all Link could do not to spank the brat. "And you know what else, Uncle Link?"

"What?"

"You're a raving lunatic for acting like this." Tempest scooted out the kitchen door, slamming it behind her.

Link leapt to the door, and kicked it so hard the glass rattled. Then, he gripped the doorframe and leaned against the cool glass. As his anger faded, he straightened. His reflection in the glass showing unkempt hair and an unshaven face gave credence to Tempest's remark. So did the sweatshirt and jeans, which he'd worn since Valdez. If he didn't get a grip on his life, he would follow Capolucho's pattern and lose years to misery.

He went up to the bathroom and shaved. As he lathered, he remembered the smooth strokes Jacqueline used to propel a canoe. Slicing off weeklong whiskers, Link recalled the sound of her laughter. And as he rinsed the sink, he knew he would carry Jacqueline's memory in his heart until the day he died.

He showered and imagined that his heartache was going down the drain along with the suds, yet knew the bitter loss would always be with him, but somehow he had to learn to live with fate. When he applied his aftershave, the mirror reflected an older face.

It would have been nice to have a picture of Jacqueline; maybe he could ask Mavis if she had an extra.

After he dressed in clean clothes, Link wandered into his home office and tried to do some paperwork, but he couldn't concentrate.

He began pacing.

The apartment became stifling. Oppressive.

He needed air.

Link went out to his truck, climbed into the cab and backed out onto the street, then drove toward the highway.

Hours later, he parked in front of Mavis' small white clapboard house, amazed that he'd remembered exactly how to get here.

Link switched off the ignition and gazed at the dark green shutters. A curtain moved. With a sigh, he opened the door and walked toward the front porch.

The sheer curtain moved, again. A moment later, the cottage's emerald door exploded open and Mavis rushed at him. "I was about to phone the police." Mavis came to a halt in front of him, with her hands firmly planted on her hips and fury sparkling in her eyes.

"You don't have to phone the police. I'll leave."

"Over my dead body."

Link winced. "You're my only connection to Jacqueline, and— " He couldn't say any more.

"And be glad I am. Now get your lazy carcass inside before I drag you in."

Link held up his hands and shook his head.

She grabbed his hand and pushed the thumb backward. "Inside." Link went. "I've been trying to phone you for hours, but kept getting a busy signal."

"Phillip has been on the computer." Waves of pain radiated from his hand making it difficult for Link to think.

"Get a second phone line." Mavis huffed as she stomped up her two front steps, dragging him along. "Link Gavallan, you're more trouble than you're worth."

When pressure lessened on his thumb, Link was tempted to jerk free, but just then, he looked up, and saw Jacqueline's profile in the window. He stumbled and half fell against Mavis. Mavis dropped his hand and caught the railing. Link stared at the now empty window and knew he'd stepped over the edge into madness. He covered his face with his hands and blinked back tears.

"Well, the bad penny turned up," Mavis said. "Don't know what you see in the likes of him, though."

"Grandma!"

Jacqueline's face swam into sight. He blinked three times, but still saw her clutching the door. She looked different. Her hair was cut short and the left side of her head had been shaved to treat an ugly gash, which was held together with neat, tidy stitches.

"I'm leaving," Mavis said.

Link couldn't understand why Mavis sounded so pleased.

"Grandma didn't hurt you, did she?" The apparition

sounded throaty.

"Jacqueline, you're dead."

Her familiar warm laugh echoed across the porch. "No, the burned-off brows and eyelashes just make it look that way."

Link tried to focus through the tears. "I saw the newscast and knew you were dead before Mavis told me."

"I got knocked out. It's a wonder I didn't die, but all I got was a concussion." It didn't look that way. She took his hand with her unbandaged one. Her flesh felt warm. "You saved me." He wrapped his arms around her and never wanted to let go.

Link hugged her so close he could barely breath. "I wish I could have saved you." Obviously, Tempest had been right, he was a raving lunatic, but if he had to loose his mind to see Jacqueline one last time, it was worth going over the edge.

She snuggled close. "When I knew I was going to burn to death, I prayed to God not to let my last vision of this life be that glimpse of hell." She squeezed his fingers. "Then you were there, smoke swirling all around you. You put your arm around my shoulders like you did that night we walked along the river you said, 'Why don't we take a walk?'"

"You had a hallucination."

"Maybe. Or maybe it was an answer to my prayer. While you and I were walking out, I had a sort of revelation."

"Which was?"

"That I expect life to go in certain ways. But sometimes it doesn't, so I get frustrated. And sometimes I don't realize how wonderful something is, because it seems too perfect or too soon." Jacqueline shivered.

Link's arms trembled. She took a shuddering breath. Link stroked her spine in a reassuring way.

"There's a reason for everything," he said. "I'm so glad you're safe."

"It was terrifying."

"Someone called Mavis and told her you were dead."

"Nora is dead."

"Nora?" Link sat down hard on the porch's top step. Jacqueline's weight settled on his lap, her live weight.

"My freshman year roommate. At first the meeting seemed accidental and she seemed so happy to see me." Link touched her cheek; his hand trembled as he lightly traced her face. She turned her head and kissed his thumb. "Link, I should have listened to you. Nora was insane and she loved fire. She used it to kill people." Jacqueline swallowed, and snuggled against him. Link wrapped her in his arms. "If you still want me-"

"Then the answer is yes?"

She nodded. "I don't ever want to let go of you, again."

"I wish I hadn't been there, but it actually wasn't the nightmare I expected." Jacqueline frowned. "I mean it was, but it wasn't. I learned a lot from it." Her forehead furrowed. "You know how much I hate fire?"

He nodded.

"I didn't panic. Adam did. All he did was scream. If he'd stayed calm, he could have gotten himself out; thrown a chair through the window or something." Jacqueline gave him a hard hug. "Link, Adam's death wasn't my fault."

"I told you that."

Jacqueline closed her eyes, as if reliving a bad memory.

"Nora took my life so completely that she even used my folks and Grandma as people to contact in case of emergency. Can you believe it?"

"You ask me that when you've just risen from the dead?"

Jacqueline looked like she didn't know whether to laugh or cry. "They took me to the ER and treated me for burns, contusions and smoke inhalation, when I insisted that I was me, they admitted me to the Psychiatric Unit."

"Why?"

"Nora worked there and the ER nurse knew her. My ID burned in the fire. Word got around that Nora had burned to death and I was burned, too. The police thought I'd killed her, and tried to steal her identity." Link didn't know what to say. Jacqueline's shoulders shook. "Wasn't that ironic?"

Link kissed her. "I love you, Jacqueline Cardew."

"And I love you, Link Gavallan."

"Are you two idiots through making a spectacle of yourselves on my front porch?" Mavis demanded. "The neighbors are talking."

Jacqueline scrambled off his lap, and Link hopped to his feet, grabbed Mavis and kissed her. "I love you, too, Grandma."

www.ingramcontent.com/pod-product-compliance
Lightning Source LLC
Chambersburg PA
CBHW062023170626
46813CB00001B/272